CW01650707

# Bella Vista

Catherine Jinks was born in Brisbane, Queensland, in 1963. She grew up in Papua New Guinea and later spent four years studying medieval history at the University of Sydney. She has previously published four adult novels, including *An Evening with the Messiah* and the acclaimed *Little White Secrets*.

After working for several years as a journalist, Catherine now lives in Leura, New South Wales, with her husband, Peter, and their daughter.

Also by Catherine Jinks

For adults:

*An Evening with the Messiah*
*Little White Secrets*
*The Inquisitor*
*The Notary*

For children:

*This Way Out*
*Pagan's Crusade*
*The Future Trap*
*Pagan's Vows*
*Pagan's Scribe*
*Eye to Eye*
*The Secret of Hermitage Isle*
*Piggy in the Middle*
*The Horrible Holiday*
*The Stinking Great Lie*
*You'll Wake the Baby*
*What's Hector McKerrow Doing These Days*

CATHERINE JINKS

# BELLA VISTA

PENGUIN BOOKS

All characters in this novel are fictional and any resemblance to any person, living or dead, is entirely coincidental.

Penguin Books Australia Ltd
487 Maroondah Highway, PO Box 257
Ringwood, Victoria 3134, Australia
Penguin Books Ltd
Harmondsworth, Middlesex, England
Penguin Putnam Inc.
375 Hudson Street, New York, New York 10014, USA
Penguin Books Canada Limited
10 Alcorn Avenue, Toronto, Ontario, Canada M4V 3B2
Penguin Books (NZ) Ltd
Cnr Rosedale and Airborne Roads, Albany, Auckland, New Zealand
Penguin Books (South Africa) (Pty) Ltd
5 Watkins Street, Denver Ext. 4, 2094, South Africa
Penguin Books India (P) Ltd
11, Community Centre, Panchsheel Park, New Delhi 110 017, India

First published by Penguin Books Australia Ltd 2001

1 3 5 7 9 10 8 6 4 2



Designed by Cathy Larsen, Penguin Design Studio
Typeset in 12/16 Bembo by Midland Typesetters, Maryborough, Victoria
Printed and bound in Australia by Australian Print Group, Maryborough, Victoria

National Library of Australia
Cataloguing-in-Publication data:

Jinks, Catherine, 1963– .
Bella vista.

ISBN 0 14 100134 8.

I. Title.

A823.3

www.penguin.com.au

*For my father, who taught me that there's politics in every facet of life.*

## Acknowledgements

*With thanks to Nick and Margaret Howlett of Kanangra Lodge, Blackheath, John O. Ward and Kevin Rooke.*

*This project has been assisted by the Commonwealth Government through the Australia Council, its arts funding and advisory body.*

# CHAPTER ONE

Late one morning, when all the guests had gone, Avril found a hair in the third bathroom.

There was no other cause for complaint. Clean towels had been hung and stacked with mathematical precision. Two small bottles of conditioning shampoo sat snugly together on the antique marble-topped washstand in which the spare toilet paper was customarily concealed. Miniature bars of virgin soap ('Australian Wildflower Collection') had been carefully positioned beside the brass taps of the vanity. Steven had even remembered to replace the discreet little packets of sanitary napkins that were kept, in accordance with Avril's instructions, on a shelf to the right of the door. Every tile gleamed, and the toilet smelled of jasmine.

But there, in the shower stall, lurked that trademark sign of sloppy housekeeping – a coil of pubic hair.

It was ten past eleven, and Avril had been on the job, as she liked to put it, since six-thirty. Breakfast was served between seven and nine; although she made a point of laying the table and ironing the cloth before going to bed of an evening, she was obliged to prepare most of her renowned full Victorian breakfast shortly before it was consumed. Eggs had to be boiled, and placed in the silver egg-stand. Ham had to be sliced, and arranged on the massive mahogany sideboard. In obedience to her 1879 copy of *Cassell's Household Guide*, Avril also chose to put the bread and butter on the sideboard, although the sugar basin, milk ewer and toast rack went on the table. Napkins, of course, were of damask, rolled and placed in silver rings. The preserves were homemade. Avril's only concessions to the twentieth century were muesli and cornflakes (disguised in a couple of Liverpoolware soup tureens), together with an electric warming plate, which kept the porridge and bacon from growing cold.

This morning she had also made stewed kidneys, served on buttered toast. The lady from Brisbane had sampled them, before pronouncing them a little too heavy for breakfast, but Avril had not been offended. Indeed, she rather enjoyed the stunned looks that normally greeted her scalloped sheep's brains, hashed mutton or mackerel pie. What cast-iron stomachs those Victorians must have possessed! Although it had to be admitted that certain European visitors, accustomed to starting their day on herring or caviar or suety dumplings, were only too pleased to work their way through a good hearty meal before trudging off, in a fine mist, for an energetic day of bushwalking or rock-climbing. Such guests, Avril had noticed, were always the ones well furnished with heavy boots, state-of-the-art rain protection and indestructible Thermos flasks. No need to tell *them* to wear a hat, or take a bottle of water. You were more likely to see them setting off for Mount Hay wearing a hobble skirt and bustle than a pair of high-heeled summer mules.

Not like some people. There were certain visitors who, while they may have booked accommodation for two nights only, found themselves spending a whole week in the Blue Mountains – most of it on the premises of the Blue Mountains Hospital. Not that any of Avril's guests had suffered anything more serious than a broken wrist, or a mild case of sunstroke. But one had to be prepared for the worst. Running a guesthouse in Leura was not unlike running a guesthouse at Bondi Beach – except that, in Avril's case, there was a statistical probability that one of her tourists would fall off a cliff. At Bondi

Beach, the tourists were more likely to drown in a rip-tide.

It must be confessed that Avril had very little sympathy for grown men and women who fell off cliffs. She herself had never been close enough to an unfenced precipice to lose her balance. In her opinion (and it was one carefully concealed), people who took life-threatening risks – people who went hang-gliding and parachute-jumping and potholing – had to suffer the consequences.

After brushing away the traces of the morning's breakfast with her grandmother's lacquered crumb collector, Avril had cleared the table and washed the dishes. Owing to the fact that she usually employed a set of Edwardian Royal Doulton side plates and oatmeal bowls, as well as a lot of old silver, she did most of this work by hand. Then, while the couple from Brisbane made their leisurely preparations for a day of antique-shopping, she had straightened the bedclothes on her own bed, thrown open the curtains, finished off the stewed kidneys, and retired to the bathroom for approximately ten minutes, while Steven built up the drawing-room fire. It was his job to fiddle about with tongs and newspaper and kindling and ironbark, dressed in a creamy Fair Isle pullover and rather tight jeans, making lord-of-the-manor noises and cheerful remarks about the weather, while the guests trickled out of their rooms, looking for advice. Where was the Paragon Cafe? How long would it take to drive to Blackheath? Was there a taxi service, in this neck of the woods?

Steven was very good at dealing with such questions. He was naturally gregarious, an enthusiast, energetic and well informed. People liked him. They liked his wide, mobile face under its thatch of silver hair. They liked his high colour and guileless blue eyes, his intense sociability, and his peculiarly inappropriate presence in that big old Edwardian house, with its rich and sombre colour scheme, its ox-blood leather and black-walnut furnishings, its long, dark corridors and sepulchral hush. A breath of fresh air was how one guest had described him, in Avril's hearing, not long before. A breath of fresh air. Not like Avril, who might have been born and raised in that house, so well did she blend in. But the guests liked Avril, too. They liked the way she drifted in and out of the dining room at breakfast time, calm and contained, with her hair pulled back in a chignon and a string of pearls around her neck. She knew that she inspired confidence – even awe. She had grown smugly accustomed to that look, compounded equally of reverence, horror and disbelief, cast at her by women of almost every age when they learned that she made her own quince jam, raised and dried her own potpourri, and had sewn the little lace and muslin potpourri sachets that scented the drawers in the guestrooms.

Avril prided herself on her housekeeping accomplishments. She saw herself as highly skilled in a world that, having largely abandoned its hard-won expertise in such things as floor-waxing and bed-making, was now willing to pay for the opportunity of experiencing a properly waxed floor and a well-made bed at first hand. She regarded with slightly contemptuous indulgence women like Vicki Treloar, a bed-and-breakfast owner from Katoomba, who, while she used a linen service for her top sheets (and her pillowcases and towels and face washers and tablecloths), owned and laundered the fitted sheets on all of her guests' beds because it was 'so much easier to make beds that way'.

Avril, who knew how to mitre corners, used a linen service for all of her sheets – none of which was fitted. Given the time, she would have washed and starched the sheets herself, just as she laundered her own blankets and counterpanes. (No doonas were permitted inside the Bella Vista Guesthouse.) But she knew her own limitations. It was hard enough keeping up with the blankets and pillows, especially in mountains weather. That morning, for example, she had been obliged to air the pillows from the Blue Room, because Mr Petzl smoked. They now hung in the little glazed verandah off her own sequestered sitting room, while the Larssons' towels whirled around in the dryer, and the dishwasher churned away in the kitchen, and Avril thrust newly delivered bottles of milk and cream and local apple juice into the fridge.

It was not her job to clean the bathrooms. It was Steven's job to clean the bathrooms – all five of them, including their own – because he was more vigorous than she was, and had a stronger stomach. Cleaning the bathrooms was, in fact, Steven's main role as host of the Bella Vista Guesthouse. Normally this task kept him busy for a good two hours, if all of the rooms had been occupied, and all of the guests were leaving that day. Yet this morning he had rushed through his duties, swearing and clattering, because he had made some kind of appointment with some kind of aggrieved ratepayer, and the result was skimped work. Sloppy housekeeping. A hair in a shower stall.

It was, as Avril later remarked, the hair that broke the camel's back. God knows, she had been patient, not to say accommodating. For three years, ever since Steven's election to the Blue Mountains City Council, she had put up with council meetings and committee meetings and board meetings and ceaseless telephone calls that ate into Steven's time until he could barely find a minute to keep the accounts in order. Not only was he a city councillor; he was also on the board of Upper Mountains Tourism Limited, and part of an advisory taskforce for the highway revitalisation, and secretary to the Getaway Association, which was a small group of local guesthouse owners who shared a very specific commercial and professional agenda. Not that Avril had any problems with the Getaway group. She and Steven had joined it shortly after purchasing the Bella Vista five years ago, and she had always admired its insistence on certain high operational standards among its members. These standards ensured that the group was small, exclusive and well regarded. They also ensured that its members could refer their guests to each other without fear of disappointing anybody. At least 20 per cent of the Bella Vista's business was obtained by means of such referrals.

But standards have to be kept up. And, gazing at the pubic hair in her shower stall, knowing that it was unforgivable to confront any guest with such evidence of previous habitation, Avril thought: This is the beginning of the end. We'll be thrown out of Getaway, if he's not careful. Doesn't he realise that our *livelihood* depends on *keeping things clean*?

The lawn needed mowing, too. Would he expect her to do that? Would he expect her to chop kindling, and take the car in for a service, and have a sharp word with the neighbours about their dog?

Certain tasks were not in Avril's domain. She didn't have the time for them, let alone the inclination.

Something, she knew, would have to be done.

A little later, Avril was standing at the checkout line in her local department store. She deplored this particular retail outlet, but certain items were not readily available anywhere else. Sixty-watt candle globes, for instance. Small kitchen appliances. Inflatable paddling pools. She could understand that the population of the Upper Mountains had little alternative, when it came to department stores; given the choice between this one and a rather long drive, people were naturally indolent.

But why come to eat at the department store cafe? Why hang around outside its bank of glass doors, amid screaming infants and clouds of exhaust fumes? Avril was continually astonished at the attraction that this utilitarian structure seemed to exert, sitting as it did in an unlovely car park not ten minutes' drive from a stupendous vista of plunging sandstone cliffs and smoky blue valleys. Of course, when the clouds settled onto the mountains, it *was* too damp and chilly to stay outside. But there were innumerable cafes, and pleasant ones too; there was the library and the youth centre and, in any case, why weren't some of these children in school? Or at home, where they surely belonged?

No doubt, however, some of their homes left a lot to be desired. Avril was by now accustomed to what Steve called the hippy element. After living for seventeen years in Sydney's North Shore region (Pymble, to be exact), on a street lined with tall trees and gracious homes, amongst lawyers and bankers and doctors and orthodontists, Avril had been taken aback to discover that hippies still existed. Ferals, her daughter called them. Men with long matted hair, dressed in embroidered Indian waistcoats and ragged trousers; women with pierced noses and Celtic tattoos, sometimes barefoot, their babies blinking over their shoulders in a stunned sort of way, or bouncing up and down on tie-dyed knees. Most of these people were young, naturally, but there were some older men too, with bushy beards and craggy faces and fierce expressions. Always striding along at a good clip, sandals flapping, shoulder bags weighed down with earth-coloured clothes and home-grown legumes.

As for older *women* – well, there were only a few of them. Vera Rudkowski might have been classified as one, for she certainly had the hippy vote. She must have been about forty-five, but favoured trailing chiffon skirts, layers of crocheted cardigans, and three or four earrings in each ear. Perhaps, working at the local neighbourhood centre, she saw no reason to invest in a modest woollen suit, or a silk blouse – though for council meetings, and when canvassing votes, she did tend to dress more conservatively. On these occasions, Avril had seen her wearing jeans and a jacket. Even so, it seemed like something of a miracle that she had been elected. Why vote for such a woman? Granted that she was a forceful presence, big and articulate, with an extremely wide circle of acquaintances and a history in the mountains that went back thirty years. But why vote for someone so loud, so overbearing, so conceited and aggressive? Why vote for someone so stubbornly blind and wilfully obtuse?

Avril wondered this as she stood in the checkout queue, watching Vera at the next station. Vera was buying – what? Silicon sealant. Batteries. Men's underpants (for the young artist she lived with?). A packet of handkerchiefs. She looked morose, her heavy face set in a frown as she fished around in her worn leather wallet. Her dark hair, flecked with silver, was caught up inexpertly between two mismatched tortoiseshell combs; strands of it dangled over her neck and ears. She was wearing purple shadow on her eyelids, and chunky bracelets of wood and bone and beaten silver on her thick brown arms.

Then she looked up, and saw Avril. Their eyes met. Without so much as a blink, Vera turned away, even as a tentative smile was forming on Avril's lips. It was a snub, and a brutal one. Vera knew Avril. They had been introduced on election day.

But Steven was a sworn enemy, so why waste a smile on his wife?

You horrible woman, Avril thought, her gaze on Vera's ample behind. You're the cause of all this. If it weren't for you, Steven wouldn't have run for council. If it weren't for you, and what you did to poor George, it would never have even crossed his mind.

Poor George. Poor George Lovecek. On her way to the post office, Avril passed the arcade in which George's little computer shop was concealed. Steven had first met George in the course of buying various pieces of computer equipment (the exact nature of which remained a mystery to Avril, who ignored computers as thoroughly as she ignored fuse boxes, Whipper Snippers and air-pressure gauges). The two men had discovered that they enjoyed each other's company; indeed, George and his partner, Dianne, were the first good friends that Steven and Avril had made in the mountains – despite the fact that Dianne was rather formidable, in a brisk, efficient, well-groomed sort of way. One always sensed that she was reluctant to waste time. Occasionally her bright, smooth social manner even struck Avril as being a little false. It was as if, behind her beautifully applied make-up, Dianne was secretly stewing over an invoice or tax return or consignment of toilet paper. For she worked as purchasing manager at the Fremont Resort, and the Fremont Resort was a big operation.

George, in contrast, was a soft little man. He carried a fraction too much weight around his stomach, his thinning hair was slightly unkempt, and his large, gentle brown eyes seemed inadequately defended by a pair of steel-rimmed spectacles. Of course he was clever, and well organised, and better positioned financially than Steven was. Yet Steven always spoke of him with a certain degree of fond indulgence, as if he were not quite fully grown. And it had to be said that, in many respects, George was a follower. Dianne appeared to dictate his actions on the home front. Steven set the agenda for both himself and George in council. As for the Grevillea Lodge affair, which had moved Steven to action in the first place – that had been the result of certain activities undertaken, not by George, but by George's former business partner, Geoff Searle.

Avril had never quite understood what happened to Grevillea Lodge. It had been Geoff's brainchild, his baby – an ecotourism development somewhere out near Mount Victoria. George had simply invested a large amount of money in it, impressed as he was by Geoff's ideas, by his enthusiasm, and by his commitment to doing the right thing the right way. There had been surveys and letter drops and community consultation, a $35 000 master plan, long meetings with council staff, all of it occurring long before Steven's arrival in Leura. But still there were problems. Steven, upon hearing all the details, had regaled Avril with accounts of environmental impact statements and catchment committees and designated developments. She recalled a period of months when the Land and Environment Court had been involved. But she had been busy with her newly purchased guesthouse at the time, and had paid little heed to Steven's blow-by-blow descriptions of Geoff's war with the Blue Mountains City Council.

At last the money had run out. Geoff's option to purchase the Mount Victoria land had expired. Various other difficulties to do with a building approval conspired to shake his resolve. After two-and-a-half years of fighting, he had given up – having spent more than $100 000.

'And all because of people like Vera Rudkowski,' Steven had remarked one night, as he and Avril lay in bed. 'I mean, Geoff's credentials – there's nothing wrong with 'em. He knows what he's doing. He cares about the bush. But people like Vera, they won't have a bar of it. She won't *say* as much, but she doesn't want a thing going up. No development of any kind. Scared shitless, no imagination, doesn't seem to realise that we're all dependent on the bush up here. What tourist's going to pay money to look at a dirty-great construction site? There are sustainable ways of doing this, as long as guys like Geoff are in charge, but Vera can't see it. Can't see past Elkington and that other idiot waving their petitions. And Elkington raises bloody cattle! What a farce! Buckling to a squatter, I *ask* you.' A pause. 'They talk about conservatives. *They're* the conservatives. Can't abide change.' Another pause. 'I tell you, we're in trouble with that mob in charge.'

Shortly afterwards, with the help of certain sympathetic locals, Steven had decided to run for election in Ward One. He had persuaded George, who lived in Wentworth Falls, to run in Ward Two. But although they had both won places on council, Steven had not defeated Vera Rudkowski.

She remained entrenched, causing him much dismay and irritation, which he customarily brought home from the council chambers and dumped in Avril's unwilling ear.

Vera Rudkowski, she thought: I could cheerfully shoot her. And no-one, what's more, would ever suspect that I'd done it. Not with all the enemies she's made.

At the post office, Avril bought stamps and a birthday card. While standing in line to make her purchase, she was accosted by a woman named Stella Swann. Stella was a staunch conservationist, and a stalwart presence at council meetings. She lived in a broken-down weatherboard on the fringes of Katoomba, wore the most extraordinary assortment of hand-knitted, vegetable-dyed clothes, and appeared to have no means of support. Her incoherent letters (mostly about dogs and cats) were often to be seen in the *Blue Mountains Gazette*; she made a point of haranguing councillors whenever they came into her orbit. On average, Steven received two telephone calls from her every week.

And when no councillor was available, she happily settled for the next best thing.

'I've just been to Kale's Nursery,' she informed Avril, an electricity bill clutched to her chest. 'I've been looking at their stock.'

'Oh?' said Avril. With a sinking heart, she counted seven people in the queue ahead of her.

'Do you know what they're selling, there? Cherry laurel. *Cherry laurel*. I said to them, don't you know that's classified as a *weed*? And convolvulus! Can you believe it?' Thrusting her face into Avril's, she exhaled a cloud of onion-scented breath. 'There ought to be fines. *Big* fines.'

'I'm sure,' Avril murmured.

'Last week I was in Bullaburra, and do you know what I found being sold there? Spanish heath. Unbelievable. And Scotch broom! That's not only a weed, that's a *noxious* weed!'

The line moved at a glacial pace. At last, however, Avril was served, and joyfully left Stella fiddling about with grubby notes and change. Honestly, she thought: it was a typical example of what she'd had to endure since Steven's election. Bailed up at the post office! As if *she* had anything to do with what you could or couldn't buy at a nursery!

'. . . but they pass these resolutions,' a breathless voice suddenly declared, just behind her, 'and what happens? Damn all! Take the tree preservation order. What are they doing to enforce that? Nothing, as far as I can see. A perfectly good silver birch down the road from my house – beautiful tree, introduced, of course, but no trouble to anyone – and where's that gone, I'd like to know? With whose permission?'

Though small, Stella was quick on her feet. All at once she was at Avril's elbow, babbling on about the iniquitous practice of cutting down hollow trees and tree stumps ('Where are the possums supposed to live, I'd like to know?') while Avril cast about frantically for a means of escape. Then she remembered George. Though vulnerable to attack when he was working – because he couldn't just walk out of his shop – George had never been bothered there by Stella. 'Maybe it's the odour of hot plastic,' he said. 'I don't think she likes technology.' Hoping that this was indeed the case, Avril turned into the arcade where George's shop presented a bland facade to passers-by, and walked through the door on which the words 'G. L. Business Systems Pty Ltd' had been painted in a small, neat, golden script.

Sure enough, Stella stopped at the threshold. 'Well . . . I'll have a word with your husband about it,' she muttered, before charging off to find fault somewhere else. Avril plotted her progress through a window display of corporate-grey monitors and modems.

'Hiding out?' asked George, emerging from behind the counter.

'From Stella Swann.'

'Ah.'

'You're quite right. She won't come in here, will she?'

'A Stella-free zone. It's like waving garlic at a vampire.'

'I just don't know what she expects from me. Of course it *is* dreadful that the nurseries sell convolvulus, but I don't see what *I'm* supposed to do about it.'

'You're supposed to get your husband to do something about it,' George offered. 'The power behind the throne . . .'

'As if I could get Steven to do anything,' said Avril, turning away from the window. She smiled at George, wishing, as always, that he would do something about his *hair*. He was really quite a presentable-looking man, behind those dreadful polyester shirts and that straggling fringe. Why didn't Dianne take him in hand? 'You should see our lawn,' she continued. 'It looks like a hayfield. But Steven's always so busy, going to works inspection meetings or whatever it is you people do.'

'Oh.' George's smile was a little embarrassed. 'Yes.

Well, I guess . . . there's a lot on these days. And Steven is very conscientious.'

'I know,' Avril sighed.

'Of course, it's all this warm weather,' George continued, turning the conversation somewhat. 'I had to mow *our* grass yesterday, and the daffodils are coming up everywhere!'

'Yes, I'm seeing a lot of bulbs.'

'Would you like some of my clippings, Avril? I have all the mulch I want.'

'Oh, no.'

'Really, it's not a problem. I could drop over some time – leave you a couple of bags. You were saying that you needed something for your rhododendrons.'

'Well I do, of course, but –'

'That's a hell of a lot of mulch. Especially if you want to cover that eastern corner.'

'I'll see. It's very kind of you. I'll see how we fare with our own clippings.'

'Just give me a call, then.'

They discussed gardening for a while, before the appearance of a gangling youth with bad skin and some obscure computer-related question recalled George to his duties. Avril left the shop. She was very fond of George. Such a *nice* man. So easy to talk to. And for someone who was professionally associated with computers, he had a remarkably broad range of interests. Conversing with George wasn't like conversing with – oh, with his assistant Kyle, for instance. Avril had once been obliged to exchange small talk with Kyle, over drinks at George's house. What a painful experience that had been! When he was not babbling on about C-drives and software, Kyle seemed unable to string four coherent words together.

George was different. He liked opera. He liked birds. He liked gardening. Indeed, it was he who tended the garden of the house that he shared with Dianne – and he did it beautifully. He had a solid library of gardening books, an enviable collection of first-rate gardening tools, and a real talent for growing new plants from cuttings. All of Avril's white hydrangeas had been grown from George's slips.

Of course, he was barely even competent when it came to housekeeping, but in Avril's opinion, the house should have been Dianne's job. After all, George had a shop to look after, and a garden too. Yet it was he who sometimes telephoned Avril with inquiries about cockroach baits and stain removers. Was it any wonder that, during her visits to George's house, she had often noticed grease caked on the rangehood filters, and soap scum on the glass shower screens?

Poor George: he did his best. And his priorities were right. Although he, like Steven, was a city councillor, he would never have dreamed of leaving his edges untrimmed.

If only, Avril thought, if *only* Steven could be like that!

The mist cleared that afternoon, and a watery sunshine succeeded it. Avril was therefore able to induce Steven to mow the lawn, at long last; although at first reluctant, he was soon singing and swearing exuberantly over his aged Victa, just as Avril had expected he would. Essentially, her husband was a man of action. Give him something energetic to do, and he would throw himself into it with gusto.

Meanwhile, Avril made lemon drops. She liked to leave a small dish of homemade sweets in each of the guests' bedrooms: lemon drops, ginger drops, peppermint drops. She also liked to serve little cakes to the guests when they first arrived – cakes and hot drinks. Steven often shook his head over such time-wasting extravagance, but Avril pointed out that, like the Bella Vista's roaring fire, the smell of baking was a foolproof way of making people feel thoroughly at home. And the sweets cost nothing, really: a little sugar, a little grated lemon. She always wrapped them in strips of greaseproof paper, twisted into fans at both ends.

When the 2:54 p.m. train arrived, Avril went to meet it. Normally Steven picked up guests from the station, but she had no intention of allowing him to walk away from a half-cut lawn. Knowing Steven, it might be days before he managed to finish the job. So she checked the book, familiarised herself with the names inscribed therein (Amanda Vukic and Robin Sternbeck – not married, obviously), and drove at a majestic pace to Leura Mall, where the flowering cherries were budding.

When Steven had been retrenched from the bank, and had received a severance payout based on thirty years of faithful service, it had been Avril's idea to open a high-class guesthouse. At first her sights had been set on Bowral. But her initial glimpse of Leura Mall, carpeted in drifts of cherry blossom, had changed her mind. Granted, the busy little retail strip did contain a takeaway food outlet, an auto-accessories shop, and a food-distribution warehouse. But it also featured several up-market boutiques, a jeweller, a bakery store renowned for its sourdough bread, numerous attractive cafes, and a very good bookshop that Avril regarded as a genuine ornament, though she never went inside. When she wasn't thumbing through homemaking magazines, she had recourse to a small, personal library of well-loved novels, which she liked to read over and over again. *Pride and Prejudice* was one of them; *Rebecca*, another.

It was chilly on the station platform, and Avril was relieved when the train arrived. She was also relieved to discover that the new guests were not sporting silver nose-studs or spikes of green hair. In the past five years, guests of this dubious kind had only once presented themselves, and had subsequently proved to possess amiable and peace-loving natures, which quite belied their ferocious appearance. (Avril had grown quite fond of them, in fact; they had known a great deal about fertilisers and rose-pruning.) Nevertheless, she still approached every new encounter with a faint sense of trepidation, and was relieved to discover that, in this case, her fears were groundless. Amanda Vukic and Robin Sternbeck were dressed with perfect propriety in expensive-looking pullovers and jackets (Country Road?), though the rest of their possessions were concealed in rather shabby gym-bags. They must have been in their late twenties or early thirties, Avril decided; Amanda wore an aggressive shade of lipstick, and smelled of smoke, while Robin's fair, bland, smooth-jowled face seemed specially designed not to give offence. Amanda yelped enthusiastically all the way back to the guesthouse. Robin interjected a few suave comments about State Rail and imported coffee. They had been referred to the Bella Vista by a friend, and appeared to know exactly what to expect. Once inside, Amanda pounced on Avril's lemon drops with delight, and demanded to know what she proposed to give them for breakfast. Calves' liver? Sheep's brains?

'I don't know,' said Avril cautiously. 'Is there anything you'd particularly like?'

'Julie had some kind of curried omelette.'

'Devilled omelette. Yes.'

'But she said you cook all kinds of things. Victorian-type things. Bits of liver and spleen.'

'I do a proper lamb's fry, if you want one. Heart, liver, kidneys and onions. Butchers don't generally sell spleens anymore. Not like in the old days.'

'Please don't go to any trouble,' Robin observed. 'No matter what you cook, she won't eat it. She can't face a fried egg in the morning, let alone a pig's liver.'

'Oh, but you're such a big *man*,' said Amanda. 'You'd have no trouble polishing off a haggis or something, right?'

Avril left them chaffing each other fondly over one of Avril's quilted counterpanes. She prepared a tray in the kitchen, with coffee in a silver pot, teacakes on a willow-patterned plate, and milk and sugar in two heavy pieces of Stuart crystal. She was preparing to take this elegant afternoon tea out to the drawing room when Steven appeared, and told her that Pat Baldwin had rung.

'Said she wants to drop by this afternoon,' he observed, 'and discuss something with me. I don't know what.'

'Can't she talk to you over the phone?'

Steven shrugged. He was plastered with wet grass. His face was flushed.

'Maybe she just happens to be heading up this

way,' he said, peering into the fridge. 'Don't ask me. Where's that fizzy lemon stuff?'

'You finished it. What time is she coming?'

'Soon. About five, she said.'

'Well – I'd better save some of these teacakes, then.'

'Sweetheart, you don't have to feed everyone who sets foot in the place.'

'Pat Baldwin is the *mayor*, Steven. I think we might make a bit of an effort for the *mayor*.'

'If you say so.'

'Besides, it's no trouble. I've already done the baking.'

Steven grunted. Then, at Avril's suggestion, he went to change his clothes and splash some water over his face and arms. By the time he emerged into the drawing room, wearing a tweedy jacket over a knitted vest, the couple from Brisbane were chatting genially with Amanda and Robin, who had discovered Avril's teacakes and were uttering cries of delight.

'How fabulous,' Amanda exclaimed, scattering crumbs. 'Still warm, too! Fantastic.'

'So have you been on any walks?' Robin inquired politely of Mrs Petzl, an elderly woman with the wind-buffeted look of someone who had been striding around on bluffs for an hour or two. 'We were thinking about doing one now.'

'Oh, it's getting a bit late for that,' Steven remarked. 'Wrong time of year to set out after four.' He was crouched in front of the fireplace, expertly wielding a poker. 'Unless you just want to stroll down to the Gordon Falls lookout or something.'

'I need to work off what I've just eaten,' Amanda muttered indistinctly, through a mouthful of cake. 'And what I'll be eating tonight. I'm told there are some pretty good restaurants around here – is that true?'

The Petzls responded enthusiastically, and Avril deduced, from long experience, that although much would be *said* on the subject of bushwalking, not one metre of national park would be traversed that afternoon. Instead, Amanda and Robin would sit in front of the fire, discussing their plans, until it was time to eat again. Then they would go off and gorge themselves at a fancy restaurant, come back in a taxi, drink several glasses of Steven's port, and throw themselves into bed, from which they would only emerge when the smell of morning coffee tickled their nostrils. Slightly hung-over, they would pick at Avril's lavish breakfast, and become submerged in the newspapers until lunchtime, when a mounting appetite would drive them to overeat at one of the more fashionable cafes. When they finally did decide to go for a walk, it would probably be raining. Therefore they would spend their afternoon hovering in giftshops, and eating Devonshire teas, until it was once more time for dinner.

People often came to the mountains for a spot of bracing exercise, but returned home feeling distinctly liverish, perceptibly heavier, and a trifle out of sorts when they considered the money they had spent on what had been planned as a low-cost weekend.

Sure enough, Amanda and Robin were still in the drawing room, peering at brochures, when Pat arrived.

'Steven,' said Avril, poking her head around the door. 'Steven, Pat's here.'

'Oh. Right.' He had been declaiming on the subject of poorly maintained walking tracks. 'If you'll excuse me . . .'

'Yes, of course,' said Amanda.

'No sweat,' said Robin.

'Thanks so much for your help,' said Amanda, her raised voice pursuing her host down the corridor. In the kitchen, Pat was waiting, a plump and placid woman with short, straight grey hair. The wind had nipped at her nose and cheeks, turning them pink; otherwise her complexion was pale – almost livid. Bundled up in a chunky hand-knitted cardigan, she looked much larger than she normally did.

Poor Pat, thought Avril. Those varicose veins!

'Getting a bit nippy out,' Steven proffered. 'The weather's been so warm lately, and now look at it.'

'Yes,' said Pat. She wasn't a garrulous woman. When she spoke, it was in a quiet and measured way, as if she were thinking hard. Avril had never regarded her as being particularly intelligent, though she was well furnished with commonsense. What she did have was a certain kind of earnest gravity, and an ability to keep order, without resorting to violent means, which must have been derived from her experience as a mother of four sons.

She had been mayor now for seven years, and such was the confidence she instilled that her success at the next mayoral elections was pretty much taken for granted. 'Good old Pat,' was the general opinion among the councillors. 'She's got no vision, and she'll never set the place on fire, but at least she's honest.' And reliable. And conscientious. And willing to listen.

'Would you like coffee, Pat, or tea?' Avril inquired, offering the mayor a plate of cakes.

'Oh. Thank you, Avril, tea would be nice.'

'Just come into the sitting room,' Steven suggested, guiding Pat through the door and into one of Avril's precious wing-backed chairs. The sitting room was a snug little refuge, all Axminster carpet and Laura Ashley chintz. Avril and Steven's bedroom opened off it. 'I might have a cup of that myself, Avril, if I could,' he added.

Obediently, his wife slipped away to switch on the

electric jug. When she returned, Pat was staring at her feet, while Steven talked about something called the Blue Mountains Bioindicators Project.

'Are you all right, Pat?' asked Avril, after Steven had expressed his views, and Pat had responded with a grunt. 'You look a bit under the weather.'

'Oh, *I'm* okay,' came the reply. 'But I'm afraid Frank isn't.'

'Why?' Steven leaned forward. 'What's the matter?'

'He's been having problems . . .' Pat trailed off. Then she blinked, and straightened, and proceeded in a brittle voice: 'It's prostate cancer. We just got the test results.'

Appalled, Avril was almost relieved when the electric jug shrilled its high-pitched warning. She hurried out of the room to turn it off, leaving Steven to grope for the right words. He was much better in these situations than she was, perhaps because the sight of other people's distress didn't really seem to upset him. As she made the tea, Avril could hear his low-pitched voice rumbling away with easy sympathy.

Thank God for Steven, she thought. Thank *God* for Steven.

'. . . if there's anything we can do, just give us a yell, Pat,' he was saying, when Avril returned with the teacups on a silver tray. 'I mean it. Anything. Is he going into hospital?'

'Tomorrow.'

'God. Up here, or . . .?'

'Nepean.'

'Right. Right.' Steven nodded solemnly, and reached for his tea. His hand hovered for a moment over the plate of cakes; then he withdrew it, as if embarrassed to eat in the presence of tragedy.

'I'm so sorry, Pat,' Avril murmured.

'Thank you.'

'It's – I mean, the prognosis can be pretty good, for this kind of thing. Can't it?' Steven asked.

'I don't know.' Pat sounded tired. 'The boys have been terrific. And Frank's semi-retired, of course, so it won't make a huge difference as far as – well, income, and so on. But I don't know . . .' She shook her head. 'It's something we'll just have to cope with.'

Sympathetically, Steven patted her hand. Such gestures had always come naturally to him; he felt comfortable slapping people on the back or throwing his arm around their shoulders. Watching him as he sat there, so well put together in his slightly stuffy clothes (that vest was a mistake; where on earth had he found it?), Avril felt a thrill of fear. How long was it since he'd had his prostate checked?

'The thing is,' Pat was saying, 'I'm going to have to cut back on my council commitments. Not altogether, but some of my committees –'

'Of course,' Steven interposed. 'Don't worry about it, Pat. Everyone will understand.'

'And I won't be running for mayor,' Pat concluded. 'I couldn't possibly.'

'No, no. We wouldn't expect you to.'

'That's why I wanted to have a word.' Pat's gaze rested on Steven for an instant, before roaming away. 'I know you're new to council, but you've made an impression. Everyone says so. Well – not Vera, of course, but most of the others. And the staff – I've had nothing but good reports from the staff. And you can see both sides of an issue, I've always thought that.' Nodding gravely, Pat made a visible effort, and looked Steven straight in the eye. 'You're not always losing your temper. You don't *like* a barney – not like some of them. I've seen you trying to resolve disputes. You speak up, you've got your opinions, but you're not always sniping and finding fault for the sake of it. What I'm saying is, it's not a personal thing with you.'

'Well . . . thanks, Pat.' Steven seemed puzzled, but alert. 'It's nice of you to say so. Personally, I've always been very impressed by your performance, too.'

'People don't realise how hard it is, being mayor,' Pat said; then added, with a smile, 'though it's not as hard as being a mother.'

This remark was directed at Avril, who smiled in response. She was beginning to feel uneasy.

'Some people are mayor because they want to rule the roost,' Pat went on. 'I just wanted to make sure that everyone got a fair hearing. It's important that everyone gets a fair hearing.'

'I know.'

'You strike me as the sort of bloke who wouldn't ride roughshod, Steve. And I like your attitude towards the community – towards your role in the community. That's why I've decided to nominate you for mayor. What I'm saying is, you've got my vote. If you want to run, that is.' Solemnly, heavily, Pat leaned back in her chair. 'Do you?' she asked. 'Do you think you could handle being mayor, Steve? Because *I* think you could.'

# CHAPTER TWO

Pat left around five o'clock; the mood thereafter was solemn. Avril put on a long face and said very little. Once, during dinner, she asked Steven if the doctor had checked him out recently. Once she remarked, in her gentle way, that Barry had called from Upper Mountains Tourism. At first, Steven was thinking too busily to notice the atmosphere. He was thinking that he already had three votes in hand: his own, Pat's and George's. Vera would probably run against him; she had run against Pat the previous year, without success, though she'd had the support of Gareth Cleves and Maeve O'Meagher. Three votes for the Greens, in other words. And if the Labor faction fielded a candidate – Bert, perhaps? – then Bert would have another three votes. But what would Allan Purchese do? Allan was a dyed-in-the-wool Liberal, and Sue Schaarf, who had run second on his Ward Four ticket, was known as The Doppelgänger. She'd jump the way Allan did. Steven had a good chance of securing both their votes.

As for Celeste . . . well, she was a wild card. No telling *what* she'd do. Celeste was all over the map.

There was no doubt about it, though: she did like Steven. Perhaps he could use that to his advantage.

'We should send a card,' said Avril.

'Hmm? What?'

'We should send a card to Frank. At the hospital.'

'Oh. Yes. Right.' Slowly, as his wife cleared the kitchen table, Steven became aware that she was brooding. Because of Frank? Possibly. But she'd only ever met him once. Watching her as she scraped plates, her head bowed, her lips pursed, her gaze turned studiously on whatever she happened to be doing, he thought: Bugger.

'So,' he said, throwing down the gauntlet. 'What do you think?'

'About what?'

'About Pat's suggestion.'

A pause. She removed her wedding and engagement rings before dragging a pair of rubber gloves over her narrow hands.

'Well?' he prodded.

'I think it's absurd.'

'Why?'

'Because you have enough to do as it is.'

'Getaway elects a new executive in January. The Revitalisation Taskforce won't be hard to pull out of. The board's a bit tricky, but I can probably ease off a little.' Didn't she realise what a chance this was? 'Avril, I'd be *mayor.* Mayor of the Blue Mountains. I think it's worth the effort, don't you?'

'Why?'

'Why? Because I might make a difference, that's why. I mean, it can be so frustrating. You know how it is, I've told you often enough. As mayor, I'd have the casting vote. I'd be able to chair any meeting I turned up to. God, I might actually get something *done.* Improve the quality of life around here.'

'Whose quality of life?'

'What do you mean? Everyone's.'

'Not mine. I don't want to do the bathrooms.'

Steven delivered himself of an exasperated sigh. 'You wouldn't have to do the bathrooms,' he said. 'I'll keep doing the bathrooms, all right?'

'I don't see how.'

'Don't you? Well, maybe that's because you're a little bit blinkered. I mean, you're not really looking at the big picture, are you? You're sort of focusing on all the little things. Making mountains out of molehills.'

'Little things, yes. Like the hair I found in one of the shower stalls this morning.'

'What?'

In a clipped sort of way, carefully rinsing crystal glasses, Avril acquainted him with the details of her discovery. It was so bloody typical. For five years now he'd been cleaning the bathrooms, and this was the first time she'd caught him out. The very first time.

But he was patient, because he knew how she baulked at new ideas.

'Well . . . that was a slip-up,' he confessed. 'It won't happen again. I'll make sure it won't happen again.'

Although she said nothing, her silence was eloquent.

'Avril, has it ever happened before? No. I think you're making a big issue out of it, when . . . well, frankly, it's not worth worrying about.'

Cutlery clattered into the dishwasher.

'What about our standards?' she said at last, in a small voice.

'What about them?'

'They'll slip. They're slipping now.'

'No, they're not.'

'And it's foolish to say that your being mayor won't have some kind of effect on what we do.'

'All right. Okay. I'll admit that you'll have to make a few adjustments.'

'Like cleaning the bathrooms.'

'*No.*' Picking up a tea towel, Steven reminded himself that she was always at her worst when her domestic arrangements were under threat. 'Look, maybe the trick is to start focusing on essentials. And not to spend so much time on what doesn't really make much difference.'

Avril raised her head, like a deer scenting danger.

'What do you mean?' she said.

'You know what I mean. The stewed kidneys. The baking. The best china. The homemade Christmas wreaths. It's not *necessary*, Avril.'

'Yes, it is.'

'Sweetheart, the guests would be quite happy with stainless steel.'

'No, they wouldn't. Don't you remember what Mr Pettingell said? He said he loved coming here, because he always got the real thing.'

'That's because he's a poncey interior decorator,' Steven pointed out.

Avril's cheeks were flushed. She took several deep breaths, resting her wet, gloved hands on the edge of the sink.

'All these things,' she said, in a slow, strangled voice, 'are part of our reputation. They're the *essence* of Bella Vista. Without them, we'd have no competitive edge at all.'

'Competitive edge!' Steven snorted. Where on earth had she picked that up from? The *Women's Weekly* guide to running your own business? 'To be competitive, Avril, you have to have built-in cost-effectiveness. Making mackerel pie for breakfast is *not* cost-effective. No-one bloody eats it, for starters.'

She didn't reply. She never did, when he employed profanities. Aware that he was beginning to lose his temper, Steven threw down his tea towel and went to put the garbage out for collection.

Wouldn't it be nice, he thought, if *just this once* she'd said, 'That's wonderful, darling.' Just this once. But no. The house might suffer. And anyway, she can't stand it when I have my own interests.

That was the problem, of course. Those so-called slipping standards were simply an excuse. Avril wasn't worried about bookings and takings. She was worried that he'd found something interesting and rewarding to do outside the domestic sphere. As he dragged their big, green bin up the driveway, and positioned it near the letterbox, he recalled two previous occasions on which Avril had prevented him from pursuing certain activities that took him out of the house. Not work, of course; she hadn't objected to the bank – how could she? But she'd kicked up a hell of a stink over that golf-club committee, moaning and complaining and brooding and slamming down plates of food until he'd been forced to give it up. And then there was his charity work. She'd objected to that, for some reason.

Selfish cow.

Well, she wouldn't stop him running for mayor. Strolling back towards the looming bulk of the Bella Vista, his arms folded against the chill night air,

Steven reflected on her probable tactics. She would give him the silent treatment. She would refuse him his conjugal rights. She would drift out of the room whenever he entered it, but in a pointed manner, leaving no doubt as to the fact that she was being intentionally rude. Avril rarely raised her voice. They were not a couple who habitually engaged in competitive door-banging and crockery-smashing. There might have been the occasional shout, but on the whole, their disagreements were muted. Repressed. Though not in any way less vicious, for all the restraint displayed when it came to the use of foul language.

Sighing, Steven let himself in through the front door. What on earth did she expect, for God's sake? She knew what he was like. They had discussed all this before buying the guesthouse. He'd spent twelve years as a lending manager. His days had been full of meetings, interviews, phone calls, conferences, and confabulations in the toilet or the tea room. He wasn't the sort of bloke who could sit at home all day. They had agreed that he would be responsible for liaising with the local community, because he was an outgoing sort of person, and she was so shy.

Now she was complaining that he'd done exactly what they had intended he should do. After all, you had to liaise with the local community if you were going to serve it.

The drawing-room fire had collapsed into a heap

of smouldering embers. With a few prods and thick sticks and twists of newspaper, Steven managed to revive the blaze (he was an expert with fires), in order that his guests, when they returned from their respective dinners, should have leaping flames to sit in front of while they drank their port. He was toying with the notion of pouring himself a modest glass when the telephone rang, and he heard his wife answer it.

'Oh – hello, George,' she said.

George! He had to tell George the big news.

'No, I – I'm afraid I haven't given it much thought.' Avril looked up as Steven entered the kitchen, then looked away. 'Yes, I suppose so . . . are you sure it won't be any trouble? No? All right, well . . . thank you. That would be very kind. Yes. Yes. I know. George, Steven's waving his arms at me, so I think he wants to talk to you.'

Steven grabbed the receiver. 'George! Mate! Have I got some news for you!' He proceeded to recount the details of Pat's visit, making a great effort not to skim too breezily over the fact that Frank was ill. After all, Steven's good fortune was Frank's bad luck. It wouldn't be right to sound overly enthusiastic. 'So,' Steven concluded, after relating the essence of Pat's offer in grave tones, 'that means I've got Pat's vote, your vote, and mine, which makes three. The question is: who else will be standing? Have you heard any whispers?'

At the other end of the line, George was silent.

'No,' he said at last. Then: 'Vera, maybe.'

'That's what I thought. Who else? Bert?'

'Perhaps. But only if he's heard that Pat's not standing.'

'Pat was going to call him tonight, after she'd spoken to me. Which means that everyone will know by tomorrow night.'

'Probably.'

'I reckon I've got a good chance with Allan, don't you think? And I might get Celeste's vote, if I try hard. Because on a personal level, you know, we get along okay.'

'Yes,' George agreed cautiously. 'But Celeste gets along even better with Bert. So if Bert runs –'

'I know. It depends on the Labor caucus.' Steven pondered. Avril was scrubbing furiously at a crust-caked frying pan, but he knew that she was listening. 'Maybe I'll call Bert myself tomorrow. And Maeve. If Vera's planning something, Maeve will tell me.' For Avril's benefit, he added: 'Maeve's a lovely girl.'

'She's not going to vote for you, though,' said George. 'Not if Vera's running.'

'Well . . . maybe not. But if I can get Allan, I'll get Sue. And Celeste makes six.'

'If Bert's running, you won't get Celeste.'

'No, but I'll still be ahead of the pack. I'll have five votes, Bert will have four, and Vera will have three. So Vera will be knocked out, and who will the Greens vote for then?'

'Gareth will vote for a mayor in his own ward,' George remarked, and Steven remembered, with an inward curse, that Gareth Cleves, like Bert Plummer, represented Ward Two.

'Well . . . maybe,' he said. 'I'll have to work on him. Suppose I offer him deputy mayor? That might do the trick.'

There was another long silence at the end of the line. Frowning, Steven wondered if George wanted to be deputy. Surely not? No-one else would vote for George, even if Steven did. Gareth was a much likelier candidate – and if he secured two votes from Steven and George, he might return the favour, and support Steven as mayor.

With Gareth as deputy, Steven might even win Vera's vote.

He tried to explain this to George, who eventually agreed that, if matters turned out as Steven had predicted, making an offer to Gareth would be the best strategy. They concluded their conversation on amicable terms, and Steven hung up feeling that he had taken his first step towards the mayoral office.

Avril was drying glasses with a martyred air, which her husband chose to ignore. After all, if she wanted to be unreasonable, and set the table with crystal stemware instead of nice thick, serviceable, dishwasher-proof glass, then it was she who should suffer the consequences.

'What was George ringing you about?' he inquired.

'Mulch.'

'Mulch?'

'He's going to drop over some grass clippings.'

'Oh.' More gardening stuff. 'Right. He's a nice bloke, George.'

'Very.'

'Reasonable.'

No reply.

'He's going to support me when I stand for mayor,' Steven announced. Whereupon Avril turned on her heel.

'Well, I'm not,' she retorted, and marched into the laundry with her wet tea towel.

As Steven had anticipated, Avril refused to talk to him in bed that night. She rolled away from him, curling herself into a tight little knot on the far side of the mattress, her curved back communicating exactly how she felt about his decision.

The first of many such nights, no doubt. But Steven didn't have enough energy to protest. He simply vented his feelings by putting his wet glass of water directly onto the polished mahogany of his bedside cabinet. (*How* she would fume, when she saw that he hadn't used a coaster. There was every chance he'd committed the cardinal sin of damaging the woodwork!) Then he settled under the blankets with a sigh.

He was asleep within minutes. He'd never in his life had trouble getting to sleep. Furthermore, he usually slept straight through the night, waking early in the morning – between six and half past – without the aid of pills, hot drinks, or weird relaxation techniques. Not like Avril. Avril was a very light sleeper. She'd once leapt awake at the sound of a cockroach scritch-scratching over a birthday card in the adjoining room.

That night, however, he did wake up. So did Avril. So did everyone else in the house, because it would have been difficult to sleep through the uproar that suddenly broke out at 1:15 a.m.

It sounded as if someone was trying to smash the front door down.

'For Christ's sake,' Steven protested, groggily pushing himself upright. Avril was shaking his arm.

'Steven!' she whispered. '*Steven!*'

'Get off.' He nudged her hand away, swung his legs out of bed, and stood up. Someone was shouting incoherently.

'Call the police!' Avril exclaimed.

'Hang on.' He was putting on his glasses. 'Let's just see who it is, first.'

'But –'

'Maybe it's Robin. He might be pissed. He might have lost his key.' It seemed unlikely, but after all, Amanda and Robin did appear to be night owls. As far as Steven knew, they hadn't returned by the time he'd locked the front door, at ten past eleven. 'Just take it easy, will you? Calm down.'

'Be careful, Steven.'

'Yeah, yeah.'

'Get that old walking stick. The one in the umbrella stand.'

'Avril, please.' Though it wasn't a bad idea, on reflection. Yawning and bleary-eyed, Steven staggered to the front door, which was rattling under the blows of a furious fist. On his way, he passed a tousle-headed Robin emerging from the second guestroom.

So that was one theory put to rest, anyway.

'Who is it?' Robin inquired, his eyebrows working.

'I dunno.' Steven pulled his father's heavy walking stick from the umbrella stand. 'Whoever it is, they'd better watch out. Hey! *Hey!* Who is it?'

'Open up!' came the muffled reply. Peering through a stained-glass panel, Steven could just make out a large, blurred shape in some kind of coat.

'Tell me who you are, and what the hell you think you're doing!' he barked. 'Do you know what time it is?'

'Open up! Open this *door*!'

Steven glanced back, and saw a scattering of faces. Avril was standing at the far end of the corridor. The Petzls were hovering near the umbrella stand, pale and disconcerted. Amanda was blinking in the lamp-light, her expression drowsy and resentful.

'Tell him to piss off,' she croaked.

'I'm really sorry,' said Steven. 'I don't know who it is.'

'Perhaps you should call the police,' Lena Petzl suggested nervously. Then Robin stepped forward.

'Open the door,' he told Steven. 'I'll stand over here, and if this guy tries anything, I'll jump him.'

Steven suddenly realised that he was cutting a rather unenterprising figure in front of his guests – two of whom were female. Therefore, to prevent Robin from taking control, he raised his walking stick and threw open the front door, braced for any eventuality.

He found himself face to face with a drunken young man wearing a goatee, heavy boots, and layers of black clothing.

'Where is she?' the intruder demanded, but without lunging at Steven, or in any way threatening violence. On the contrary, he looked a little unsteady on his pins, Steven thought.

'What do you mean?' There was a strange car in the driveway, but no-one else in sight. 'Where is who?'

'Natasha! I know she's here! Where is she?'

'Natasha?' Steven looked back at Avril, whose expression disclaimed any knowledge of their daughter's whereabouts.

'I *know* she's here!' the strange man yelped. 'Her and that bastard Busso! She said she was coming up to the mountains, she told her flatmates!'

'Well she didn't come here,' Steven replied through his teeth. 'Now I suggest –'

'But *he* told his secretary! Oh, he lied to his fucking *wife*, of course – told her he was going to fucking Melbourne, or some bloody thing –'

'Mate, I don't care who told you what.' It was getting cold, standing on the doorstep; Steven's breath turned to steam as it hit the air. 'The fact is, it's one o'clock in the morning, Natasha isn't here, and if you don't get off my property, I'll call the police.'

'But she *must* be here!'

'She's not. Now go away, and if you're lucky, I won't tell Natasha that you came stumbling around here like a drunken bum in the middle of the night, with drool stains all down the front of your shirt.'

Surprised, the intruder dropped his gaze, whereupon Steven slammed the door shut. He turned, and was about to apologise again when there was a sound of knocking.

'Okay, that's it –' he began. But before he could reach the phone, Avril stopped him.

'Wait,' she said. 'Wait. Don't call the police.' She looked very fragile in her clinging silk robe; even in winter, she could never be persuaded to wear a layer of good, thick flannelette. 'We don't want *that* kind of reputation.'

'But –'

'There must be a way, Steven. Let me talk to him. We don't want to make him cross or he might damage something.'

'I don't know,' Steven grumbled.

'Please. It's all right. Really.'

So Steven opened the door again, and Avril addressed the bearded intruder in a soft, sweet voice, explaining that she was Natasha's mother.

'I don't think we've met you,' she said. 'What's your name?'

'Fergus,' the young man replied. He looked suddenly rather deflated, as he stood blinking at Avril's fluttering satin and lace.

'I see.' Avril picked nervously at the breast of her robe. 'Well, if you want to, Fergus, you can come in and have a look at Natasha's room. It's quite empty. The bed's made. She hasn't been up here in at least two months.'

'But she said she was going to the mountains . . .' he muttered.

'Well, she never told *me* she was coming. And I'd like to think that she would at least drop in, if she did come.' A pause. 'Perhaps, if she shows up, I could say that you were looking for her?' Avril tentatively suggested.

An incoherent mumble was the only reply.

'The thing is, Fergus, it's very late. And we have guests here. Paying guests. Couldn't you – I don't know – maybe sort this out with Natasha somewhere else? Please? It really has nothing to do with us. Unless, of course, you'd like to see her room.'

But Fergus didn't want to see Natasha's room. In the absence of Natasha – in the absence of any kind of resistance, and in the face of Avril's disarmingly hesitant demeanour – he backed down the front steps, stumbling a little, and returned to his car.

Admiringly, Steven put a hand on Avril's shoulder.

'Come on,' he said, pulling her inside. 'You'll freeze to death.'

'He shouldn't be driving.'

'As long as he doesn't take out the front gate.'

'Steven, he might *hurt* someone.'

'Well what do you expect me to do?' Closing the door, Steven swung around to face his guests. 'Sorry about that, folks, I'm . . . believe it or not, we don't normally get people trying to bash our door down in the middle of the night.'

'Who's Natasha?' Amanda inquired.

'Natasha's our daughter.' Noting the looks that the Petzls were exchanging, Stephen went on to say: 'I'll be taking $50 off the cost of your rooms tonight. This kind of thing – it really isn't on.'

The prevailing atmosphere immediately lightened. Robin looked pleased; the Petzls muttered an acknowledgement. After wishing each other good-night, they all withdrew, whereupon Avril followed Steven back to their own quarters.

Here she paused beside the silver-framed photograph on the dressing table. It was a photograph of Natasha at her twenty-first birthday party. There had been a string of disgruntled males on that occasion too, as far as Steven could recall. Natasha was twenty-four now, but hadn't changed much.

'Up to her old tricks,' he remarked.

'I'll have to ring her,' was Avril's response.

'Not *now*, for Christ's sake.'

'No.'

'She won't be at home anyway. Judging from what old Fergus said.'

'Oh, she wouldn't come up from Sydney without at least giving me a call.'

Steven grunted. In his opinion, there was no telling what Natasha would do. Not that she was trouble-some, exactly. She had a good job (marketing), no obvious addictions, no chronic illnesses and no out-standing debts – or so it appeared. Steven assumed that she was in no pressing need of money or comfort, because since her teenage years she had never come to her parents for help. She rarely approached them for anything. They hardly saw her from one year to the next, and when her mother spoke to her on the telephone, it was almost always Avril who initiated the call. Natasha was casual and uncommunicative. Like her mother, she took refuge in silence. But unlike Avril, she had a hard, dismissive, hostile way of holding her tongue. Steven didn't quite know what to make of Natasha.

He loved her, of course. That went without saying. And he was proud of her, too; she was a smart girl. Attractive. A credit to him, really. But he was hurt by the manner in which she'd shut them both out of her life, pulling a blank face down over her thoughts at the age of thirteen, and never once, since then, permitting him a glimpse of her true feelings.

For this reason – and because he sensed, uneasily, that her relations with men were not entirely honourable – he preferred not to think about Natasha. It was too upsetting.

'The last boyfriend I heard about was Daniel,' Avril murmured, as she climbed into bed. 'But that was a while ago. She's never mentioned any Fergus.'

'Don't worry about it.'

'I hope she'll be all right.'

'Avril, Natasha can look after herself.'

'He didn't look very nice, did he? Not at all the kind of person you'd expect her to take up with.'

Steven grunted. He had no wish to engage in a conversation about Natasha's romantic entanglements at one-thirty in the morning.

I need my sleep, he thought drowsily. I need my sleep so I can get in there and charm the socks off Celeste Whitfield.

He could do it, no question. She was a simple soul, in many ways. And Maeve O'Meagher – Maeve was a lovely girl. Lovely. Straight as a die, and so earnest it fairly broke your heart.

Reflecting on the manifold good qualities of Maeve O'Meagher, Steven went to sleep smiling.

It was a busy weekend, not least because the guesthouse was full, and the weather miserable. When rain lashed the treetops, and southerlies howled up Leura Mall, tourists tended to congregate in front of warm fires, sipping cups of coffee and demanding entertainment. Though Steven sent his own guests to the cinema, and to Katoomba Plate World, and to various galleries, bookshops, cafes and antique stores, he was nevertheless obliged to spend a lot of time chasing up weather forecasts, demonstrating the mechanics of the video player, hauling loads of wood, locating spare umbrellas, and talking endlessly about the Blue Mountains.

He talked knowledgeably, though he had only been a resident for five years. During his first year in Leura he had joined a bushwalking club, to familiarise himself with all the tracks thereabouts. During his second year, he and Avril had joined the Getaway Association, which met at a different restaurant once every month in order that its members should become aware of which establishments to recommend. At the end of that same year he had been elected to council, and had been plunged into a world of civic functions, local dignitaries, contentious issues and public services of which he had hitherto been ignorant.

So it was that, after five years, he considered himself a bit of an expert on the region. He could answer most inquiries himself and knew where to find the answers to most others. He had memorised the bus and rail timetables. He could name all the local taxidrivers, a large number of the council employees, and a fair number of concerned residents. He could also identify quite a few species of weed – thanks to his wife's tutelage – together with a respectable range of native plants. He read the *Blue Mountains Gazette* from cover to cover (Avril barely glanced at it) and made a point of chatting with receptionists, shop assistants and checkout operators. Gradually, he had even managed to build up a useful fund of mountains-related gossip.

The result was that he supplied his guests with a degree of assistance and insight that they could have obtained almost nowhere else. Yet Avril persisted in regarding his council-related activities as being detrimental to business. It didn't seem to matter that the tradespeople they used had been recommended to Steven by residents whose homes he had visited, while seeking their opinions on issues relating to Ward One. Avril still regarded his sporadic Saturday-afternoon door-to-door treks as a waste of time. If people had complaints or suggestions, she said, they could always contact him. Why bother them at home? Everyone would think that he was a Jehovah's Witness.

But Steven liked pressing the flesh, as he put it. He liked to get about, show his face, and hear what people thought. He liked their astonished expressions when they realised that he really was interested in what they had to say. Sometimes, of course, he encountered snorts of disbelief, furious tirades, or brusque rebuttals. Once he had been attacked by a dog. On the whole, however, people were amazingly kind, or, at the very least, civil; even when they were busy, they accepted his card with expressions of gratitude, and many invited him into their homes.

He had drunk tea with numerous little old ladies, who were grateful for an opportunity to talk, and who were generally under the confused impression that he was their local MP. He had sipped strange herbal concoctions amid dangling crystals and incense burners, flat lemonade amid roaring toddlers, and percolated coffee in beautifully decorated rooms full of silk upholstery and objets d'art. He had heard complaints about rates, roadworks and tip fees, about car parking and garbage collection, about dogs and skateboards. Sometimes he would be asked 'What on earth are you in it for?', and he would laugh, and say that he liked the community; he wanted to make sure that the Blue Mountains got a fair deal.

But the truth was that he missed intimate contact with strangers. He missed visiting people's homes, discussing their dreams, and helping them to fill in their loan application forms. He missed the grateful looks on their faces, whenever he managed to unpick a particularly nasty financial knot on their behalf. He missed many things about his old job, not least the sense of careless expertise that naturally accompanied thirty years of banking experience.

That was why, on Saturday afternoon, he went to Blackheath for two hours, ignoring Avril's accusing look as he walked out into the rain. Although he was only able to visit seven houses during that time, he came away feeling that he had scored a few points. Blackheath residents tended to see themselves as virtually ignored; Katoomba and Leura were regarded as the favoured townships. Blackheath voted for Vera simply because she lived there, and not necessarily because support for her views was widespread.

'Oh. So you're our councillor too?' one dazed-looking young mother, in a run-down rented house, had said to him. 'I thought it was just that woman who lives here. What's her name?'

Another woman, neat and elderly, in a fibro cottage with manicured lawns and lovingly tended beds of violas, had remarked: 'I've never much *cared* for Vera Rudkowski, I don't like her *manner*, or that *fellow* she's taken up with, but at least she did something about getting the footpath repaired up there near the station.'

An interesting afternoon, all things considered. Illuminating. Steven had gone home feeling very satisfied with himself, and had spent most of the evening in conversation with a terrific young bloke from Scotland, who'd had everyone in stitches with his stories about Scottish football fans. The next day he cleaned all five bathrooms with meticulous care, before rushing off to the official opening of a new children's playground. This was not an entirely successful event, thanks to the weather; a damp mist meant that there was no crowd of brightly clad children clambering up and down slippery dips, to gladden the heart of the *Gazette* photographer. But at least the occasion served to keep Steven's thoughts occupied, as he tried to forget the fact that the Labor councillors would be meeting that afternoon.

Bert had told him as much the previous day. 'Only just heard from Pat,' Bert had said cautiously. 'We'll have to consider all our options.' Now, upon encountering each other in the drizzly playground (for Bert made a point of ensuring that there was always a Labor presence at such events), the two men touched only briefly on the topic of mayoral candidates. Hunched beneath an ancient umbrella, Bert remarked quietly that it was a damn shame about Frank Baldwin.

'Poor old Pat,' he said, in his gravelly voice, and they both glanced at the mayor, who was chatting with the president of the local branch of the Lions Club.

'Yes,' Steven replied.

'She's a reasonable sort of mayor, all things considered. Bit slow on the uptake, but her heart's in the right place.'

'You're not wrong.'

Bert peered up at Steven from under his bushy grey eyebrows. At sixty-eight he was the oldest councillor, but he remained pretty vigorous, despite some recent trouble with skin cancers. A stalwart Labor man, he was also a member of Rotary, a supporter of local senior citizens' groups, and a frequent visitor to most of the retirement homes in the Upper Mountains. He was small and nuggety, with a preference for slightly oversized grey suits, and very old, very conservative ties.

'Think you'd do as well as Pat has?' he asked.

'I'd certainly try. Bert –'

'Any damned fool can try.' Looking away, Bert added: 'I'll let you know what we decide to do.'

'Thanks.'

'Can't promise anything.'

'No.'

'Pity about the rain.'

Shortly afterwards, the crowd dispersed. Steven went back home, where he updated the Bella Vista's webpage, sorted out a few bills, and helped George to unload three large bags of grass clippings from the boot of his car. A quick drink with George, a telephone call from a troubled tour operator, and all at once the afternoon had faded into evening. Restlessly, Steven roamed about the house. He poked at the fire and rearranged the brochures. He unloaded the dishwasher. He couldn't seem to settle to any work; his council business paper remained unread on his desk.

At dinner, he was jumpy and distracted, hardly listening as Avril informed him, in a flat little voice (was she still moping?), that she hadn't spoken to Natasha yet. When at last the phone rang, he fairly leapt to his feet and flung himself across the kitchen.

'Yes?' he gasped, lifting the receiver. 'Bella Vista Guesthouse?'

'Oh.' It was Bert. 'That you, Steve?'

'Hello, Bert.'

'Thought I'd better let you know – just out of courtesy.' Bert cleared his throat. 'Finlay's running for mayor.'

'*Finlay?*'

'Chris likes the idea of a Labor mayor, and with Finlay we'll get the Green vote.'

'You're kidding.'

'He's done a deal with Vera. Pretty damn quick off the mark, I'll say that for him.'

'But Jesus, Bert, I mean – *Finlay*.'

'He'll toe the line. Has to.'

'You really want *Finlay* for *mayor*?'

There was a pause at the other end of the line. Steven could hear the tinny yelp of a television or radio announcer in the background.

'Gotta go with the majority, Steve,' Bert said at last. 'It's the way things work. He's not a bad bloke, when you get to know him.'

'Bert –'

'Sorry, but I'll have to sign off. Me tea's on the table. See you Thursday.'

He rang off. Dazed, Steven put the phone down. Finlay Gascoigne? *Finlay Gascoigne?* The place would go to hell in a handcart.

Returning to his chair, Steven surveyed the plate in front of him, before pushing it away. He had lost his appetite.

'There are apricot muffins,' said Avril.

'What? Oh – no, thanks.'

'Cup of coffee?'

'No. Thanks.' Finlay Gascoigne! Finlay was a dubious piece of work – an opinionated, self-satisfied, sneaky little bastard, who called himself a teacher and considered himself an intellectual. The arts were his platform; he turned up to every concert, gallery exhibition and literary lunch in the mountains. Not that there was anything wrong in that, of course. But it was the supercilious *way* he did it, parading around with his face almost permanently set in a sneer (unless he was balefully sulking about something), his 23-year-old girlfriend hanging off his arm like an accessory, his wardrobe proclaiming that he was *of the moment*, his long, pasty cheeks clean shaven except at the line of his jaw, along which a thin, pretentious hedgerow swept up to meet his narrow moustache near the corners of his mouth. Ageing and balding, but fighting this process every step of the way, he favoured berets and panama hats and other distinctive varieties of headgear that Steven found deeply annoying. It was rumoured that he had been a member of the Communist Party in his youth.

On being informed that Steven had once worked as a bank manager, Finlay's cautious air had immediately been transformed into a patronising one. He patronised most people – Avril because she was a housewife, Maeve because she was so young, Bert because he was so old, Celeste because she went to church on Sundays, George because he wore pink polyester shirts – and those he didn't patronise he tended to treat with barely veiled hostility. Allan, for instance. Sue Schaarf. Chris Diacopoulos, who, being handsome, well groomed, sharp, successful and thirty years old, was difficult to patronise, despite the fact that he was a real-estate agent, with no justifiable claim to any kind of artistic insight or humanist sensitivity.

The only councillor who seemed to be on Finlay's wavelength was Vera Rudkowski. Although they had numerous reservations about each other, they also shared many of the same opinions when it came to fast-food outlets, medium-density housing, tourist coaches, arts funding, property developers, public spaces, tree-preservation orders and chain stores. Possibly, Finlay regarded Vera as a little extreme; possibly, Vera regarded Finlay as a bit of a Labor sell-out. But on many things they saw eye to eye.

No wonder they've cut a deal, Steven thought. The amazing thing is that Bert and Chris went along with it. Surely they can't believe that having a Labor mayor is worth the price of Finlay calling the shots at council meetings?

*Not a bad bloke when you get to know him.* My arse, he isn't.

'Bert says that Finlay's running for mayor,' he told Avril mournfully, 'because he's got the Greens in his pocket.'

Avril said nothing. She was carefully cutting up her last potato.

‘Well? What do you think of that?’ Steven wanted to goad her into making some kind of remark. ‘Bit of a bloody disaster, isn’t it?’

Avril forked a fragment of potato into her mouth, chewed it and swallowed it before replying: ‘I don’t see why.’

‘*You don’t see why?*’

‘He seems intelligent enough.’

‘He’s a prick.’

‘Just because he doesn’t share all your opinions –’

‘That’s *not* why he’s a prick, and you know it!’

‘Don’t shout at me, thank you.’

‘You’re just saying this,’ Steven observed, in a sudden flash of inspiration, ‘because you’d rather anyone was mayor but me.’

‘I’m saying it,’ Avril replied, ‘because being mayor isn’t like being a president, or a generalissimo. Whoever’s mayor, it won’t make much difference.’

‘It will to me!’

‘And to me,’ Avril said quietly. ‘But not to anyone else around here. That’s why nobody cares. Except you people on council.’

Then she rose, and picked up the plates. God, she could really be crushing. Steven scowled at her slim, straight back.

Nice to know where the voters stand, he thought crossly.

## CHAPTER THREE

On Monday evening, Natasha answered her phone at long last. She listened silently as her mother described Fergus's brief visit; it was not Natasha's habit, during telephone conversations, to reassure her interlocutor with little exclamations of assent, or grunts of understanding. As a result, Avril often found herself wondering if the line had gone dead. She would say: 'Natty? Are you there?' And Natasha would say: 'Yes, Mum. I'm here', in a tone that almost, but not quite, seemed to suggest that she would have preferred to have been just about anywhere else.

When Avril had finished, Natasha remained silent for a moment longer. Then she remarked that she was sorry, but really it wasn't her fault. Fergus was a lunatic. That was why she had broken up with him.

'Oh! So you're not going out together?' Avril exclaimed, with relief.

'Not anymore.'

'He didn't look like much of a prospect.'

'He isn't.'

'I wonder why he thought you were staying up here?' Avril asked, not wishing to put the question more directly. When Natasha replied, her tone remained slow and calm and just a little flat.

'I've no idea,' she said. 'I did go away, but I went to Canberra.'

'Did you? That's nice.' Avril wondered who might have accompanied her. 'Did you enjoy yourself?'

'I suppose so.'

'Did you go to the National Gallery?'

'No. We were visiting friends.'

'We?'

'Me and Malcolm.'

'Oh.' Malcolm what? Malcolm Busso? 'I don't think I've met Malcolm.'

'No. You wouldn't have.'

'Is he nice?'

'Yeah. He is.' Quite unexpectedly, Natasha added: 'Fergus is freaked out. He won't accept that I don't want to see him anymore. I've told him a million times, but he's so up himself – he just won't believe it.'

'Oh dear.'

'Next time he shows, just call the police. Honestly.

It's the only way to handle him. Stupid jerk.'

'But he's not *bothering* you, Natty?'

'I can deal with it.'

'Are you sure?'

'Mum, I'm fine.'

'Well – you call me if there's any trouble. Or call the police.' Avril hesitated as she juggled phrases in her head. How would she ask? 'Was Fergus deliberately lying, do you think?' she finally queried. 'When he said that your flatmate had told him you were up here?'

'Oh sure. He lies all the time.'

'So when he said that you were . . . um . . . involved with a married man named Busso – that was a lie, too?'

There was a pause. Avril heard the sound of a long, exhaled breath at the other end of the line, and wondered if Natasha was smoking.

'Malcolm's name is Busso,' Natasha drawled. 'Malcolm Busso. But he's not married.'

'He's not?'

'No.'

'Oh. Well. That's good.' Avril girded her loins, and said: 'Separated?'

'No.' For the first time, a trace of expression crept into Natasha's voice. It sounded like amusement. 'Is that what you're worried about, Mum?'

'Well, why not? Married men are a dead end, Natty.'

'I know.'

'They're not worth the trouble.'

'I know.'

'So everything's all right, otherwise?'

It was. As usual, Avril failed to extract very much from her daughter as far as recent activities were concerned. Natasha had bought a beautiful pair of shoes – $160, but they were beautiful; she had walked out of the middle of a lousy movie; her flatmate had broken the video player. Nothing about her job, her friends, her plans, her love life. The conversation wasn't long. Before hanging up, Avril asked Natasha if she was smoking.

'Not right now.'

'Oh, Natty . . .'

'Don't worry, Mum. It's under control.'

Under control. That was certainly one way of describing Natasha, who never seemed to let anything slip. Avril herself was a fairly self-contained, organised sort of person, but Natasha always made her feel slightly shrill. As if a dithering hysteric, visible only to Natasha, were lurking just beneath Avril's reserved facade.

'That was Natasha,' Avril informed Steven, who was sitting at his desk. This desk had been placed on the back verandah, which was protected from the elements by a bank of rattling windows. 'She said she wasn't up here on the weekend. Apparently Fergus is a bit touched. He won't believe that she doesn't want to see him anymore.'

Steven grunted. He was poring over his council business paper.

'Steven? Did you hear me?'

'What? Yeah, I heard you. What about it?'

'Well . . . I just *thought* you might like to know.'

Another grunt. Honestly, he was impossible. When he wasn't absent in the flesh, he was absent in the spirit. But one had to be thankful for small mercies; at least when he was actually at home, he could be relied upon in a crisis. The following night, for example, he went off to a board meeting, leaving Avril to look after the only guests in the house. They were two men from Sydney, Paul and Gene, who shared the same bed. Avril wondered how they managed to sleep, because they were both very large, and the bed was only a double – but that didn't seem to trouble them. In fact, like a good many of the male couples who found their way to her guesthouse, they were scrupulously clean and deeply impressed by Avril's attention to detail, sighing with envy as they surveyed her quilts and her samplers. (Avril always welcomed such men serenely into her house for that very reason, and was particularly attentive to their needs.)

Shortly after seven o'clock, Paul and Gene went out to dinner. Avril subsequently spent some time applying a mixture of boiled soft soap, soda and bleach to the smoke-stained marble mantlepiece in the drawing room. She then ironed and laid the cloth for tomorrow's breakfast table, set out various pieces of highly polished silverware, unloaded the dishwasher, and sat down to watch television. At nine, Paul and Gene returned. By 9:15, Gene was vomiting frantically, his arms around the toilet bowl in the second bathoom.

'Food poisoning!' Paul cried, upon summoning Avril. 'It must be food poisoning!'

'Oh, no. I don't think so,' Avril demurred. 'You went to Carmen's, didn't you? They've a very good restaurant there. Top-class chefs. I'm sure they're terribly careful . . .'

'Well, what else could it be?!'

'I don't know.' Avril's own stomach was churning at the smell. 'A virus, perhaps?'

'Call a doctor!'

'No, no,' Gene groaned. 'No doctor.'

'You've got to have a doctor!'

'I don't know any doctors around here who do house calls,' said Avril in a small voice. 'But I'll try.'

Escaping thankfully to the telephone, she tried an after-hours number, and had to leave a message. After forty-five minutes, when the stink of vomit and diarrhoea in the Blue Room was almost impenetrable, her call was returned – and she was advised that, if things looked very bad, then Gene should report to the hospital's emergency room.

Gene was adamant.

'Not the hospital,' he gasped. 'No way.'

'He can't go to the emergency room!' Paul exclaimed. 'He'll puke all over everything!'

'I think it's getting better.' Gene's hoarse voice echoed strangely, for he was speaking into the toilet bowel. 'It's not so bad . . .'

'Don't you have any Maxolon or anything?'

Avril had to confess that she didn't, in fact, have any Maxolon or anything. This went down rather badly. So did the information that none of the local chemists was open after nine o'clock. Wiping up vomit with one of Avril's bathmats, Paul pointed out that a guesthouse ought to have a fully equipped first-aid box with antinausea medication, while Gene retched and sobbed and groaned. It was all most unpleasant.

At twenty past ten, Steven returned – just as Gene's symptoms were beginning to abate. He was still vomiting, but at more widely spaced intervals. While Avril hovered helplessly in the background, Steven hastened to offer comfort in the form of reassuring words, sympathetic jokes, a strong arm and an old packet of Gastrolyte, which happened to be lurking at the back of the medicine cabinet, behind his after-shave lotion.

By half past eleven, Gene was safely tucked into bed – though every hour or two thereafter, until about four o'clock in the morning, Avril was awakened briefly by the sound of a flushing toilet.

'If only you'd been here!' she exclaimed the next morning, while Steven was getting dressed.

'I don't see what *I* could have done,' he replied, 'except hold the poor bugger up.'

'But you're so good with sick people. You don't have a weak stomach.'

'Rubbish.'

'You know what to say.'

'It's not what you *say*, it's what you *do*.'

'You should have been here. What if he'd died?'

'Avril.' Steven turned, one sock dangling from his fingers. 'I can't always be here.'

'No. But it would be nice if you were here *sometimes*.'

'I am.'

'When?'

'Yesterday afternoon.' He had assumed the patient, patronising tone that resulted from years of dealing with fifteen-year-old customer-service officers. Avril found it deeply insulting. 'Didn't you see me?'

'I saw you,' she retorted, 'but you weren't here. Your body was here, but your mind was somewhere else.'

'Rubbish.'

'Oh. I see. So that's going to be your response to everything I say, is it? "Rubbish".'

'Avril . . .' He was pulling on his jumper. 'It's too early for this. Okay? And we've both got a lot to do.'

'Well I'm sorry, but I have to take advantage of your presence when I can, Steven.'

'God,' he said, and sighed. Then he sat down and began to tie his shoelaces. 'You know, this isn't going to work. Not this time.'

'What do you mean?'

'You know what I mean.'

'No, I don't.' In fact she had an inkling, but wasn't going to admit it. Not when the whole argument was so unreasonable – so *outrageous* – that it didn't even deserve to be acknowledged.

'Avril, it's always the same,' he said calmly, but in a measured way that spoke of hidden tension. 'You don't like me going out and finding things to do. That's what it is. It was the same with –'

'Not when you've got a business to run!'

'It was the same with the golf club,' he continued inexorably, 'it was the same with the Smith Family, now it's the same with the council. It's got nothing to do with the business. It's you.'

'That's so –'

'Just because *you're* completely focused on this house doesn't mean that *I* have to be. I can't sit around here all day. You know that.' He rose. 'Now

I'm going out to start the fire, and I suggest you get stuck into breakfast, or it isn't going to be ready in time. Not,' he added, 'that Gene's going to be eating very much, poor bastard. I just hope the hashed mutton doesn't make him start vomiting again.'

Whereupon, having thoroughly denigrated Avril's culinary skills, Steven strode from the room before she could protest. It was a cowardly action. He knew that she couldn't pursue him – not when there were guests in the house. But he had fled, she was certain, because he didn't want to hear her obvious retort.

The fact was, Steven only went out and found things to do when he wanted to escape from something at home. His interest in the golf club had surfaced when Avril was helping to nurse her terminally ill mother. His charity work had coincided with Natasha's arrival; she had been a difficult, colicky baby, though not as difficult as Steven, who had resented the broken nights, the late dinners, the endless crying and the absence of sexual intercourse. So bitterly had he resented these things that he had absented himself, for longer and longer periods, until Avril had been forced to complain – to *insist* upon his attendance. Whereupon he had fought back, with great success, by proving to be utterly incompetent in the kitchen, the sickroom and the nursery. Bottoms had been burnt out of saucepans. Thermometers had shattered at the sound of Steven's approach. Natasha's dirty nappies, whenever her father bore the responsibility for them, had forever been sliding messily off her chubby behind, or turning up under sofa cushions. Avril couldn't decide whether Steven's lack of skill was deliberate or not, but whatever its cause, the result was all he could have desired. Rather than expose Natasha to the risk of gastroenteritis, or her mother to the clumsiness of Steven's ministrations – which might result in soiled sheets, or incorrect dosage, or even a fall from bed – Avril had finally relieved her husband of his duties. So although he'd not returned to his golf or his charity work, he had been left with an inordinate amount of spare time, which he'd devoted to the construction of a fish pond in which Natasha nearly drowned at the age of three. (It had subsequently been filled in, at Avril's insistence.)

Now, Avril felt sure, Steven was trying to escape from their business. He'd never managed his own business before; he had always been an employee. Obviously the stress of the undertaking was beginning to affect him. Obviously, for Steven, it was far easier to advise other people on the functions and financing of *their* businesses than it was to keep on top of his own. Too many petty details, probably; he'd always been a bit of a big-picture man.

Well – if he won't give it his best shot, Avril thought, then things can only get worse. He's got to be made to see that. He's got to understand that we *can* pull this off as long as we *work together*.

As long as we agree that the business comes first.

On Wednesday the skies cleared, and some wedding guests arrived. They were not, to Avril's disappointment, the bride's immediate family; she did not have an opportunity to view the gown, the bouquets or the going-away outfit. Instead she had to satisfy herself with two plastic-wrapped dresses of somewhat skimpy design, one mauve, one teal, which were hung in her own wardrobe (because the cupboards in the guestrooms would not accommodate their trailing skirts). These two dresses belonged to the girlfriends of the groom's two attendants, who were raucous young men, without, as far as Avril could see, anything to recommend them except healthy constitutions and an ability to drive cars. One of them shared a room with his girlfriend; the other was constantly trying to invade the privacy of the second girl, who had evidently, and understandably, insisted on a room of her own.

This girl seemed nice enough. She kept her room clean, and complimented Avril on the beauty of the house. Her companions, however, joked about Avril's breakfast spread, broke one of her teacups, and left their bathrooms in such a mess that by the end of their three-night stay Steven was muttering that they should be charged extra. Within an hour of meeting them, Avril was beginning to worry about her counterpanes, not to mention the glassware that stood on the marble-topped commodes.

She rather feared for the solemnity of the wedding, with such young people in attendance. Would they let off firecrackers? Would they put whoopee cushions on the pews, or pass out from the effects of strong liquor while the vows were bring exchanged? Anything was possible.

On Thursday, when she was hanging out the laundry (having first cleaned the line with a notched cork, as was her habit), Avril reflected on her own wedding. It had been a triumph, and an event to remember. Endless planning had resulted in flawless execution. Despite the fact that Avril's parents had not entirely approved of Steven – who was, after all, a bus-driver's son – they had been lavish with their financial support. One hundred guests had been invited to a stone church decked with white roses: afterwards, the reception had been held at a former seminary, with prawn cocktails in crystal glasses served on linen tablecloths, and piano music, and dancing to the easy-listening repertoire of a band dressed in bow ties and white dinner jackets. Beautiful. Graceful. Elegant.

And in the midst of it all had been Steven, so handsome in his black-and-white suit (thank God she hadn't let him wear one of those dreadful brown seventies abominations!), his smile big and white in his lean, tanned face. Contrary to bridal tradition, *he* had been the radiant one. Avril had been too sick with relief and anxiety to enjoy the occasion much. She had been worried that something would go wrong: that the reception would be undercatered, that she would stumble during the bridal waltz, that her skin would break out, that Steven would turn to her at the altar and say, 'There's been a mistake.' For Steven had been a catch – no doubt about it. Not rich, of course, but handsome and charming and clever and attentive and so beautifully *easy* in his dealings with everyone, male and female, young and old, high and low. No company appeared to intimidate him; no-one seemed impervious to his wide grin and his bright, questing gaze and his pleasant conversation. Even Avril's father, a crusty old journalist, had succumbed in the end. After Steven had once dealt competently with a shredded fanbelt when Avril's parents' car had broken down, Avril's father had declared Steven to be 'a good man'. 'I reckon there's nothing that bloke can't handle,' he'd said, and Avril had agreed. She had seen Steven cope with all the things that she couldn't cope with: fanbelts, tap-washers, irate motorists, insurance forms, mortgage contracts, boisterous teenagers, even tearful great-aunts. She hadn't known, when she married him, that he couldn't cope with long-term stress. With the dreary minutiae of everyday existence.

Well, she knew it now. And she had suffered for it. And he had the *gall* to accuse her of holding him back, when all he wanted to do was escape from his more taxing responsibilities!

The phone rang. Because it was hanging off her belt, Avril was able to answer it immediately. George Lovecek was on the other end of the line.

'Oh. Hello, George,' she said.

'Hello. How are you?'

'Fine. And you?'

'Great. Listen, I found the name of that landscape bloke. The one who repairs stone walls. Remember you were asking?'

'Yes, of course. Thanks so much. You're very kind.'

'Do you want the details? Now?'

'Hang on a minute. Just let me go inside and find a pen.'

'You're outside? Lucky you. It's a beautiful day, isn't it?'

'Lovely.'

'When I think of all the gardening I have to do . . . and here I am, stuck in the shop.'

'Oh, you'll get it done. I know you. Your garden never suffers. Not like ours.'

'What do you mean? What's wrong with your garden?'

'Oh, just the usual. I have to transplant that rhododendron, and feed the roses, and prune all those daisies, and do *quantities* of weeding, and when am I ever going to get the time?' Arriving in the kitchen, Avril picked up a pen and stood poised over the Laura Ashley memorandum pad. 'I'm inside now, George – do you want to give me those details?'

He did, then asked about the rhododendron. What rhododendron? And why did it have to be moved?

'Oh, didn't I tell you? It's sitting out in the blazing sun. Not doing well at all, now that we've cut back all that ghastly honeysuckle. But it's quite big, you know, which means I'm going to need help – and Steven's always so busy . . .'

'Would you like me to help?'

Dear George, she thought. What a *nice* man.

'No, no,' she said. 'I wouldn't dream of asking.'

'You didn't ask. I offered.'

'But you've got all your own gardening to do. You just told me.'

'Yes. And you just told *me* that I'd get it done.'

Avril laughed. 'Well, you know you're always welcome,' she said, 'no matter what you do when you get here. Of course I'd love to have your help. But don't put yourself out on my account, please.'

'I won't. It's good exercise. Is Steven around?'

'No, I'm afraid not. I don't know where he is.'

'Oh.'

'But I certainly hope he shows up soon, because I've got a nasty feeling that one of our guests is going to start lugging cases of beer into the bedroom, or something.' Avril went on to describe the new guests in scathing terms, before making George laugh with an account of Tuesday night's gastric attack.

'It was so disgusting,' she finished mournfully. 'Having to deal with the laundry, I mean. The towels, and so forth.'

'But the linen service . . .?'

'Only picks up my white towels. I wash all the coloured bathmats and facecloths. Besides, the linen service only comes once a week. You can't have dry vomit sitting in the laundry basket for three days.'

'No. I suppose not.'

'I wish Steven had been there. I'm so *hopeless* at that kind of thing.'

'I bet you aren't.'

'Yes, I am, George, really. And Steven's so good at dealing with people. And now he wants to go off and become mayor! When I hardly see him as it is!'

There was a pause. Avril wondered if she should perhaps have stayed off the subject. But George said: 'Yes. I didn't think you'd be too thrilled about that,' and sighed.

'It's just that there are some things I can't deal with,' Avril confessed. 'I'm pathetic, I know, but I simply can't. Cars and things. Neighbours. Dianne would take it all in her stride, she's so competent, but I'm incapable of changing a car tyre. Or drilling a hole.'

'I know what you mean,' George replied, with slightly awkward humour. 'Dianne's so capable she makes me feel inadequate most of the time.'

'Of course I know I ought to learn,' Avril went on, 'but how can I, when I've got so much else to do? Oh dear. And here I am, moaning into your ear, George. I'm so sorry.'

'No, no. It's all right.'

'And you've probably got people lining up there, waiting to be served. Well, I'll get off, now, and leave you in peace. Unless there's anything else you wanted to ask?'

'No. Not really. Though I . . .' He hesitated. 'I probably should mention that Dianne saw Natasha on the weekend. At the Fremont.'

'What?' Avril was so shocked, she actually had to sit down. 'You mean *my* Natasha?'

'Yes.' There was another pause. 'The thing is, she didn't seem at all put out when Dianne said hello. Not as if she was hiding or anything. I thought – I mean – you did know that she was staying there, didn't you? Dianne thought you must have, but you didn't say a word to me. Though it's none of my business, of course.'

'No. I mean, I didn't know.'

'Oh.' He sounded crestfallen. 'Sorry. I probab shouldn't have –'

'Please. It's all right. Why shouldn't you?'

'Damn it. I wish I'd – now I wish I hadn't said anything.'

'George, it doesn't matter. Really. Sometimes children just don't want their parents around.'

'She didn't ask Dianne not to say anything.'

'She's an adult. If she wants to come up here for a romantic weekend, she's free to do so without having her mother breathing down her neck.' Avril laughed gently, all the while thinking: she lied to me! 'I know that *I* wouldn't have wanted *my* mother around, in those circumstances. Would you?'

'No. Perish the thought.'

'Well – I'd love to chat, but I've a raft of things to do. So I'll see you later, shall I?'

'Saturday?'

'What?'

'Saturday. I could come and help you transplant that rhododendron on Saturday.'

'Oh. All right. Lovely. After you close the shop?'

'Fine.'

And he hung up. She lied to me, Avril thought, mechanically tearing the top page off the memo pad, and pinning it to the cork board that hung near the refrigerator. Why would Natty lie? Because she knew that I wouldn't like the boy she was with?

didn't want to hurt my feelings, Avril se she came up here, and knew that wouldn't want to meet us (what boy- unless he was being considered as a law?), and she didn't want to tell me in case I was hurt that she hadn't dropped in.

It seemed a reasonable enough explanation. Avril pondered it for a while, became satisfied that it must be the truth, and felt much happier. She wouldn't tell Steven. Steven would make some hurtful remark. He found it difficult to understand why Natasha should value her independence so much, not realising that an only child must always fight harder to loosen the parental bonds. Natty has to prove to herself that she's her *own person*, Avril thought. And after all, she's still very young. And maybe she meant to drop in on her way back home, but ran out of time at the last minute.

Unless, of course, Malcolm Busso really *was* unsuitable?

Reflecting on the infinite number of possible flaws that might distinguish Natasha's new boyfriend (married? elderly? teenaged? a biker?), Avril returned to her pegs and her washing line, one ear cocked for the crash that she half expected to hear from the bedrooms currently occupied by those two raucous young men.

Still snoozing, of course, though it was practically midday.

Really, you couldn't blame Natty for avoiding her parents' home. Why not, when it was always full of loud-voiced yobbos who left blood-spotted ribbons of toilet paper on the bathroom floor after they had shaved in the mornings?

Steven went to a council meeting that night. He returned at half past eleven, waking Avril by dropping his shoe (on purpose, she felt sure) and subsequently pouring breathless speculations into her ear as she groped under the pillow for her handkerchief. Pat, he told her, normally gave Celeste a lift back to Warrimoo after council meetings. Tonight, however, Chris Diacopoulos had offered Celeste a lift – and she had accepted. Now why was that? Was Chris trying to influence Celeste? Would he try to persuade Celeste that Finlay would make a good mayor?

'Maybe I ought to call Allan,' Steven fretted, sitting on the edge of the bed. 'I've been holding off, because I figured – well, who's Allan going to vote for, except me?'

Avril grunted.

'I thought that if *I* called *him*, then he might expect me to make some sort of offer. In return for his vote,' Steven continued. 'I mean, he'll probably expect it anyway, but I thought that if I waited for *him* to make a move, then I'd be in a slightly stronger position. Don't you think?'

Avril sighed.

'And I need to keep my deputy vote in reserve. I don't want to promise it to Allan if I don't have to. And I shouldn't have to. Like I said – who else is he going to vote for?'

'Steven,' Avril said at last, plaintively, 'I don't *care*. I really don't care. Now turn off the light and go to sleep.'

'How could Chris persuade Celeste about Finlay, of all people?' Absorbed in his meditations, Steven didn't seem to notice Avril's tone. He did, however, change into his pyjamas, turn off his bedside lamp and slip under the covers. 'Celeste hates Finlay. She knows he wants to ban cats from the Blue Mountains. What makes Chris think she'll come round?'

Avril kicked him drowsily in the kneecap, and he was silenced for a time. Just before drifting off, however, she heard him mumble something about Ward Three. Was he talking in his sleep now? Would she have to start buying earplugs?

The next morning, he tried once again to interest her in the question of what Chris Diacopoulos was up to. Should he call Bert? Should he call Celeste? Should he call Allan? At last, Avril could take it no longer.

'Call anyone,' she said. 'Just stop asking me what to do. How should I know?'

'Just thought you might have an opinion . . .'

'Well, I don't. Now could you take this porridge out, please? I'm running late – here.' Not that it mattered much, since the raucous wedding guests would probably miss breakfast again, and the French couple had ordered their breakfast for a quarter to nine. 'What do you think? Should we light a fire? I think it's going to be quite warm.'

Steven declared that no fire would be necessary. As he ladled porridge into the big tureen, he told Avril that various developments had been approved by council the night before, including one medium-density retirement community in Hazelbrook. 'Which really put Vera's nose out of joint,' he said with satisfaction. 'It doesn't seem to occur to her that older people might need smaller homes, and lots of company.'

'Where's the biggest frying pan? Oh. There.'

'I said to her: "Perhaps you'd prefer our senior citizens to move out of the Blue Mountains, Councillor?" That got her back up.'

'I'm sure. Excuse me.'

'She said she wasn't satisfied that the proposal met with requirements laid down by Development Control Plan No. 10, but I know that's only an excuse. She doesn't want to offend her hippy mates.'

'Steven, would you *please* get out of my way? I'm trying to get into that cupboard.'

'Bert was over the moon,' Steven concluded, wandering out of the kitchen. 'I think he might want to move into that complex himself, when he gets a bit older.'

The French couple were charming. Small and spry, and beautifully turned out, they couldn't open their mouths without praising fulsomely everything that Avril had to offer. They loved the food. They loved the house. They loved Leura and the mountains and the light and the *untouched* quality of all that bush, that endless, blue-green bush, so wild and yet so tame, not threatening at all, though it had such a remote aspect.

'Perhaps because it contains no cougars or grizzly bears?' Mme Vourzay remarked. 'No blood-soaked history? One doesn't feel that hostile eyes are watching one's descent.'

'Well . . . there are some pretty nasty snakes,' said Steven. 'And spiders.'

'Oh, yes. In your garden, Steve?'

'Sometimes.'

'How strange. To have death lurking in that garden.' Mme Vourzay glanced out the window. 'Such a civilised garden. No wild trees at all. Is it a great effort to keep the bush at bay? Must you beat back encroaching eucalypts?'

Steven glanced at Avril, who was bringing in the sweetbreads. 'I don't know,' he said uncertainly. 'You'd better ask my wife.'

'It's the introduced species that are the problem,' Avril observed. 'Privet and ivy and so forth.'

'Ah. So this quiet garden, with all its foreign plants so neatly trimmed – this garden is the aggressor? Are all its pollens and berries creeping into the bush?'

'I . . . I suppose so. In a way.'

'How odd.'

The other guests emerged some time around eleven, banging doors and laughing loudly. They were going off to a cafe for brunch, before attending a wedding rehearsal. Fortunately, the Vourzays had already left; Avril shrank from exposing them to all the very worst aspects of Australia. As she had foreseen, the Vourzays left their bathroom in almost immaculate condition. Certain other guests appeared to have spent the night executing finger paintings on their vanity mirrors with hair mousse and shaving cream.

Steven was on his knees in a shower stall, complaining about this, when Pat rang.

'Well, Pat,' said Avril, who answered the phone, 'he's a bit busy, right now –'

'It's okay.' Steven appeared suddenly at her elbow, splashed with water and out of breath. 'I can take it.'

Avril pointed at her watch, but Steven chose to ignore the fact that it was already a quarter past twelve, and he had only cleaned two bathrooms. What would happen if the new guests arrived early? They were actually due at half past one.

'Oh, yes. Right. Uh-huh.' Damn him. He was frowning, his gaze on the floor, as he responded to the faint gabble issuing from the telephone receiver. Suddenly he stiffened. '*What?*' he exclaimed. 'You're joking! She can't be serious . . . what? But for Chris-sake . . . yes. I don't believe it. I do *not* believe it . . . Pat, this can't happen. Finlay for mayor and her for deputy? I mean . . . I know. I know. *Un*believable. Jesus . . . But no-one's going to have a bar of it, surely? You reckon? Bloody hell . . .'

Sighing, Avril went to her bedroom. Here she divested herself of her wool skirt and cotton blouse, replacing them with a frayed pair of trousers and one of Steven's old shirts. It looked as if *she* would have to clean the bathrooms now.

'. . . So what if he'd be the first Lower Mountains mayor in twenty years, or whatever?' Steven was saying, when she returned to the kitchen. 'What's the point of having a Lower Mountains mayor if he's against everything that you campaigned for? I don't understand. It's ridiculous.'

Upon entering the bathroom, Avril began to wipe the tiles that Steven had so promptly abandoned. She scrubbed various patches of grouting with a tooth-brush, and removed a sliver of soap from the ceramic soap dish set into the wall. As she worked, she could hear her husband talking.

'. . . I hope you pointed out . . . yes. She said what?

Oh, come on. Pressure? What kind of pressure? Once he's in, that's it. She won't have an ounce of leverage. Not with that guy. He doesn't know the meaning of the word gratitude. What's that? Oh . . .'

He went on for exactly twenty-three minutes. By the time he'd finished, Avril had passed from the shower stall to the toilet bowl. She was wiping off urine stains when he addressed her from the bathroom doorway, leaning against it as if shock had deprived him of his sense of balance.

'Celeste,' he announced dramatically, 'is going to support Finlay's bid for mayor.'

Avril said nothing.

'Pat ran into her at Springwood this morning. Celeste said that Chris offered her deputy. He told her it would be good for them both if Finlay became mayor, because Finlay's Lower Mountains. He said Bert would make Finlay toe the Labor line, and not go crazy. Can you believe that?'

Still Avril remained silent.

'Deputy mayor! Celeste! My God, they must be desperate.' There was a pause; Steven appeared to be lost in a series of complex calculations. 'Celeste is the key,' he said at last. 'With Celeste, they've got seven. Seven votes. Unless Maeve has second thoughts. She might. She and Finlay don't get along.' Another pause. 'I'd better phone George about this. See what he thinks.'

Avril was so furious that she had all but lost the

power of speech. As Steven strode away, however, she recovered the use of her tongue, and called sharply: 'Steven!'

'What?' his voice echoed back along the corridor; he hadn't stopped moving.

'*Steven!*'

No reply.

Avril threw down her sponge, ripped off her gloves, and marched into the kitchen. Steven was already punching out George's number on the telephone keypad.

'Are you going to finish the bathrooms?' she inquired, with what she considered to be commendable restraint.

'What? Oh. In a minute.' He was holding the receiver to his ear. 'George? Mate? Listen, you won't believe this, but Pat just called . . .'

Stifling an impulse to wrench the receiver from his hand and stuff it down his throat, Avril returned to her half-cleaned toilet. While Steven conducted a thorough inquiry over the phone, making at least three more calls, she wiped and polished and scrubbed and sprayed and generally made sure that the bathrooms looked presentable. She was preparing to mop the very last floor when Steven approached her again, this time looking flustered and apologetic.

'Sorry about that,' he said. 'My fault entirely. I just had to settle a few things.'

Avril refused to talk to him, savagely wringing out the mop before slapping it down on the floor again.

'Here. Let me.' He reached for the handle, which she let drop, so that it clattered onto the tiles at their feet. Once again, she removed her rubber gloves.

'I'm sorry,' Steven pleaded. 'I'll make it up to you.'

'When?'

'Whenever.'

'You mean when you haven't got a council meeting or an interview or a works inspection.'

'Avril.'

'Do you really think,' she remarked, in shrill exasperation, 'that I won't be cleaning bathrooms when you become mayor?'

'*If* I become mayor.' He made a wry face. 'It doesn't look good at the moment. Unless I can somehow convince Celeste that she's being a goddamn fool.'

'Augh!' Avril threw up her hands. She left the bathroom with Steven in pursuit, hurrying to change her clothes before the new guests arrived.

'Look – Avril – I'd get paid extra for being mayor.' He followed her into their own quarters. 'We could use that money to hire someone. Someone who'll clean the bathrooms.'

'Huh!' She snorted. 'As if we could find anyone who'd do it properly!'

'Of course we could. Why not? I'm not the only

chap in the world who can disinfect a toilet.'

'It seems to me,' said Avril, unbuttoning her shirt, 'that money like that would be better spent on other things. Like a mirror for the mantlepiece – a good one. Or new cupboards in the laundry.'

'Avril, first things first –'

'That's right! I agree! First things first!'

Steven began to look annoyed. 'You know,' he said, 'believe it or not, this house doesn't happen to be the most important thing in life.'

'Oh yes it is, Steven. It's our livelihood.'

'Just because you're bloody obsessed with the place –'

'I am not!'

'I've seen you *mooning* over it.'

'I don't *moon*. I simply pay proper attention to detail . . .'

The doorbell rang. Breathing heavily, Avril and Steven stared at each other.

'The Mitchells,' said Steven.

'You get it,' said Avril. 'I'm not presentable.'

'They're early,' said Steven, and went off to greet the newly arrived guests, leaving Avril to fume as she donned her hostess clothes again. How dare he call her obsessed! It was sour grapes, that was all – sour grapes, pure and simple. He just couldn't bear it when her attention was diverted from him.

And he wondered why Natasha never came home!

Had it ever occurred to him that poor Natasha was sick of competing? That she didn't want to fight for every bit of notice paid to her?

He was jealous. Jealous of the house, because it was just as handsome as he was, and attracted equal amounts of attention.

What a child.

# CHAPTER FOUR

Steven felt mildly guilty about the bathrooms. Avril might be obsessive, but she was quite right: he should have done the bathrooms on Friday. They were his responsibility, after all. So on Saturday morning, after the young larrikins had left (earlier than usual, and looking uncharacteristically well groomed – though awkward and uneasy – in their wedding tuxedos), he tackled his cleaning routine with great energy and enthusiasm, singing Gilbert and Sullivan choruses in a baritone that always sounded much better when it was bouncing off a tiled wall.

The sun was shining. It was going to be a beautiful day. Perhaps he would take the guests on a bushwalk that afternoon. Many people appreciated his company when it was offered to them, especially in view of the fact that he was familiar with all the best walks. Some guests, of course, liked to be left alone. The Mitchells, for instance, appeared to be just a little stand-offish. But those other two – Cindy and Maynard – looked ready for anything, though they must have been pushing seventy.

I hope I'm like that when I'm seventy, Steven thought. I probably will be. Avril, on the other hand, ought to watch herself. She doesn't get out enough.

'Steven!' He suddenly realised that she was standing at the door; his noisy rendition of 'A Wandering Minstrel, I' had masked the sound of her approach. 'George is here,' she said, 'if you want to say hello.'

'George?' He was lost, for an instant. 'What for?'

'Don't you remember? I told you last night. He's come to help me transplant that rhododendron.'

'Oh.' More gardening stuff. He seemed to recall her mentioning something about George, but his mind had been on the Local Environmental Plan at the time, and he had not paid much attention. 'Tricky sort of job, is it?' he asked, assuming that it must require an elevated level of esoteric horticultural expertise.

'Well . . . it's a heavy one,' Avril replied. 'It's quite a big plant.'

'Will you need me for anything?'

'No.' She spoke firmly. 'No. You just finish the bathrooms.'

'All right. I will,' he said, deciding that he wouldn't take offence at her tone. It was too nice a day for domestic tension. 'I'll just say hello to George, though. Quickly. Don't want to put him off side.'

George was standing in the garden, short and tubby and looking (Steven decided with amusement) not unlike a mushroom in his wide-brimmed Akubra. He wore baggy, dirt-encrusted pants and a pair of leather gloves. A stack of highly specialised gardening equipment lay on the grass beside him.

'G'day,' said Steven.

'Hello,' said George.

'Turned out pretty nice, eh?'

'Very.'

'So.' Folding his arms, Steven regarded the rhododendron. 'This is the blighter, is it? Looks a bit sick.'

'That's why we're moving it,' Avril pointed out. She too was dressed in gardening clothes, but, unlike George, managed to invest them with a certain degree of weathered elegance. Trousers always looked great on Avril. 'We have to move it out of the sun a bit.'

'I see. Well. Good luck.' Steven turned back to George, who gave the impression of being ever so slightly uncomfortable. (Why?) 'I'm afraid I can't help you, mate – I've been ordered to finish the bathrooms.'

'Oh, don't worry. We'll be fine,' said George. 'It's not that big a job.'

'If you say so. I tell you what, though – when you're done, we'll have a beer together.' Glancing from George to Avril, and back again, Steven was suddenly struck by a faint suspicion. Jesus, he thought, sourly diverted: this looks a bit familiar. Then, to tease, he said, 'How's Dianne, by the way? Everything all right there?'

'Absolutely,' George replied.

'Good. Good. Well, back to the bathroom. Give me a yell if you need anything.'

Which they won't, he reflected sardonically, returning to his scourers and disinfectants. Suddenly he wasn't cheerful anymore. He no longer felt like singing; instead, as he scrubbed furiously away at patches of soap scum, he cursed Avril and her underhand methods of coercion. People regarded her as being so defenceless, with her delicate bones and her fading voice and her gentle manner. What they didn't know was that she used these characteristics strategically in her battles with Steven, coming on so helpless, so incapable, that she triggered the protective instinct in any other male who happened to be in the vicinity. And she did it on purpose. She did it whenever Steven found something to do away from home – whether it was charity work or public service or even a series of golf tournaments – so that the next thing he knew, every time he turned around there was some bloke lurking in the background, changing fuses or ferrying her to hospital with a sick child.

It had happened twice before. It was one of the techniques employed by Avril to reel Steven back in. Obviously she was using the same method again, only this time she'd picked the wrong target. George, of all people! Steven had to laugh. Previously, she had cast her net at a neighbour and at Steven's cousin Paul. On both occasions, she had thrown her gasping, floundering catch back into the water as soon as Steven repented. Oh, there had been nothing *physical* about her relationship with either man; Steven was sure of that. She just had a way of making things seem more intimate than they really were.

Now it looked as if she might have George in her sights. She didn't realise that, unlike Paul or that idiot with the toupee, George was Steven's good friend. It was highly unlikely that George would succumb to Avril's wiles; the guilt would make him too wretched. He was an honourable man, was George – a man who, in any case, was firmly under Dianne's thumb. George needed a strong woman like Dianne to give him that extra bit of backbone. Avril could never supply him with enough support.

Besides, mused Steven, I've rumbled her little game. I know that she wouldn't have the guts to actually take George to bed. She just wants to flirt and languish and jiggle him under my nose for a while. Well, she can jiggle all she wants; I won't bite. I'm going full steam ahead with this campaign. And if she doesn't like it, she can cry on George's shoulder.

The telephone rang. Scowling, Steven went to answer it. He was surprised to hear Allan Purchese pronounce his name.

'Hello, Allan,' he said. 'What's up?'

'Ah . . . just been thinking, Steve. About some news I've heard.' Allan generally spoke slowly and softly. He was fifty-two, only a year older than Steven, and part-owner of a pine furniture warehouse in Penrith, together with a restaurant in Glenbrook. (His wife managed the restaurant.) A prominent member of the Blaxland Chamber of Commerce, he was always leading the pack when it came to small-business issues, industrial parks, budgetary questions and market permits. Although Steven rather liked him, he didn't trust him entirely – for Allan, who rarely lost his temper or even raised his voice, was reputed to be a behind-the-scenes manipulator. A political animal. A bit of a dark horse.

But Steven appreciated the fact that Allan was at least professional when it came to his duties as a councillor. Despite the fact that he was overweight, he always dressed neatly and appropriately. He seemed to grasp the essentials of every item on the council agenda, and religiously attended every meeting of every committee to which he'd been appointed. Indeed, he was practically omnipresent, a large, smooth, benign feature of the council chambers, articulate, unflustered, and reliably (though not noisily) opposed to everything that fell from Vera Rudkowski's lips.

Steven did wonder, though, about his principles. They seemed a bit elastic sometimes.

'What news is that?' he asked, whereupon Allan replied: 'I hear that you're running for mayor, Steve.'

'Oh. Right.'

'And Finlay is too, I hear.'

'Yes.' Steven waited.

'Interesting choice. On the one hand, Steve, you're a bloke I can talk to. A reasonable bloke.' There was a brief, ruminative silence. 'On the other hand, Finlay happens to represent my ward. Mine and Sue's. You can see our dilemma.'

'Not really,' Steven retorted. 'Looks like a pretty obvious choice, to me.'

'Well – on a *personal* level, I agree with you.' Allan's voice was soothing. 'Finlay's not an easy guy to get along with, on a personal level. But in our situation, we have to think of the bigger picture, don't we? We have to think of the residents. And I can't help wondering if the residents of Ward Four might do better with Finlay as mayor.'

'If you say so, Allan.' Swallowing his anger, Steven refused to make the obvious response. He knew that Allan was simply trying to manoeuvre him into making an offer – or why bother ringing at all? 'I guess you've got to vote the way your conscience dictates.'

'Yes.' There was another pause. Steven decided that he had managed to startle Allan, and was pleased by his own cunning. 'Of course,' Allan continued, 'the residents of Ward Four would probably be just as well served if you were mayor and I was deputy. That's a possibility worth considering.'

My arse it is, thought Steven.

'Well . . . I dunno, mate,' he said, feeling quite certain that Allan Purchese would rather forego a large chunk of his quarterly profits than see Finlay Gascoigne as mayor. 'I mean, even if I had your support – and Sue's, as well – it would still only give me five votes. And I'd need at least six to stand a chance. How am I going to get six votes, unless I can offer the deputy as a sweetener? Besides,' he added, 'you'd only have my vote and George's. I dunno what Pat would think about having you for deputy, Allan. I mean – this isn't meant to be a slight, you understand . . .'

'Oh, I understand.'

'. . . but I just don't know how Pat would feel. I haven't asked her. I can't guarantee anything.'

'No. Of course not.'

'The thing is, Allan, I've no objection myself. Personally. But I need the ammunition. If I'm going to persuade, say, Maeve O'Meagher to come on side – well, I know it's a pretty remote possibility.'

'Maeve? As deputy mayor?'

'I'm not saying it's certain, I'm just saying that she does think for herself, sometimes, and we get along. Whereas she doesn't get along with Finlay. That's all I'm saying. And if I can offer her my vote for deputy, then maybe it'll be enough to push her over the line. See?'

'Maeve O'Meagher,' Allan said thoughtfully. 'Well, it's an interesting tactic, Steve, but I don't know if it'll work.'

'Worth a try, I reckon.'

'You think so? Maybe. In my opinion, though, your best bet is Celeste.'

'*Celeste?*' Steven had to laugh. 'Mate, where have you been? Don't you know that Chris has got his hooks into Celeste? She's going to vote for Finlay – because Finlay's offered *her* the second spot!'

Allan laughed softly. 'Yes,' he said, 'I know that's the situation *at the moment*. But if I could persuade Celeste that you were a better choice, Steve, then perhaps you'd reconsider giving me your vote?'

Steven was surprised. He shifted uneasily. What was going on?

'What do you mean, "persuade"?' he inquired. 'What are you talking about?'

'I'm saying I think I could persuade Celeste that

Finlay isn't the right man for the job.' Allan sounded amused. 'I'm not going to threaten her with violence, Steve, if that's what you're worried about.'

'No, but –'

'I have some information, is all. Information about Finlay. He happens to teach Sue's daughter.'

'Oh.'

'So if I do manage to turn her around, I have your assurance that you'll vote for me? You and George?'

Still Steven hesitated. He was loath to commit himself.

'Why should Celeste switch sides,' he asked, 'if we can't offer her the deputy's spot ourselves?'

'Because there are some things that Celeste won't compromise on.'

'Like?'

'Like certain issues that I won't go into now, but let me assure you, they're close to her heart. Now – have we got a deal? If not, then I'll probably vote for you, but it won't do much good. Because Maeve O'Meagher is a long shot, Steve. She *might* give you her support, but she's more likely not to. Vera leads her around by the nose.'

'Oh, I wouldn't say *that*,' Steven protested, stung by this criticism of Maeve. He had to admit, however, that Maeve was, indeed, a long shot. Whereas, if he offered Allan his vote for deputy, it would only be after he had secured Celeste's support. 'You reckon you could really get Celeste on side?'

'I think so.'

'But even then, it would only mean an equal split. They'd have to draw it out of a hat.'

'Your decision, Steve.'

Steven considered his options. Really, it wasn't much of a choice. And there was always the remote chance that Maeve might give him her vote *without* a sweetener. Hell, she might not even want to be deputy!

'Okay,' he sighed. 'You're in. If you can turn Celeste around, you can have my vote.'

'And George's?'

'And George's.'

'Excellent. Well then – I'll get onto it straight away.'

As he hung up, Steven glanced through the kitchen window. He saw George, at the bottom of the garden, manfully chopping away at a patch of soil that looked as hard as rock. Avril stood beside him, supporting the trunk of the sick rhododendron, which had obviously been dug out of the ground. Half the garden appeared to have been removed along with it; there was a vast amount of dirt adhering to its lower portions.

Poor bastard, Steven thought, watching George's straining backside. Shall I tell him about Allan's offer? Not now, perhaps. Later. When Avril isn't around.

Returning to his bathroom duties, he tried to persuade himself that he'd done the right thing. It wasn't hard. With Celeste on side, he'd at least have a fighting chance. And although Allan wouldn't have been his personal choice for deputy, he was probably a better prospect than Gareth Cleves, who currently held the No. 2 position. Steven didn't much like Gareth. At first sight, he was just a small, dry committee man, blessed with the kind of methodical brain that can find its way easily through legal documents and the Local Government Act. (People often mistook him for a lawyer, although he was in fact a semi-retired orthodontist whose son had pretty much taken over his Wentworth Falls practice.) On closer inspection, however, Gareth had proved to be an almost virulently passionate Greenie, utterly uncompromising and obsessively well informed on such things as catchment systems and bushcare programs. It was Gareth's view that the residents of Ward Two had elected him to protect their environment – so, by God, he was going to respect their wishes. Steven found him to be verging on the monomaniacal when it came to questions of drainage and creeks. The man had drainage on the brain.

Gareth, in fact, seemed to believe that the local water authority was involved in some kind of dark conspiracy with various government departments and mountains committees.

Steven regarded him as a very tiresome sort of bloke.

'Steven!' Avril's voice came echoing down the corridor. 'Steven, George is going now! Do you want to say goodbye?'

Puzzled, Steven downed tools and went out to the garden, where George was throwing shovels and trowels and half-empty bags of fertiliser into the boot of his car. He was red-faced and sweaty, and looked as if he could use a cold drink.

'George!' Steven exclaimed. 'Where are you going? What about that beer?'

'Oh – I can't, Steve, honestly. I've got loads of things to do. And you're busy enough yourself.'

'Rubbish.' What had Avril been doing? Telling George not to interrupt Steven while he was cleaning the bathrooms? Probably. 'I'm just about done. One more floor.'

'No, really –'

'Come *on*. Look – I'll finish the floor while you wet your whistle. It won't take five minutes.'

'But I can't go inside,' George protested, gazing down at his loam-caked apparel. 'I'd mess the place up.'

'Then Avril can bring something out to you. She's not dirty.' Avril, in fact, was looking remarkably spruce for someone who had just spent an hour or so gardening. A little loose dirt on the gloves, a speck or so on the knees – clearly she had been playing spectator, for the most part. 'Don't tell me you couldn't murder a middie, George.'

'Well . . .'

'Attaboy.' On his way back inside, stopping at the screen door (where Avril was removing her garden shoes), Steven turned to his wife and said, in a low voice: 'Were you going to send that poor bugger home without a drink, for God's sake?'

'He didn't want to stay, Steven.'

'Because you asked him not to?'

'Don't be silly.'

He pursued her into the kitchen, where she began to drag ice trays out of the freezer.

'I see you got *him* to do all your dirty work,' Steven continued, goading her a little, though in a jocular fashion. 'Poor old George. You've really got him where you want him, haven't you?'

Avril sighed.

'What on earth are you talking about?' she said, with irritable condescension. 'He's a gardener, Steven. He likes gardening.'

'Is that why you didn't ask me to do this job of yours? I'm bigger than he is, in case you didn't notice.'

'Yes – and you also seem to be busier. I never know when you're going to be around.'

'Listen.' Steven took her arm, which felt immensely delicate in his grasp, like balsa wood wrapped in layers of silk. He could smell the cool, flowery scent of her perfume. 'Don't start this. Okay?'

'What? Start what?'

'You know what.'

'I'm sorry – I've absolutely no idea what you're talking about.'

Steven regarded her puckered brow, her wide eyes, and her astonished, disdainful expression.

Cute, he thought.

Then he touched the tip of her narrow nose with his forefinger.

'This time,' he said, with a half-smile, 'it's not going to work.'

And he didn't look back as he left the kitchen.

It was raining on Sunday, not just a misty veil of droplets but a really heavy rain – the kind that sent cataracts pouring down the steep incline of Leura Mall. Once again, Steven had to drag out his spare umbrellas, his gallery brochures and his fund of cheery small talk. Once again, he had to dance attendance on the drawing-room fire. Happily, however, his guests were all well adapted to a civilised indoor existence. The wedding yobbos had been replaced by a delightful Sydney couple, Mark and Gay Sternberg, who were up in Leura for a two-night stay. Mark was a rather quiet chap with a droll sense of humour; Gay was a cracking blonde, not very young but stylish and articulate. They had arrived late the previous evening, and emerged for Sunday breakfast shortly after the Mitchells left for church. (Steven, of course, had been able to supply them with service times for every denomination.) Gay immediately endeared herself to Avril by exclaiming with knowledgeable enthusiasm over the Bella Vista's antiques and architectural features. Mark, for his part, threw himself onto the bacon, accepted – with gratitude – Steven's offer of percolated coffee, and declared, in heartfelt tones: 'Thank God it's raining.'

Steven laughed.

'That's a new one,' he remarked. 'None of our guests has ever said *that* before.'

'Oh, I was counting on it. My idea of a holiday is lounging around in front of the TV with a lot of food and alcohol within easy reach. Now that it's raining, my wife won't expect me to go tramping through the wilderness.' Selecting a boiled egg, Mark added: 'I'm up for a pub crawl, but if it's views she wants, then I'm sure they're just as nice through the windows of a decent cafe.'

When Cindy and Maynard appeared, the conversation flowed easily, and soon the dining room was noisy with laughter. It was exactly the kind of company that Steven liked. He was drawn into a debate about traffic congestion, and eventually found himself sitting beside Gay, discoursing on the Megalong Valley. She was a confident, glamorous woman, the sort of woman who would be at home anywhere, from a five-star hotel in Paris to a pitched tent in the outback. She wasn't at all like Avril.

She was quite voluptuous, for one thing.

When the Mitchells returned, their fellow guests were still in the dining room, talking. Steven heard the crackle of car tyres on gravel; peering through a window, he recognised the taxi drawing up outside his front door, and sprang to intercept the car's driver before she could pull into the street again.

It was Maeve O'Meagher, fresh-faced and cheerful, wearing a pink cardigan and, in her hair, a gauze scarf.

'Hello, Steve,' she said, beaming. 'How are you?'

'Fine, thanks Maeve, would you like some coffee? It's a bloody awful day to be out.'

'No, no. Thanks, but I can't. I'm working.'

'On a Sunday?'

'I'm filling in. Go inside, Steve, you'll get soaked.'

'Actually, I'd like a word with you some time. If you've got a moment. Over coffee, or something?'

'Sure. I'll ring you.' She flashed her wide, white smile again before shifting gears and craning around to reverse the car. Steven, retreating, wondered if she would need help, but of course she didn't; her vehicle surged up the driveway without mishap, and was soon bumping into the street.

The horn sounded sharply, twice. A hand waved. Then the taxi was gone, and Steven went back inside.

Here he found that the Mitchells, responding to the convivial atmosphere in the dining room, were already singing the praises of 'that lovely taxidriver'. Apparently her services had been secured with the aid of a mobile phone; she had picked them up at the church, and had driven them almost as far as the Bella Vista when Bea Mitchell had suddenly realised that she'd left her umbrella under a pew.

'So she turned around and went back,' Bea recounted, 'and it took me ages to find the thing, because someone had already given it to the priest, but she didn't charge us for the time she waited. She was so *nice*.'

'The taxidrivers here are all pretty nice,' Steven volunteered. 'They'll pick up your shopping for you – they'll even deliver it into your house, if you give them the key. I've known that to happen.'

'Goodness!' said Gay. 'A bit different from Sydney!'

'Of course,' Steven added, 'Maeve is a *particularly* nice girl. She's on the council, you know. The Blue Mountains City Council.'

'Really?'

'She's only twenty-four, but she's a damned good councillor. I know how good she is, because I'm a councillor myself.'

'*Are* you? For heaven's sake!'

There followed the usual flurry of questions, as Avril silently padded about on her long, thin feet, serving the Mitchells with fresh coffee. Steven always enjoyed describing his civic duties to his guests, who were usually astounded that he had the time, much less the inclination, to serve on a local council. He liked to think that they were subsequently able to picture him outside the narrow confines of his domestic sphere, making decisions that affected the whole community. It was gratifying when they laughed, and shook their heads, and said it was amazing, they'd never have guessed, he looked like such a *laid-back*, *well-balanced* individual.

'Well, all I can say is, if *you're* on the local council, then it must be a lot better here than it is where we live,' Bea Mitchell observed. 'Our local council is a *shambles*.'

'Is she a full-time taxidriver? That girl?' Mark inquired, whereupon Steven revealed that no, she wasn't; she was studying at the local TAFE, part time, with the aim of becoming a dental assistant.

'You've got to understand, she's an absolute fixture around here,' he said. 'Everyone knows Maeve, and Maeve knows everyone. She's been a community figure since she was about sixteen years old, running church charity drives and protesting against silicon smelters and I don't know what else. She's part of an enormous family – they pop up all over the place. And being a taxidriver, she gets to talk to a lot of people. She gets to *help* a lot of people. Like Bea here.' Steven laughed. 'Hell, I practically voted for her myself,' he added, with a sly glance at Avril. 'She's such a charmer – and she looks so good in her mug shots. You can see why she got elected.'

'I didn't get a look at her,' said Mark, whereupon Bea helpfully provided a thumbnail sketch of Maeve O'Meagher: dark brown hair, pale complexion, strong eyebrows, freckles across her nose . . .

Then the telephone rang, and Steven went to answer it.

'Steve. How are you?' Allan Purchese's suave greeting caused Steven's heart to skip a beat. 'It's Allan. Allan Purchese.'

'Yes. Hello, Allan.'

'You'll be pleased to know that Celeste has changed her views. She's decided that you're the right mayoral candidate.'

Steven swallowed. For a moment he was speechless.

'Steve? Hello? Did you hear me?'

'Yes. But –'

'The deal's still on, isn't it?'

'Yes, of course. But how did you –'

'Do it? No problem.' A soft chuckle. 'Did I tell you that Sue's son Matthew is in Finlay's English class? Poor kid hates his guts, of course. Well apparently he told Matthew's class that all cats should be shot – and followed up with a story about how he'd shot one himself with an air rifle. It was only wounded, but he finished off the job by drowning it in a bucket of water.'

'Jesus.'

'Strong stuff, eh? Myself, I don't think he really did it. It doesn't seem to me like he'd have the balls. But I didn't say that to Celeste, naturally.'

'You told Celeste?'

'Sue told Celeste. And Celeste told Sue that it was disgraceful. She was going to write to the headmaster. A man like that shouldn't be teaching children. He *certainly* shouldn't be running for mayor.' Another laugh. 'Can't say I disagree with her. Sounds like a bit of a sicko, to my way of thinking.'

'But will she vote for *me*, Allan?'

'Looks like it. Sue told Celeste that she was voting for you, and Celeste said that you were a decent enough fellow. I mean, she doesn't have much choice, does she?'

'Maybe I should buy a cat,' Steven remarked jovially, as a sense of elation stole over him. 'Bloody hell, Allan – good *job*!'

'I know.'

'Did she say she was going to call me?'

'Celeste? She said she wanted to "speak" to you.'

'Then she probably will. Call, I mean.' Steven

found himself laughing. 'I'll get Avril to make cat noises in the background, shall I? Bloody hell, Allan. Bloody hell. You've certainly got my vote!'

As Steven hung up, he punched the air. Take *that*, Finlay Gascoigne! He wanted to tell someone – Avril? No, not Avril. She'd throw ten kinds of fit. George? Yes, George. He'd have to tell George anyway.

But before he could lift the receiver, the phone rang again.

'Hello?' he said, having pounced on the receiver. 'Bella Vista Guesthouse?'

'Oh. Hellew.' A mincing female voice. 'Is thet Steven Lockhart?'

'Yes. Is that you, Celeste?'

'It is. Yes.' Her slow, strangled delivery, with its gravelly lows and nasal highs, was unmistakable. She was a couple of years younger than Steven, but behaved like someone ten years older, dressing in pastel tracksuits and dowdy printed frocks, wearing her glasses on a chain, and having her hair set in a fossilised perm. Because her interests were wholly centred on the needs of respectable suburban residents, she was not always easy to pigeonhole: on the one hand, she campaigned for safer streets, better playground equipment, no medium-density development and increased funding for children's holiday activities; on the other hand, she favoured curfews for teenagers, larger car parks, and much harsher penalties for disturbing the peace. She was bitterly opposed to the microchipping of cats, when (as she frequently pointed out) poisonous snakes were allowed to roam free, unmolested, because they were classified as protected wildlife. She was, in effect, a woman who didn't appear to notice that she was living in the middle of a gigantic national park.

Steven always felt that she would have been much more at home close to the city, in a suburb where neat brick boxes stretched as far as the eye could see.

'I hope I'm not disturbing you,' she said, whereupon Steven assured her that she was not. He could hardly contain his amusement; what on earth was she going to say?

'I hed a word with Sue Schaarf last night,' she continued, then stopped.

'Yes?' Steven prompted.

Celeste cleared her throat, and approached the subject from a different angle.

'Steven,' she said, 'I would like to know, truthfully, how you stend on the issue of benning cats in the Blue Mountains.'

'*Banning* cats?' Steven echoed. In fact, he had no strong feelings either way. He could understand that cats were a terrible pest. On the other hand, he sympathised with the little old widows who had nothing else on which to lavish their affection. 'I didn't know that it *was* an issue,' he said cautiously.

'I mean, no-one's given any serious consideration to a ban, have they?'

Celeste muttered something about Gareth and the 'green dictatorship'. Then she said, in her creaking, constipated way: 'I jest want to know where you *stend*, Steven.'

'Well . . . if it came to the crunch, of course I couldn't support a ban. It would be unfair, I think.'

'*Thenk* you.' There was a sound of heavy breathing. 'Thenk you.'

'What's up, Celeste?'

'We-e-ell, the fect *is*, I've been approached by Chris Diacopoulos and asked to support Finlay Gascoigne's bid for mayor.' A pause. 'And I've been approached by Pat Baldwin on *your* behalf.' Another pause. 'And I *don't* approve of Finlay's attitudes.'

'Ah.'

'So I think I'll vote for you, Steven.'

'I see. Well – thank you.'

'Which means thet I would expect you to hear me out on certain metters, when they arise.' She spoke so slowly that Steven was overcome (as always) with the desire to finish her sentences for her. 'Vera and her crew heve always been *very dismissive* of me.'

'Yes, I know. I'm sorry.'

'There's such a thing as common politeness.' More heavy breathing. 'And there's such a thing as the democratic *pro*cess. And I would expect the mayor to remember thet at all times.'

'Of course.'

For several more minutes, Celeste explained to Steven exactly what he would be expected to do as mayor of the Blue Mountains. Normally, he would have extricated himself with a few excuses; this time, however, he felt constrained to listen to her rant on, shifting from foot to foot as she moaned about the mayoral secretary and the three-minute speech restriction at ordinary council meetings and the fact that she was always apologising for the rudeness of council staff, who once left her friend Janet waiting on the telephone for twenty minutes before cutting her off, so that she had to ring again, even though she was on a pension . . .

Steven clicked his tongue, and made sympathetic noises, and smothered his yawns, until at last Celeste was interrupted by her own doorbell ('Oh! Thet must be Trish!'), and bade him a hurried farewell. Thank you Trish, he thought, putting the receiver down. Whoever you are, you just saved my bacon.

Then he called George Lovecek, left a message on his answering machine, and strutted back into the dining room, his spirits soaring.

He found his guests all clustered around one wall, upon which Avril had arranged a selection of family photographs.

‘Is this your daughter, Steve?’ Julie asked, indicating a snapshot of Natasha, aged sixteen.

‘Natasha. Yes,’ he replied. ‘She’s older now.’

‘How old?’

‘Twenty-four.’

‘No other children?’

‘No.’

‘Steve, is this *you*?’ Gay was peering at a wedding portrait. ‘My God, you look like Hugh Grant! Except for the haircut.’

‘Oh please.’ Though flattered, Steven pretended to wince. ‘Don’t talk about that haircut.’

‘Wasn’t he a looker, Mark?’ Gay turned to her husband, then seemed to hear herself, and added, smiling at Steven: ‘Still is, of course.’

‘Well – I haven’t lost *all* my teeth. Yet,’ Steven laughed. He could barely contain his sense of exhilaration; he knew that he was fairly sparkling with it. His campaign was back on track! One more vote – just one more – and he’d have it in the bag!

Avril was eyeing him suspiciously.

‘Oh, don’t talk about teeth,’ Gay was saying. ‘My dentist told me the other day that my gums were receding. He said that when they creep back far enough, your teeth start to rattle. Rattling teeth! Something else to look forward to. Along with the hump and the hair loss.’ She sighed theatrically. ‘All I can do is stick my finger in the dyke, I suppose.

And desperately try to hold back the tide.'

'Well, you're holding it back magnificently,' Steven declared, cutting a glance at Avril. Her face could be difficult to read, but he sensed that she was on the alert. Something about the tautness of her neck told him so.

Good, he thought. Serve her right.

And he went on to supply the assembled party with a brief but comic account of his life so far, noting as he did so that Gay, in particular, was enjoying his self-deprecating humour very much.

She had a gratifying way of applauding his jokes, and then elaborating on them. He liked the warm, smooth, honey-coloured slopes of her decolletage. He liked the go-to-hell opulence of her golden jewellery.

But most of all, he liked to see Avril stacking dirty dishes with grim forbearance, a flush of colour on her normally pale cheeks.

# CHAPTER FIVE

Steven disappeared from the house shortly before eight on Monday morning – and for this his wife was thankful. Whatever the reason behind it (and Avril couldn't remember the excuse he had offered, though she knew it had something to do with council business), his absence meant that she didn't have to put up with his sickening behaviour at breakfast, when Gay Sternberg appeared. He had been all *over* that vulgar woman the day before, and Avril was determined to avoid witnessing any heartfelt goodbyes. Thank heavens Gay was going! Though, to be fair, it wasn't really her fault. She might have been a little crass, with her gold jewellery and her loud voice and her lavish make-up, but she hadn't set out to dazzle Steven – or anyone else, for that matter. It was Steven who had practically crawled down the front of her dress. And why? Because he had a *ridiculous* notion in his head about George Lovecek, and wanted to punish Avril for something that was clearly the product of his overactive imagination.

Once again, he was being unreasonably jealous. It had happened before, when he had absented himself for long periods; then, as now, Avril had been forced to seek help from other people. Help – not pleasure. But Steven had chosen to regard her frantic efforts to cope as attempts at seduction, and had reacted accordingly. The way he'd shouted at poor Eric! The way he'd stormed about, accusing her of 'making eyes' at his cousin, when all she'd done was to ask Paul for a discount on a washing machine! (He'd been managing a whitegoods store at the time.) Steven had caused such a ruckus, with his baseless accusations, that Eric and Paul had made themselves scarce, leaving Avril – once again – to cope on her own. She'd had to soldier on with her old washing machine, which had lost its ability to switch from the 'rinse' to the 'spin' cycle without manual assistance.

And now, even to imply that she was attempting to ensnare George . . .

It was worse than ridiculous. It was insulting.

Of course, being jealous of George didn't mean that Steven was more in evidence. Oh no. He had gone off yet again, leaving Avril to serve breakfast, clear up after the guests, and probably even clean the bathrooms, though he'd promised to be back before ten. Was this fair? Was this reasonable? It would serve him right if I *did* get involved with George, she thought savagely, as she stripped the Sternbergs' bed. It would serve him right if I abandoned the housework, and went off to visit George in a seedy hotel room.

After all, a person could do far worse than George. He wasn't exactly a sex symbol, but at least he was sympathetic. At least he was there when Avril needed him. Though she wouldn't have needed him for anything, if Steven had been around a bit more.

Or if he hadn't been drooling over the female guests whenever he did happen to be at home.

Not that he'd been genuinely interested in Gay Sternberg. It had all been for show. Gay Sternberg was far too vibrant for Steven's taste; though he enjoyed the company of dominating women in small doses, he didn't really like to compete. He liked to be the centre of attention, and he couldn't ever be that when Gay was around. He liked to impress, and to charm, and to take the lead – more and more so as he grew older.

No. The whole Gay Sternberg thing was a ploy. A device. A trick to make Avril feel jealous – when all it had done was to make her cringe. The embarrassment of it! The dreadful baritone chuckle he had employed! The wry smile on Mark Sternberg's face, and the Mitchells' puzzled glances! Appalling. Unendurable.

I shan't take him to task, Avril decided. It's what he wants, and it will only compromise my dignity. Besides, it's a secondary issue.

The bathrooms are what this is *really* about.

At this point the phone rang. Expecting yet another council-related call, Avril was tempted to let it ring. But her sense of duty (which had always come to her rescue, even in the toughest circumstances) once again drove her to put her sulks and grudges aside. Reminding herself that she was running a business, she went to the drawing room and picked up the receiver.

'Bella Vista Guesthouse,' she said. 'May I help you?'

There was a noise at the other end of the line. It sounded almost like a sob. But no-one said a word.

'Hello?' said Avril. 'May I help you?'

'Is . . . is that Mrs Lockhart?' The voice was female, high, unsteady, and thick with emotion. Avril didn't recognise it.

'Yes,' she replied. 'This is Avril Lockhart. Who am I speaking to?'

'Janelle Pearce.'

Not recognising the name, Avril said nothing. There followed a few sniffs and snorts from Janelle, before the mysterious caller finally remarked, 'You've never heard of me, have you?'

'No.'

'But you are Natasha's mother?'

'Yes.' Fear shot through Avril like a dose of fast poison. 'What is it? What's happened? Is she all right?'

'Oh, *she's* all right!' Janelle squeaked. 'I just thought you'd like to know – I just *thought* you should *know* – that I'm – I'm . . .' More smothered, gurgling noises. 'That I'm seven weeks pregnant,' she continued, with an obvious effort, 'and that Malcolm Busso and I have been together for *six years*, and that you're daughter is busy *ruining* my *life*! I just thought you should know that, Mrs Lockhart!'

Dazed, Avril sat down on the shield-backed chair provided for long telephone conversations. She remembered what Natasha had told her about Malcolm Busso.

'You're not married, are you?' she asked breathlessly.

'No we're not,' Janelle sobbed, 'but we might as well be! We live together! We bought a house together! I'm having his *baby*!'

'But –'

'He has commitments, Mrs Lockhart! We had a perfectly good relationship, until Natasha came along and *threw* herself at him, and got him drunk and dragged him into bed one night –'

'Oh, come now,' Avril interrupted, barely thinking

before she spoke, 'surely he's a grown man? You make him sound like a sozzled teenager.'

'He's my partner!' Janelle shrieked.

'But not your husband.'

'Augh!'

There was a sharp, explosive clatter; Janelle had hung up. Avril, who had been about to point out that, in any case, this had nothing to do with her, put her own receiver down more gently.

Living together was all very well, but it argued a lack of commitment. And babies required commitment. Avril didn't approve of having babies out of wedlock. It was all very well for the parents, but what about the children? Surely they had a right to some security?

She thought for a while, still shaken by this unexpected attack. How extraordinary, that Janelle should have seen fit to communicate her feelings to Natasha's *mother*, of all people! For what purpose? To what end? Surely she couldn't be deluded enough to expect that Avril would take it upon herself to correct Natasha? Chide her? Threaten her? Certainly it was unfortunate – the whole thing was unfortunate – but really, if one was going to have babies out of wedlock, one was taking an inevitable risk. The man wasn't actually married, after all. Natasha's behaviour was no more immoral than Janelle's. And what kind of woman would telephone her rival's mother, for the purpose of defaming her rival? What did this say about Janelle?

An unstable woman, Avril decided. Out of control. Perhaps deluded. I should very much like to hear Natasha's side of the story.

But when she called Natasha's work number, she was informed that her daughter was 'in a meeting'.

The girl who answered was very nice. Very apologetic, in fact. She wanted to know if Avril would like to leave a message. Perhaps have her daughter return her call? Avril hesitated, but finally decided against this offer. Uncertain whether employees of Natasha's firm were permitted to make long-distance calls from work, she replied that she would call again in a little while. Then she went back to her chores, which included a load of laundry, a batch of scones, a grease spot on the dining-room carpet, and a telephone call from Celeste Whitfield, who wanted to talk to Steven. Avril explained that Steven was out. She took a message, and went back to her mixture of magnesia and fuller's earth, which had to be spread on the carpet and allowed to dry.

Was it all, perhaps, a hoax? Was Janelle lying about her pregnancy? Anything was possible. Six years together . . . she had sounded quite young. Possibly it had been a teenage romance. Avril wondered if Janelle had been aware of Natasha's visit to the mountains. Was that why she had called Avril?

Because she was under the impression that Avril had welcomed Malcolm Busso into her home?

I'd certainly like to have a word with that gentleman, Avril thought crossly. It occurred to her that Natasha herself was very possibly ignorant of his relationship with Janelle. What could be likelier? Natasha was a bright, sensible woman, with a vigorous sense of self-esteem. Why would she get involved with a man so emotionally entangled, unless she was unaware of his life with Janelle? Or unless that relationship was not as well established as Janelle had implied?

Or unless the baby itself was a fiction.

Steven returned when Avril was carefully brushing dried paste off the dining-room carpet. (It had worked, too: the grease spot was gone.) He blew into the dim, silent house like a gale-force wind, banging cupboard doors, throwing keys around, and splashing about in the kitchen sink as he washed his face and hands – which he dried on a tea towel. He explained to Avril that he had been inspecting an overgrown laneway; local residents had been demanding for some time that the council cut back all the blackberry and cotoneaster – without any discernible results. 'Oh my God. Celeste?' he moaned, when Avril had drawn his attention to the message on the cork board. 'Just my luck. But I'd better keep her happy.' Whistling, he then went off to spend thirty-eight minutes on a call to Celeste, while Avril coped with an annual council inspection that had utterly slipped her mind. A rather morose young man arrived on the doorstep, with a card and a clipboard; he examined the extinguishers, the fire alarms, and the thermostat on the fridge, went through the cupboards and the cutlery drawer, lifted the toilet seats, poked about in the laundry, and finally, with a few grudging words of approval, handed Steven several printed forms defaced with splashes of illegible handwriting.

Apparently, the Bella Vista was considered safe. The Lockharts had passed their annual inspection.

'Looks like I greased the right palms,' Steven remarked to Avril, with a wink, when the inspector had departed. But she wasn't impressed.

'I haven't done the bathrooms, Steven,' she replied coldly. 'I've been busy doing other things.'

'No worries. It's only eleven. Plenty of time,' was his response, as he bounced away to collect his buckets and disinfectants. Glowering, Avril attended to her scones, which were slighty burnt, thanks to the Blue Mountains City Council. She would have to make a new batch. And she wouldn't tell Steven about Janelle – not, at least, until she'd spoken to Natasha. Steven always took the worst view of Natasha's love affairs. He seemed to regard her as being of a somewhat *predatory* nature, just because she knew her own mind, and wasn't afraid to make the first move. Steven didn't seem to realise that girls were different nowadays. For better or worse, they were all more assertive when it came to their own needs – more assertive than Avril's generation, at any rate.

Natasha will be able to explain, Avril thought. I just know this whole thing is a storm in a teacup.

But once again, when she called Natasha's firm, her daughter was unavailable.

'I'm going to have lunch with Maeve O'Meagher,' Steven declared soon afterwards, upon finishing the bathrooms. Avril was eating her own lunch by that time (a slice of Swiss cheese on brown bread, a few sardines, a handful of pickled onions and a scone with jam and cream, washed down by two cups of strong coffee). 'I want to have a word to her about Finlay Gascoigne,' he explained.

'Oh yes,' said Avril, with chilly politeness. She noticed that he had changed his shirt, combed his hair, and reapplied his deodorant.

'Just so you don't think I'm doing it behind your back,' Steven continued, winking again, but in a somewhat sly and defiant fashion. 'Just so you know it's purely business.'

Avril folded a piece of brown bread between her fingers, chewing meditatively.

'I think I might be able to persuade Maeve that Finlay's a bad choice,' Steven went on. Then, with a grin, he added, 'I reckon I might charm her into my way of thinking. *If* I try hard enough. What do you think?'

Avril swallowed. 'You're fifty-one years old, Steven,' she said at last, dryly.

'What's that supposed to mean?'

'It means that you shouldn't delude yourself.'

He snorted.

'You think I'm deluding myself?'

'You're certainly embarrassing *me*.'

'Oh, I don't know.' His tone was slightly arch. 'Gay Sternberg said I was still a looker.'

'That's what I'm talking about.'

Another snort. He poured himself a glass of soft drink, and drained it in a matter of seconds. 'Some women like a bit of give and take,' he said reflectively, but with a touch of smug condescension that Avril found *revolting*. She got up, and began to stack dirty crockery.

'So – anything you want, while I'm out?' he asked.

'No.'

'No shopping?'

'No.'

'Don't worry – we're not going anywhere expensive,' he said. 'Just the Cherry Tree Cafe.'

Avril was tempted to retort: Make sure you sit up front, where everyone can see you. But she restrained herself. It would be fruitless to suggest that Steven was just stoking his ego, taking a 24-year-old girl to lunch. He would simply deny it, even to himself. And she didn't want him to think that she was jealous, since the whole point of the exercise was clearly to make her so.

He still had a bee in his bonnet about George – that much was obvious. And nothing that she said or did would persuade him that he was wrong.

'Okay. Well, I'll be going,' he finally remarked, after waiting (in vain) for her to comment. 'I'll be back in an hour or so. When are the new guests due?'

'There's only one. He's due about four, I think.'

'Right. Okay. Good,' said Steven, and left. Avril heard him singing as he climbed into the car. Please God, she thought, don't let him embarrass poor Maeve. That poor girl doesn't know what she's letting herself in for.

On reflection, however, it occurred to Avril that Steven was unlikely to do anything too gauche in his wife's absence. His charm was founded on a very clear and intelligent appreciation of other people's responses to it; he could read an audience with great precision. He didn't need to flirt, or ogle, or generally disgrace himself – not unless he was deliberately trying to enrage Avril. He was far too smart to do anything clumsy like that.

It's a quarter to one, Avril mused, glancing at the kitchen clock. I won't call Natasha now; she'll probably be at lunch. I'll wait until . . . let's see . . . I'll wait until two.

The wait seemed very long. Avril put a piece of

Albinoni on the stereo, and did a bit of dusting. Outside, it was overcast; the grey sky was cross-hatched with naked branches. The ground, however, was bright with spring colour: puddles of pink blossom from the flowering cherries; blazing daffodils and jonquils; the intense, almost purple blue of the grape hyacinths. Avril noted, with satisfaction, that her tulips were beginning to show themselves – and that her apple tree was budding. George was envious of her apple tree, which produced fruit quite good enough for stewing (as long as she kept the parrots away). His own tree was a blighted, wizened old thing. He called it Hepzibah.

Avril cut some flowers, and distributed them throughout the guests' bedrooms. She rearranged the magazines and brochures on the drawing-room sideboard. Her footsteps echoed on the polished floor; her cherished grandfather clock chimed in the hallway.

Its Big Ben signature tune was followed by a pair of long, tolling notes. Two o'clock. Avril went to the telephone.

'Hello, Marketing Services.' A sing-song salutation. 'Natasha speaking.'

'Natty? It's me.'

'Oh. Hi.'

'I wouldn't be interrupting, only I just had a call from a girl named Janelle.' Silence. 'She said that she was pregnant with Malcolm Busso's baby, and that you were ruining her life.' Another silence. 'Before I could reason with her, she hung up on me.'

Natasha sighed. 'God,' she said, in a flat voice.

'She told me she wasn't married –'

'She isn't.'

'. . . but that she'd been living with this fellow for six years.'

'Mum.' Natasha spoke calmly. 'Don't worry about it, okay? Janelle is totally neurotic. She'd have to be, to ring you.'

'But –'

'Listen. She says they've been together for six years? It's been on and off – five split-ups. A rocky road, in other words. He always breaks it off, she comes whining back, and he's too soft to give her the boot.'

'But –'

'You think that pregnancy was an accident? She engineered it, to get him to stay. It was a last-ditch effort – she knew he was about to split. Now he doesn't know what to do, poor guy.'

'Oh.'

'Neither do I, to tell you the truth. I mean, he's nice, but do I need the aggravation? She's always screaming at me over the phone. Telling me to lay off. Like *I'm* the one who made the first move! I told her, it's been his decision, all down the line.' There was a brief pause; Avril could hear a muffled exchange, as if Natasha had covered the receiver to converse with someone else. 'Sorry,' Natasha said at last. 'It's a bit hectic here.'

'Oh, I don't mean to bother you, darling. I know you're busy. I was just concerned.'

'Don't be.' Natasha's tone sharpened. 'She's got a nerve. Jesus. How the hell did she get hold of your number? I'm going to talk to Malcolm about this.'

'You don't think – I mean, in the circumstances . . .' Avril faltered, and took a deep breath, before continuing. 'You don't think it might be best to – to back out for a while? Until he settles things? I don't want you getting hurt, Natty.'

'*She's* the one who's gonna get hurt,' Natasha replied, before adding: 'Maybe. You may be right. I'll think about it. Was there anything else?'

'Oh. Well, no . . . not really.' There was, in fact, the matter of her daughter's recent weekend visit to Leura, but Avril didn't know if she had the courage to bring it up. What could she say? *Dianne tells me you were having a naughty weekend at the Fremont*? Impossible. 'You know, Natty,' she said, after some consideration, 'if you're embarrassed or – or ashamed about anything, you don't have to worry about telling me. I won't be cross. I realise that things don't always work out the way you planned –'

'What things?' Natasha interrupted. She sounded amused.

'Well – anything. That's what I'm saying. If there's anything you've been too embarrassed to tell me.'

'Like what? That I'm into anal sex?'

'Now, Natty.' Avril refused to be aggravated. She knew that Natasha liked to shock. 'Don't be silly, please.'

'Mum, I gave up being embarrassed *long* ago. There's no advantage in it.' All of a sudden, Natasha sounded quite affectionate. 'Please don't fret, okay? I know this sort of thing freaks you out, but it's no big deal. It's just a wacko ex-girlfriend. Happens all the time.'

'Well . . . all right. But what if she calls again?'

'She won't. I'll see to that'

'How?'

'I'll tell her I'll rip her throat out if she tries it,' Natasha said indulgently. 'Gotta go, Mum – sorry. I'm due downstairs. Nothing else, is there?'

'No, I –'

'Bye, then. See you soon.'

The line crackled; there was a click, then the dial tone. Slowly, Avril hung up.

Oh dear, she thought. Oh dear, why *does* she get involved with these men? They're more trouble than they're worth. First the drunken lunatic, now the wacko ex-girlfriend. I don't understand – she's a *bright girl*. She could do better than this, surely? It doesn't make sense.

Then the phone rang, shrilling away under her hand, and made her jump. With a pounding heart, she lifted the receiver.

It was Celeste Whitfield. Was Steven at home? There was something she had forgotten to mention about parks assessment management.

Avril spent many subsequent hours fretting over her daughter's unfortunate taste in men. Sometimes she had to restrain herself from picking up the phone – for what was the point of questioning Natasha more closely? She had made her position quite clear. It was just that . . . well, Avril didn't always know whether to believe Natasha. Entirely. When it came to matters of the heart.

Then, on Tuesday evening, Natasha appeared in person. She turned up unexpectedly, with a small suitcase; Avril gasped to see her standing there under the porch light, droplets glistening in her hair and on her collar. Once again, the mist had come down, swathing every street lamp in a glowing nimbus.

'Natty! My darling!'

'Hello, Mum.'

'What's wrong?'

'Nothing.' Natasha carefully wiped her high-heeled boots on the welcome mat. 'Just felt like a break.'

'Well, isn't that nice! Come in! You're very lucky – your father's home. He usually isn't.'

Avril didn't know what to say about Natasha's hair. It had been dyed black, and in Avril's opinion the change was not an improvement, giving Natty's face an older look – a bruised, almost haggard look. Her daughter was wearing a black coat, black jeans, lots of black kohl, and a very brief, filmy purple blouse, unsuitable for the mountains in September. She favoured rather heavy jewellery, but had too much natural taste to wear more than two or three pieces at once.

Avril noticed that she smelled of smoke.

'No guests tonight, so we can have a nice, quiet family evening,' Avril said. 'Steven! Look who's here! It's Natty!'

Steven, of course, had been working on some kind of speech since dinner time; Avril hadn't managed to get a word out of him for at least an hour. He emerged from his verandah study with a slightly apprehensive look on his face, greeted Natasha, kissed her and said: 'Is anything wrong?'

'Nothing's wrong.' Avril found herself speaking sharply, as if Natasha had been accused of disorderly conduct. 'She just felt like a break.'

'Oh. Good.'

'I thought I'd take the week off,' Natasha remarked. 'What are you drinking, Dad? Port?'

'Uh . . . yes –'

'I'll have some too, if that's okay.'

She drank it in her parents' sitting room, a dark shape wedged into one of the flowery, well-padded easy chairs. There was an angular elegance in the way she held the glass, for she had Avril's long fingers, and her nails were beautifully manicured. As she drank, she informed Avril that she'd stopped to eat on the way; that the traffic had been pretty good; that the roads weren't too bad; that yes, she'd brought some warmer clothes. Then, upon draining her glass, she rose and said: 'I think I'll have a shower now. If nobody minds.'

'No, of course not.' Avril sprang to her feet. 'I'll just get you a towel. You can use one of the guest-rooms tonight, if you like – that way you can have your own bathroom.'

'Thanks, but I don't want to have to move out tomorrow.'

'Oh. Yes. No. I understand.'

'Take it easy, Mum. I'll be fine.'

Bustling in and out of her daughter's bedroom, bringing towels and turning down covers and inquiring about laundry ('Would you like me to wash these underpants?'), Avril looked forward to a cosy dialogue before bedtime, perhaps over a hot drink, when she might discover what it was that had brought Natasha to the mountains – alone. Had she split up with Malcolm over the Janelle business? Had she come home to lick her wounds? Avril felt that this might indeed be the case, but for the present, at least, her curiosity remained unsatisfied. With her wet hair concealed in a towelling turban and her make-up removed, Natasha certainly *looked* much younger, and far more defenceless. But she made it quite clear – using firm, flat monosyllables – that she wasn't going to be discussing anything with Avril that night.

It wasn't until the next morning, when Avril overheard her daughter talking on the phone, that she began to understand what was going on.

She didn't mean to eavesdrop. It happened because Natasha chose to make a call on her mobile, retreating to a sheltered spot in the garden where Avril had placed a couple of weather-worn chairs and a table, not far from her own bathroom window. The air was clear and crisp and very still, and Avril, who was pursuing her usual beauty routine (as the cosmetic pamphlets described it), was able – indeed, was forced – to hear almost every word that Natasha uttered. She began to realise that Natasha was conversing with Malcolm, that the topic of the conversation was Fergus, and that Natasha was being badly discomfited by Fergus's behaviour.

'Well I had to,' she was saying. 'What was I supposed to do? I know . . . I know . . . But he sits out the front in his car . . . Yes . . . Oh, all the time. And

I know he's the one who's been ringing up. It must be him . . . What? Oh, well that would really be useful, if you went and got charged with assault! He'd do it, too, he wouldn't miss the chance . . . I have. I went right up to him, told him to piss off. Didn't do any good . . . No. No. Oh Jesus, Malcolm, *I* don't know . . .'

Her voice cracked and wavered. Horrified, Avril stood frozen in front of the mirror, hairbrush in hand.

'. . . Up here? Who knows?' Natasha continued. 'He's been up here once. Yes, didn't I tell you? When we were at the Fremont . . . Yes, and frightened the life out of Mum and Dad, poor things . . . Maybe. I don't know . . . God, I wish you could. Really? This weekend? That would be great. I only hope he doesn't show before then . . .'

Quietly, Avril finished grooming herself. Distractedly, she moved into the kitchen, where Steven was taking his ease, the *Blue Mountains Gazette* spread across the table in front of him. It wasn't often that he and Avril could enjoy a leisurely breakfast, free from the demands of hungry guests.

He was slathering Avril's homemade jam onto a microwaved croissant.

'Steven!'

'Hmm?'

'We've got to talk to Natasha.'

'About what?' He hadn't lifted his gaze from an article on the Hawkesbury–Nepean Catchment Management Trust.

'I think she's having trouble with Fergus.'

'Who?'

'You know! That drunk who turned up in the middle of the – *Steven*. Will you *listen* to me?'

He raised his eyes.

'What?' he said wearily.

'I think Fergus is *bothering* her,' Avril whispered. 'Following her. Calling her up. That kind of thing.'

With a blank stare, Steven finished chewing a mouthful of croissant. Finally he swallowed, and said: 'Stalking her, you mean?'

'Yes!'

'Did she tell you that?'

'Well – not exactly.' Avril was about to explain when Natasha herself appeared, dressed in a very thin knitted garment, of abbreviated proportions, which in Avril's opinion could not correctly be classified as a jumper, no matter what the fashion magazines might say. She seemed perfectly serene and faultlessly groomed; her mobile phone was hooked over her belt like a weapon.

'Oh – hello, Nat,' Avril said brightly. 'Have you had breakfast?'

'I had a banana,' Natasha replied. 'But I might have a piece of toast.'

'Is that all? I've been buying a really nice muesli. Very light. I'm sure you'd like it.'

'No thanks.'

As her daughter dropped a slice of wholemeal bread into the toaster, Avril glanced at Steven. She was gratified to see that he hadn't turned his attention back to the newspaper. But he obviously didn't intend to take the lead; he was waiting for Avril to do that.

So she cleared her throat.

'Um . . . Natty?' she said. 'I hate to tell you, but I was in the bathroom when you were talking to Malcolm on the phone.'

Natasha didn't move. She had struck a thoughtful pose, her head bent over the toaster, her weight resting on one hip. Her face was hidden.

'I couldn't . . . I mean, I was . . . you know . . . on the toilet,' Avril stammered. 'I couldn't *help* overhearing –'

'Is this Fergus character stalking you, Nat?' Steven inquired bluntly. He was obviously impatient to get away.

Natasha said nothing until her toast was disgorged, in one noisy, convulsive movement. She caught it neatly, her face still concealed by a curtain of black hair, and remarked: 'I'll take care of it.'

'But Natty,' Avril protested, 'he's upsetting you. It's not right. You should call the police.'

'You should take out an AVO,' Steven advised, whereupon Avril turned to him and asked: 'What on earth is that?'

'An apprehended violence order. You know.' He wiped his jammy fingers on a piece of paper towelling. 'When the creep can't even come near you, or he'll get arrested.'

'Oh, Dad.' Natasha's tone was scornful. 'Those things are useless.'

'Rubbish.'

'They *are*. You're always hearing stories. About ex-wives who take out AVOs and then the husbands come back and beat them to death.'

'But he's not *violent*, Natty?' Avril exclaimed. 'He hasn't hurt you?'

'No, no. And he's not going to, either.'

'You should call the police,' Steven declared firmly. 'If he's pestering you, you should call the police.'

'I have.'

'And?'

'And they wanted proof. They wanted me to log phone calls and take photos and shit like that. Which I *don't* have time to do.' Natasha's toast crackled as she spread it with butter. 'Fuck him,' she concluded (making Avril wince). 'He's not going to disrupt my life. He's not.'

'But he already has,' Avril pointed out gently.

'Natasha, you came here to get away from him. Isn't that right?'

'I tell you what,' Steven interrupted, folding his newspaper, 'he'd better not show up on the doorstep again. He'd better not.'

'He won't,' said Natasha.

'How do you know? He did it once. Scared the life out of the guests – I had to give 'em a $50 refund. It's bad for business.'

'Steven!' Avril said sharply. Natasha, turning towards him, put her hand on her hip and drawled: 'Well gee, Dad. Maybe I should go. Since I'm affecting your bottom line.'

'That's not what he meant,' Avril assured her quickly. 'That's not what you meant, is it Steven?'

With a sulky look, he muttered: 'No.'

'We just don't want him turning up drunk in the middle of the night again. That's all. There must be something we can do.' Avril suddenly experienced a flash of inspiration. 'Have you actually talked to him, Natty?' she proceeded to ask. 'Have you sat down and reasoned with him?'

'There's no reasoning with Fergus.'

'But have you really tried?'

'Mum, he doesn't hear what I'm saying.'

'Perhaps that's because you're not explaining yourself properly.' Avril went on to suggest that Fergus be invited to the mountains, where Natasha and Avril and Steven could sit down with him, in a calm and comfortable atmosphere, to point out that he was mistaken in his assumptions. That he was upsetting Natasha. That if he persisted in his activities, they would have no choice but to call the police.

'He might not realise what he's doing,' Avril mused. 'He might be so upset that it hasn't sunk in.'

'Oh, Avril.' It was Steven's turn to voice his scorn. 'He knows exactly what he's bloody doing. He's trying to punish Nat for giving him the boot.'

'Yes, but what if we *reminded* him of the consequences?' said Avril. 'At the moment, all he can see is that he's getting to Natty. Because she's been angry with him – she's told him to go away. If he sees that we're all calm and sensible, and that we're going to deal with him sensibly, the way we'd deal with . . . oh, I don't know, cleaning out the gutters – if we remind him that he's always been a normal, law-abiding citizen, just like we are, and that there are civilised ways of dealing with this kind of thing –'

'What makes you think he's ever been normal?' Steven interjected. But Natasha held up her hand.

'Wait,' she said. 'Hang on.'

'At least it's worth trying, Natty,' Avril pleaded. 'You know your father's a city councillor. He's got friends in the local police force. Perhaps if we make a point of saying that . . . if we mention AVOs . . .'

Avril trailed off, aware that her daughter was thinking deeply. Natasha was leaning against a benchtop, slowly masticating a mouthful of buttered toast. Her brow was knitted, and there was a glassy look in her eyes. At last she swallowed.

'Actually,' she said, 'that's not a bad idea.'

Beaming, Avril shot a glance at Steven. He was watching his daughter with a frown on his face.

'That might just work,' Natasha continued. 'Yeah. Okay.' She looked up. 'I'll call him. I'll ask him to come over here.'

'Hang on a minute,' Steven objected. 'I don't know about *here*. Isn't there somewhere else we could go? A restaurant, or something?'

'No, no, Steven, that's the whole point.' Avril was so pleased that she could find it in her heart to be patient with his obtuseness. 'It has to be calm. It has to be quiet. There has to be a blazing fire and a hot cup of tea.'

'But what about the guests?' he asked – plaintive, now, as if he had already submitted to the forces ranked against him, and was only putting on an empty show of resistance. 'What happens if he blows up, and starts shouting? What if he starts smashing the furniture?'

'If he starts smashing furniture, we've got him,' Natasha retorted, with a rather chilling smile. 'That has to be an offence. Malicious damage, or whatever.'

'He won't smash anything,' Avril declared. 'Not if we do this properly. I'm sure he'll listen to reason. He listened to me, when I asked him to go away. In any case, Steven, I'm sure you could stop him if he did become violent.'

Steven grunted. He picked up his dirty plate and took it to the sink. Although he wasn't pleased, Avril could see that he had capitulated – no doubt because she had raised the issue of his virility.

Really, she thought. Men are such children.

'I'll ask him to come up on Saturday,' Natasha decided. 'Saturday evening.'

'That would be fine,' said Avril.

'But not for dinner,' Steven chimed in.

'Oh, but Steven, it will make him even more receptive, surely? If we feed him?'

'I'll be damned if I'm going to feed that nutter,' was Steven's determined response. Natasha regarded him with a half-smile, dusting the toast crumbs off her fingers.

'Don't worry, Dad. I know just how you feel,' she said. Then the phone rang, and Steven went to answer it.

Celeste was calling to ask whether, if Steven should become mayor, he would consider supporting a Section 356 donation to her friend Trish's new chapter of the Cat Preservation Society.

## CHAPTER SIX

Steven was cleaning bathrooms when the telephone rang on Thursday morning. 'If that's Celeste, tell her I'm out!' he yelled, before it occurred to him that Avril was in the garden with Natasha, trying to prevent Natasha from lighting up a cigarette.

As if Nat's going to stop smoking for anyone, Steven thought, ripping off his work gloves. He was surprised that she had so far refrained from smoking in her bedroom – that instead she customarily retreated into the garden, where she would sit for hours on one of the old iron chairs under the golden elm, lighting fag after fag, tipping back her head to blow smoke at the budding branches that arched above her like groin vaulting in a church.

Doubtless Avril hoped to chasten Natasha into

stubbing out her cigarette by coughing lightly as she hung out the washing. It was, in Steven's opinion, a strategy doomed to failure.

'Hello?' he said, answering the phone without enthusiasm. (He was beginning to wonder if he actually *wanted* the burden of Celeste Whitfield's support.) 'Bella Vista Guesthouse?'

'Steve? It's Maeve.'

'Maeve! Hello!' Steven's spirits instantly revived. 'How are you?'

'Good. Well . . . okay. As a matter of fact, something's happened, and it's kind of . . . well, kind of upset me a bit.'

'Oh no.' Steven was genuinely concerned. 'What's wrong? Can I help?'

'Maybe. Would I be able to come and see you? Now?'

'Of course!' God, he thought, the bathrooms. My clothes. I'll have to change my clothes. 'Whenever you like.'

'Ten minutes, say?'

'Sure.'

'Okay. I'll see you then.'

Steven was wearing a pair of paint-splattered jeans and a disgusting old sweatshirt, circa 1980, which had a hole under one arm. He quickly retreated to his bedroom, where he scrabbled through drawers full of neatly folded shirts and jumpers (you couldn't fault

Avril on her housekeeping), in search of something casual that wasn't at the same time too sloppy. He was a little apprehensive. What did Maeve want to talk about? The mayoral election, or something more personal? Their meeting on Monday had pretty much deprived him of all hope. Maeve had been bright and pleasant and sympathetic – she had wavered just a little, when contemplating the possibility of Finlay Gascoigne as mayor – but in the end she had regretfully declined to vote for Steven.

'I can't,' she'd said. 'I'd like to, but I can't. Of course you're a nicer person than Finlay, but this isn't just a matter of personalities. It's a matter of principle.'

'Maeve, Finlay wouldn't know a principle from a peanut.'

'That's not true.'

'Didn't you tell me he was involved with one of his students, at one time?'

'Well . . .' She'd frowned. 'That was a rumour. I don't know if it really happened.'

'I'll bet it did. I wouldn't put it past him.'

'I'm sorry, Steve. You'd make a good mayor – in fact I won't mind if you do end up winning – but I have to think of why I'm actually on council. You believe in compromise. Well, that's reasonable, I s'pose. But it means you have to compromise with people who don't care.' Poor earnest little Maeve! *She* certainly cared. With a puckered brow, she'd added: 'Vera cares. And she'll be pushing Finlay all the way. I reckon I should get behind her. We need to really focus on what's important. If we have to compromise with Allan Purchese or Sue Schaarf, that'll never happen.'

She had been so unhappy, poor girl; she hadn't liked to disappoint Steven. The necessity of doing so had quite deprived her of her appetite. So Steven had passed on to other topics, harmless topics, and the lunch had ended comfortably, with Maeve laughing in the sunlight, her plate cleaned of everything except a small pile of green capers, which she'd said she couldn't stand.

Now she was approaching Steven. Why? Was she having second thoughts? Or was she troubled by something else entirely – something to do with Upper Mountains Tourism, perhaps?

Steven changed his clothes. He brushed his hair. He was pondering the question of whether he should warn Avril, and deal with her reaction now, or let her find out for herself and vent her spleen after Maeve had left, when he heard a car rolling down the driveway.

Sure enough, it was Maeve's taxi – with Maeve in it. She eased to a halt; her handbrake made a strangled, screeching noise; her engine cut out and the driver door opened. She emerged wearing moccasins, corduroy jeans and a patterned pullover.

‘Can I park here?’ she asked. ‘Is this all right?’

‘Of course,’ said Steven. He wanted to get her indoors before Avril came around the side of the house, to discover who was visiting. ‘Come in. Nice to see you. Would you like a drink? Coffee? Fruit juice . . .?’

‘Just a glass of water, please.’ She followed him into the house and down the corridor, her arms folded across her chest. Steven stopped in the kitchen to pour her some water (‘Ice? No?’) before ushering her into his study – or rather, before forcing open the damp-swollen door to the verandah that he called his study. Through the wall of windows that comprised the better part of this room he could see Natasha, by herself under the golden elm, luxuriously inhaling cigarette smoke.

Where had Avril got to?

‘This is nice,’ said Maeve, looking down at his desk, with its litter of newspaper clippings and memos and correspondence. ‘What a great place to work. So sunny and comfy.’

‘Yes,’ said Steven. He arranged the chair at his desk so that it was facing the aged blue typing chair that Avril desperately wanted to throw away. ‘Sit down, won’t you?’ he murmured. ‘Sorry it’s all such a mess.’

‘Oh, it’s not so bad,’ said Maeve. She sat down. There was an awkward silence. Steven decided that she wasn't wearing make-up; her straight brown hair was pulled back, and held in place by a kind of Alice-in-Wonderland headband – what Avril would have called a barrette. She looked extraordinarily young.

Suddenly she launched into a long and complicated explanation.

'After we talked on Monday,' she began abruptly, 'I had a bit of a think. I was wondering if Finlay was really going to be any good for us. Because it's like you said – he doesn't seem to be a very *honourable* man, does he? And I mean, no matter what he might think, in the end he'll always have to follow the Labor line. Otherwise he'll get chucked.'

There was a pause. Maeve looked out the window, but didn't seem to focus on anything in the garden. Her gaze was abstracted.

Steven said nothing.

'Anyway, I had a good long think, and I didn't know what to do, so I called Gareth,' she went on. 'I wanted to ask him what he really felt, in his heart of hearts. And he invited me around. To discuss it, he said. I thought it was going to be one on one. But when I arrived, Vera and Finlay were there with him.' Another pause. 'That was last night,' she added.

Steven made a comfortable, wordless noise. He knew better than to interrupt at this juncture, despite his mounting excitement. He wanted to find out exactly what was going on first.

'It was like an ambush,' Maeve declared. She flushed, and sipped her water. She wouldn't look at Steven. 'Even Vera got stuck into me. Oh, not at the beginning. First they sort of smiled, and made jokes, and asked me what Andrew would think, if he knew I was going out to lunch with middle-aged men.' Andrew, as Steven understood it, was Maeve's long-time boyfriend – a painter from Lawson. 'They were pretty patronising. I mean, I'm used to that, just about everybody does it to me at council meetings – except you and George and Vera – but Finlay was especially bad. And then he started to bag you, Steve. He was really vicious, and I thought, well, that's fair enough. Because you haven't got much to say in Finlay's favour, either.' She cut a glance at Steven as he laughed, and a smile spread across her own face. 'Well, you haven't. Have you?' she said.

'No. I can't deny that.'

'No. So even though I don't like that sort of thing, I didn't let it worry me. But then the other two got stuck into you, and that was totally uncalled for, because you've always been fair with Gareth.' Maeve stopped, as if her last words had opened up a new avenue of thought. 'In fact, that's what I said,' she suddenly exclaimed. 'You don't always agree with us, but you don't always disagree. You're not all closed off, like Allan. I said that, and they hit the *roof*. I mean, it was like I'd said the same thing about Hitler.'

Solemnly, Steven shook his head. He maintained a calm demeanour, though inside him resentment battled furiously with a rising sense of hope.

'Finlay went totally off the deep end,' Maeve proceeded, in pensive accents. 'He accused me of selling out. Talked to me like I was some kind of kid in a schoolyard, and he was on playground duty.' She swallowed. 'Which is, I mean, *so* inappropriate,' she commented, bravely determined not to vent her childish feelings of anger and frustration. 'Then Gareth calmed us all down,' she continued, 'and reminded us that Celeste had withdrawn her support, which meant that we didn't have a candidate for deputy mayor. And he said: "Maybe you'd consider accepting our nomination, Maeve?" '

Steven raised his eyebrows. This was news. He noticed that, at the bottom of the garden, Natasha was gathering up her book and mug and cigarettes, in preparation for returning inside. Still no sign of Avril.

'As a matter of fact,' he interjected, 'I think you'd make a terrific deputy, Maeve. And I'm not just saying that.' He laughed again. 'Which is exactly what I *would* say, if I was trying to butter you up, but – oh well. You know what I mean.'

'Thanks.' She smiled shyly.

'Did you accept?'

'Well – no.' Her smile dissolved into a frown.

'That's what I wanted to tell you about. When Gareth said that, the other two just stared at him. Then Finlay sort of laughed a shaky laugh, like Gareth was kidding, and said, "Oh, I think that little carrot's a bit too important to throw away on Maeve. We have to consider winning Celeste over again. Otherwise we're not going to make it." ' Maeve bit her lip. 'Of course, what he meant was that I would probably fall in with Vera, and Celeste would need a lot more persuasion – you know . . .'

Steven nodded.

'. . . but you can imagine how he said it! And then Vera – listen to this.' She leaned forward. 'Vera started saying that if Finlay became mayor, the deputy would have to be Green. There couldn't be any arguments about that. Forget Celeste – Chris shouldn't have offered her anything the first time round, without consulting the Greens. Well, Finlay argued like hell about that. He said: "If Steve's got Celeste then he's going to win, no arguments." And Vera told him he should meet with Celeste – promise her a few things, but *not* deputy mayor – and Gareth said, "Sell out, you mean?" And Vera said that wasn't what she meant at all, that if Finlay would only be civil to Celeste, then half our problems would be over. And they got into a *huge* argument, just as if I wasn't there, and next thing I knew, Gareth and Vera were fighting over who should get the nomination for deputy mayor.'

Slightly out of breath, Maeve halted for a moment, sipping her water and flopping back into her seat. She shook her head, disbelief and distress engraved upon her small, soft, childish features.

'It was pathetic,' she said at last, staring at the floor. 'It was just pathetic. I mean, they were both so desperate! To be *deputy mayor*! Like it was some big deal!'

Steven shook his own head in sympathy, allowing a smile to play across his mouth. Some of his elation was, by this means, released in the guise of pitying amusement. He was so thrilled that his heart was racing.

'They were trying to rationalise it,' Maeve went on, 'but really it was just this sort of blind, dopey ambition. I mean, I see it all the time, but I didn't realise that *Vera* was affected. Vera! Of all people! I thought she didn't give a *monkey's*!'

'Well . . . maybe it's more of a personal feud with Gareth,' Steven opined, treading carefully. 'I notice they've had a few spats recently over that Kabala Festival thing.' Steven understood the Kabala Festival to be one of those New Age, hippy types of gatherings laced with lots of health food, tarot reading and ambient music; Vera had been sympathetic to proposals that, as part of the festival, a 'Place of Healing' be created near Katoomba, on the edge of the national park (Katoomba being, in Aboriginal tradition, blessed with powerful revitalising properties). Gareth had resisted such an incursion very strongly indeed. *A bunch of drugged-out deadbeats trampling on our native growth* was how he'd described the scenario. 'Perhaps she just feels that Gareth's had his day in the sun,' Steven concluded. 'Perhaps she feels that it's someone else's turn.'

'But not mine,' Maeve snapped, then flushed. 'Not that I care,' she added quickly. 'About being deputy, I mean. I don't feel ready yet. But you should have seen the way Vera was talking!' Assuming a saccharine smile, Maeve crooned: ' "You don't want to be deputy, do you, Maeve? Of course you don't. You've got enough on your plate as it is." '

Maeve lapsed into moody reflection, making absent-minded half-twirls on the fulcrum of Steven's shabby old typing chair, which had wheels as well as a rotating seat mechanism. Steven waited. He knew what was coming. He only hoped that Avril wouldn't interrupt at this crucial point, while Maeve was slowly and reluctantly following her instincts right into his camp.

For an instant he felt almost like a spider.

'Why do you want to be mayor, Steve?' Maeve suddenly queried, looking up. Taken aback, Steven had enough presence of mind to arrange his features into a pensive expression, while he searched frantically for a suitable rejoinder.

The reply *Because I can be* wouldn't cut it with Maeve.

'Well,' he said at last, 'I never actually thought about it till Pat brought it up. And I respect Pat. I thought: If she reckons I'd be good, then perhaps she's right. And to be honest with you, I thought Vera would probably run, which is not something I want to see happen. Vera becoming mayor.' He cleared his throat. 'I also thought Bert would probably run,' he admitted, 'before Finlay announced his plans. And though Bert's a better prospect than Finlay is, I still think they've got big axes to grind. As does Vera. The good thing about Pat is she knows how to chair a meeting. She knows how to let everyone have their say – which would be my intention as mayor. I have my views, and they tend to clash with Vera's, but when you're mayor, you're representing the *whole community*. So I'd be looking to make sure Pat's example was followed. That's all.' He spread his hands. 'I honestly don't like friction. I don't like shouting matches. I'm worried about what will happen if the mayor is someone who thrives on 'em.' Watching Maeve closely, he thought it safe enough to add: 'Like Finlay does.'

Maeve sighed. She looked out the windows again, as they rattled in a stiffening breeze. Grey clouds had rolled in from the south-west. Avril's daffodils bobbed and swayed under a silvery fir.

'You know,' Maeve said, 'I don't want to vote for Finlay. I just don't want to.'

Steven didn't reply.

'But I can't work out if it's because I know deep down that he'd be the wrong kind of guy, or because I just don't like him very much.' She laughed a little. 'Or because I'd prefer a Ward One mayor. Do you think that's it?'

'Can't help you there, Maeve. Sorry.'

'It's like with medicine. The more you hate it, the better it probably is for you. And fish and chips – they're nice, but they're unhealthy. Maybe Finlay's like medicine, and you're like fish and chips.'

'Maybe. On the other hand, maybe Finlay's like window cleaner. Tastes awful and it's pretty bloody bad for you as well.'

Again Maeve laughed. She had a sweet little laugh. Steven had always been charmed by it.

'Okay,' she said. 'You win. You've convinced me.'

Steven straightened.

'Of what?' he asked. 'That Finlay's like window cleaner?'

'Yes. Otherwise I'm going to have to sit there on council and listen to him sneer at Chris and patronise George and make fun of Celeste and pull faces at the public speakers and just – I don't know – just *poison the atmosphere*, and there won't be anyone there to tighten the reins on him. Well, you know how he is.'

'Yes. I do.'

'All right, Steve.' She rose. 'I guess that's it.'

'I'm really grateful, Maeve. Honoured, too.'

'No, no,' she protested, flapping her hand. 'I didn't do it for your sake.'

'Of course not.'

'I just hope you keep your promise. That's all.'

Steven assured her that he would. He was so elated, he wanted to lean down and kiss her – though at the same time he couldn't quite comprehend the reality of what had just occurred. She had given him the mayoralty. She had sat in his creaking old chair, in his draughty little office, and handed him the mayoralty without asking for one thing in return.

It was amazing. Incredible. She was like an angel come down to scatter blessings, an angel with a knitted pattern of windmills marching across the gentle slope of her chest.

Though the day remained overcast, he felt as if the sun had just come out.

'Hang on a second . . .' He gave the door a hard shove, then held it open and stepped back, allowing her to pass ahead of him. Given the opportunity, he would have cast his pullover into a mud puddle, so that she might traverse it without soiling her shoes. He was dizzy with an almost hysterical desire to make some gesture of appreciation. 'You sure you couldn't do with a coffee or something?' he suggested. 'One of Avril's biscuits . . .?'

'No, thanks. Goodness, is that the time?' She was

glancing at her watch. 'I've been here forever.'

'Don't worry about it,' said Steven, though he could hear an ominous clattering in one of the bathrooms. Clearly Avril had decided to play martyr again. 'It's fine. Unless you're supposed to be working at the moment.'

'Actually, I'm supposed to be studying.'

From the dimness of the corridor they stepped out onto the front verandah, which wrapped around one side of the house. (It had been extended a little, so that the guests might have French doors in their bedrooms.) Here Maeve almost collided with Natasha, who appeared to be heading inside; the two girls sprang apart, Maeve with an exclamation of surprise and apology, Natasha with a sharp, startled look and a clatter of high heels.

The contrast between them was immediately apparent. Face to face with Natasha, Maeve looked absurdly young and innocent in her childish pullover and comfortable shoes. Her brown hair shone, her nose gleamed, and her freckles seemed to mark her like a brand – like a school uniform.

Natasha, on the other hand, wore thick black make-up around her slanting eyes. Her dyed hair made her look unnaturally pale; she was wrapped in a velveteen garment of sleazy appearance, and was smoking a cigarette.

Her deadpan gaze ran over Maeve's form before

coming to rest on her face, briefly. With Natasha in high heels, the two girls were exactly the same height.

It occurred to Steven that they must be about the same age, as well.

'Uh . . . Maeve, this is my daughter Natasha. Up from Sydney,' he said. 'Nat, this is Maeve O'Meagher. She's on the council with me.'

'Hi,' said Maeve, with a smile. Natasha nodded, and smiled back – but it was a twisted smile, with more amusement in it than the situation warranted. She looked sideways at her father, and raised an arch, reproving eyebrow.

She might as well have had *Isn't this one a bit young for you?* tattooed across her forehead.

Steven was overcome by a sudden rush of fury. The little shit! How dare she make such assumptions! How dare she turn this shining moment into an awkward encounter!

'I hope you're not taking that fag inside,' he snapped. Whereupon Natasha regarded him for a moment, without expression, before replying in disdainful tones: 'As a matter of fact, I thought I'd stub it out on the Georgian sideboard, Dad.'

Then she dropped her fag-end into the dregs of her coffee, wiped her boots ostentatiously on the mat, and disappeared inside – leaving a smoky smell behind her.

Steven didn't say anything to Avril, at first. He hugged his secret to himself, glorying in it, as she spoke her mind on the bathroom issue again. He couldn't, she said, just *abandon* the bathrooms whenever some councillor decided to drop in. He had to start realising that he had a *job* to do. That they had a *living* to earn. This was a business, not just a home; you didn't see George Lovecek turning customers away every time he wanted to discuss council matters with Steven. At her mention of George Lovecek, Steven realised that he had a fantastic piece of news to impart to George, who would be delighted to hear it. He smiled as he imagined George's response.

'And don't tell me you couldn't have put her off for a few hours,' Avril concluded, her voice shrill with exasperation. 'You just didn't want to. Well – if you only knew how silly you look, standing there with that goofy grin on your face. If you only knew how *old* you must look, to a girl of her age. You're being ridiculous, Steven.'

Poor old Avril, he thought affectionately. She's actually worrying about me and Maeve.

Wait till I tell her my news; then she'll really have something to worry about.

'Now if you don't mind,' said Avril, stepping out of the shower stall that she had been cleaning, 'I'm off to finish *my* chores before the Willards arrive. And don't forget to change before you start again,

Steven – I don't want you getting Domestos on those trousers. You've already ruined too many.'

Like a good little boy, Steven obeyed. He changed back into his drudge outfit, finished his bathrooms, and put away his equipment. Then, while Avril was eating lunch (and throwing together a few rock cakes for the Willards), he stealthily took the cordless phone into his bedroom, and rang George at the shop.

It was Kyle who answered.

'No, mate, he's talking to a supplier,' Kyle rejoined, after Steven had asked if George was available. Cursing, Steven left a message; he was desperate to break the wonderful news, but realised that if he broke it to Avril, her reaction would be less than sympathetic. So he called Pat, and discovered that Pat, too, could not be reached.

Defeated, he therefore returned to the kitchen, where he allowed Avril to serve him a warmed-up dish of macaroni cheese. He ate it alone, for she obviously couldn't bring herself to sit at the same table with him; retrieving her coffee and her magazine, she retired into the sitting room. Steven watched her go without compunction, his mind on other things. He was thinking about the mayoral perks. As mayor, he would have a secretary – Lillian Ng, in fact. He would command the services of the mayoral car and driver. There were robes, too; when was the last time he had seen Pat wearing them? At some citizenship ceremony, wasn't it? Back when Stacy-Ann Keinlig, of the Willowood Guesthouse at Blackheath, had been sworn in as an Australian citizen. Steven and Avril had both attended, because Stacy, at that time, had been treasurer of the Getaway Association.

It occurred to Steven that he would look good in those sweeping robes and that big gold chain – better than Pat did, at any rate. He had the height for them. He turned over in his mind an image of the mayoral office, with its display case full of sister-city gifts from the USA and Japan, its original oil paintings of the Blue Mountains, its vast blackwood desk. He hadn't sat behind a desk like that since being retrenched from the bank. It would feel good to have an in-tray again. To have a secretary again. To have free access to a decent photocopier . . .

The phone rang.

With great presence of mind, he moved into the drawing room before answering it, closing the door behind him. If it was George on the phone, he didn't want Avril listening in. He wanted to break the news to her gently, at a favourable moment.

'George!' he said, upon hearing a familiar salutation at the other end of the line. 'Mate, you'll never guess what just happened!' Breathlessly, ebulliently, he recounted the story of Maeve's miraculous offer, relishing every detail, and becoming so ecstatic in the process that he forgot to lower his voice. 'So that's where we stand!' he exclaimed, upon concluding his narrative. 'Seven votes! George, I'm *in*! I'm in, mate!'

'Bloody hell,' said George. He didn't sound too excited.

'Well – aren't you pleased? Christ, George, I couldn't *believe* it.'

'You're not mayor yet, remember. We've still got a week to go. A week's a long time in politics – to coin a phrase.'

'I know, I know.' Steven was beginning to feel deflated. 'But you've got to admit, it's a bloody miracle. Don't you think?'

'Oh, yes. No question.'

'All right. Well . . . just thought I'd let you know.'

'Thanks.'

'Maybe we should get together with Pat some time soon. Pat and Allan. Get together and discuss things.'

'Sure. Absolutely.'

'Okay. Fine. Well, I'll see you then, George.'

'Goodbye, Steve.'

Odd, thought Steven, as George hung up. Why isn't he more thrilled? Does he know something that I don't know? Does he *suspect* something that I don't suspect?

Or is he just a tiny bit jealous?

Frowning, Steven returned to the kitchen. Upon pushing open the door, he found himself face to face with Avril, who was standing, arms folded, like some sort of accusing spectre. Like the Ghost of Christmas Past.

Her eyes were as hard as her polished granite benchtops.

'So,' she declared. 'That's what you were so pleased about.'

'What?'

'You've got seven votes. I just heard you telling George. You've got seven votes now.'

Steven sighed. Goddammit, he thought. There's no privacy in this house. Every time you turn around someone's waiting to use the phone, or poking through your CD collection.

'Yes, I have. At present,' he replied cautiously. He noticed, with a sinking heart, that she was looking very pinched around the lips and cheekbones. Always a bad sign. 'But it's early days yet. I won't know for sure until we're right on the starting blocks.'

Avril was tapping a finger against her upper arm. Steven could only assume, as the silence stretched on, that she was marshalling her ammunition.

He wondered uneasily where Natasha had got to.

'Where's Nat?' he inquired.

'Out,' was Avril's response. 'Having lunch somewhere. I couldn't go with her, because I was *cleaning the bathrooms.*'

'Avril, for Chrissake!'

'Steven, has it even crossed your mind to ask me

how *I* would cope with being lady mayoress?' Her voice quavered dangerously. 'Have you even considered what this is going to entail for *me*?'

'Well . . .' Steven was nonplussed. Lady mayoress? There hadn't been one of those for at least seven years. 'I don't know if – I mean, Frank Baldwin –'

'Isn't a wife. Steven, I spoke to Trudy Haslitt at that awful dinner we went to for the hospital – she's the widow of Bob Haslitt –'

'Yes, I know. The former mayor.'

'Well, did you also happen to know that as lady mayoress, she led a – an absolute *dog's* life, chased from pillar to post by all these female auxiliary committees and fete organisers and people arranging charity fashion shows.'

'Sweetheart, that was back in the early eighties. Things have probably changed since then.'

'I see.' She took a deep breath. 'And if they haven't? You'll be expecting me to do my bit – is that what you're trying to say?'

'Look, I've no idea what goes on in that department –'

'Obviously.'

'. . . but it's not as if *you'll* be elected. There's no law saying that you'll have to become patroness of anything. At least . . .' Frowning, he wondered if he might, in fact, have encountered at one time some sort of subclause – some kind of stray provision –

regarding the honorary appointment of the mayoress to something-or-other . . . he couldn't recall . . . he might have dreamed it . . .

'I'm not going to do this, Steven,' Avril announced. 'I'm not going to organise any stalls or join any school boards or attend any annual general meetings of the Girl Guides Association or . . . or anything like that. And I won't be attending any more dinners with you, either. Because *someone's* got to look after our business. Someone's got to make sure the clients keep coming, or we're both going to starve.'

The sanctimonious way she made this declaration suddenly ignited Steven's anger. Where the hell did she get off? But he struggled to control himself.

'No-one's forcing you to do anything,' he said patiently. 'I just think you should start looking at things the way I do. A lot of benefits flow from community service. It would be good for you to get out a bit more, and talk to people. You know how shy you are with the guests. Why not try and brush up your social skills? Learn a bit about meeting and greeting? I'm not saying you make the guests uncomfortable, but you've got to admit, you don't talk to them much.'

'No, I don't,' Avril replied coldly. 'Because that's your job.'

'For heaven's sake *why*? Why should it be my job?' In frustration, Steven raised his voice. 'You've got to start crossing these boundaries of yours, Avril! You've got to step out into the real world!'

'Don't be ridiculous.'

'I mean it! You won't do this and you won't do that – you're like a child, demanding to be looked after.'

'I am not!'

'You are! Look at that credit-card business! Always running to me, when you have to put a credit card through the machine! It's the simplest thing in the world, Avril, but you're scared of it! You don't want the responsibility!'

'Because it's *your job*, Steven!' Avril exclaimed, the pitch of her voice rising to meet his. 'I have my jobs, and you have yours! I refuse to do your jobs on top of mine!'

'But why should it be my job to hammer in a nail? Why? Can you tell me that?'

'Because it's my job to dust the pictures, that's why! And to supervise the cleaner, and to water the garden, and to prepare the shopping lists, and to do the cooking and to make the beds, and to wash the fitted sheets –'

'Fine. Okay.' He threw up his hands in defeat. 'You're twisting this around – you know what I'm getting at. But if you want to be a child, be a child. If you don't want to contribute to this community . . .'

'Oh, that's rich, coming from you!' Avril squeaked,

her voice losing force and coherence as she grew more furious. 'If anyone wants me to be a child, it's you! So you can feel like a grown-up, with all your silly schoolyard fights and your nasty little games and your . . . your . . . augh!'

She pushed past him, out of the kitchen. He followed her down the corridor, *thud-thud-thud* along the Persian runner.

'*You* should talk about little games!' he bellowed. 'Don't think I can't see what *you're* trying to do, with poor old George!'

Avril halted, just a step away from the front entrance. She rounded on him. Her cheeks were mottled with red; her hands were shaking.

'You stupid fool!' was her strangled cry.

Then she turned, flung open the door – and came face to face with the Willards.

They had to be the Willards. The man was carrying a suitcase, and the woman an overnight bag. Their car was sitting in the driveway. The woman was also clutching a well-fingered Bella Vista advertising leaflet, as if it were a lucky charm destined to protect her from wrong turns, missed street signs and unfriendly receptions.

They gawked stupidly, open-mouthed, like fish.

'Oh!' said Avril. She raised her hand to her hair. Then, scraping together the last vestiges of her dignity, she added: 'It's . . . it's Carol, is it? And Bill?'

'Ye-es,' the man replied. He didn't sound too sure. Or perhaps he wasn't too sure if he had come to the right sort of place. Peering over the top of Avril's head, Steven could see from the look in his eyes that he'd heard the shouting.

'Well!' With a jocularity that he knew must have sounded as unconvincing to his guests as it did to himself, Steven stepped forward and shook Bill's hand. 'Carol and Bill! Welcome! Welcome! Here – let me take that.'

He reached for Bill's suitcase. But Bill seemed reluctant to surrender it; was he worried that Steven might fling it at Avril's head?

'No,' he muttered. 'It's okay – it's not heavy.'

'Would you like a drink?' Avril trilled. 'Coffee? Tea? Rock-cakes?'

Bill and Carol looked at each other, hesitating. For one horrifying moment, Steven wondered if they were going to leave. He wondered if they were going to turn around, get in their car, and return to Sydney – or at least seek out other accommodation.

But the moment passed.

'Thank you,' said Bill, clearing his throat. 'Coffee would be nice.'

Then cautiously, with a sidelong glance at Steven, he crossed the threshold.

# CHAPTER SEVEN

That evening, the atmosphere at the Bella Vista Guesthouse was not as warm and cosy as it should have been. The Willards behaved like wraiths; clearly alarmed by the signs of enmity to which they had been exposed, they flitted in and out on noiseless feet, dodging their hosts, silently closing doors, and disappearing up the driveway in their luxury car, which emitted only a faint purring sound and an invisible cloud of exhaust fumes. Steven didn't bother to light a fire – in fact he spent almost the whole evening on the phone, talking first to Pat, then to Allan, then to George again, then (for some reason) to the council's general manager, Vic Rebke. Brooding over the gas burners, Avril contributed her own aura of gloom, which intensified and became more unstable – like a stormhead – upon Steven's entering the kitchen. They didn't exchange a word as he sat down to eat her veal cutlets. When Natasha joined them, Avril served up the meat with fresh beans and mashed potatoes, slammed Steven's pet jar of pickled gherkins onto the table with a calculated degree of force, and finally seated herself, scraping her chair noisily across the floor tiles.

For several minutes, there was no sound except the clink of stainless steel on porcelain.

'So,' Avril said at last, turning to Natasha. 'What did you do this afternoon?'

Natasha, who had been concentrating on her plate, lifted her eyes and said: 'Who? Me?'

'Did you go for a walk?'

'I went for a drive.'

'Really? Where?'

'Blackheath.'

'Oh, yes. Well – Blackheath's a nice place.'

Silence. Avril wondered what her daughter had done, upon reaching her destination. There were a couple of antique shops in Blackheath, but Natasha didn't seem to care much for antiques. There was a wonderful lookout, but she wasn't someone you could picture standing on the edge of a precipice, the wind in her hair, inhaling great draughts of pure mountain air while bellbirds chimed in the treetops far, far below.

She had the strained, smoky look of someone who had spent the entire afternoon – indeed, the entire year – indoors.

'Good pub,' Natasha observed, suddenly and laconically.

'What?' said Avril.

'Good pub. In Blackheath.'

'Oh.'

'I'm talking about the one on the corner. The big one.'

'Yes. I know it.'

'The owner of that hotel is on the UMT board,' Steven volunteered. 'He's a terrific bloke.'

Natasha stared. Avril didn't even afford him that much acknowledgement. She very pointedly gave him the cold shoulder, her face turned away.

'Is that where you had your lunch?' she inquired of her daughter. 'In Blackheath?'

'No. I went to Katoomba for lunch.'

'I'm sorry I couldn't join you,' Avril said sweetly. The invitation had been decidedly half-hearted, but she took comfort from the fact that she hadn't been repulsed. 'Unfortunately, I had to clean the bathrooms this morning. And you know how long they take.'

'As a matter of fact, you cleaned half a bathroom,' Steven interjected, sardonically. 'And you didn't even have to do that. I got 'em finished in time.'

Still Avril refused to speak to him. 'I never know what your father's going to be doing,' she informed Natasha. 'It's so hard to schedule anything, when he's always disappearing off somewhere.'

'Listen, Nat.' Steven spoke with forced gaiety. 'You wouldn't mind being a mayor's daughter, would you? There's a chance that I might be elected mayor. Of course, your mother doesn't like it because –'

'Okay. Stop.' Natasha lifted a hand. 'Finito.'

Confused, Avril opened her mouth. But Natasha wouldn't let her speak.

'We had an agreement, remember?' she drawled. 'We agreed that you'd leave me out of it.'

'But Nat,' Avril protested, appalled as she suddenly realised what her daughter was getting at, 'we're not trying to –'

'Yes you are. And I'm not taking sides. Forget it.' Natasha rose. She picked up her plate, her knife and her fork. 'I think I'll eat in front of the TV, if you don't mind. So you can sort it all out by yourselves.'

She spoke with just enough weary condescension to ignite Avril's temper. It was infuriating – absolutely infuriating – to witness Natasha assuming the role of offended arbiter of good taste, when Natasha herself was habitually so discourteous, so unfeeling, so graceless in her demeanour and habits. How dare she presume to talk like that?

Years ago, during that unnerving period when

Avril's mother had been dying, it had been agreed that no-one in the family would endeavour to enlist the support of anyone else in the family during a family squabble. (This understanding had been reached after Natasha – normally inscrutable – had suddenly thrown a plate of spaghetti bolognese across the room in a quite uncharacteristic display of anguish.) Stricken with guilt, Avril and Steven had promised never again to pester her with complaints about one another.

It was Avril's opinion, however, that Natasha had to some extent taken advantage of their compliance. She not only refused to endure complaints; she refused to endure anything at all that pertained to her parents' daily lives. Avril had only to say: 'Your father's bought a new computer', and Natasha would be sliding out of earshot, claiming that she needed to visit the bathroom, or make a phone call, or change her shoes. A reluctance to talk about her own life was complemented by a reluctance to engage in any aspect of her parents' lives, presumably because she found them so boring.

And what had Avril been trying to do, in this particular instance? (Steven too, if it came to the point.) She had simply been trying to explain the current situation – that Steven was exceptionally busy, that he would probably become busier, and that, as a result, Avril had been unable to join Natasha for lunch.

It had hardly been an invitation to 'take sides'.

But she couldn't unburden herself of this opinion – not to Steven, at any rate. So, as the brainless babble of a television game show trickled out of the drawing room, she and her husband quietly (and quickly) finished their meal. Then Avril cleared up, and Steven wrote letters, and they fell into bed at half past ten, without having exchanged more than three or four monosyllables since sunset. Avril was still nursing in her heart a grievance against Natasha, but before drifting off to sleep she decided to be patient. Natasha, after all, was under a lot of stress, what with Fergus and Janelle and everything.

Just this once, she decided, I'll let it pass.

The next morning, she cooked a hearty breakfast for the Willards, who barely inhaled its steam before decamping at the earliest opportunity. Avril could hardly blame them; the atmosphere was still poisonous. Steven banged through the bathrooms, then vanished without offering any kind of explanation. Natasha kept to her own room. Avril, simmering with resentment, methodically completed her chores, wondering why, today of all days, she could seem to derive no comfort from her beautiful house. Normally, when she was upset, she had only to gaze at the cornice in the drawing room, or at her pseudo-Georgian sideboard, or at the exquisite scene framed by her luxurious dining-room curtains (a scene worthy of immortalising in watercolour, with its delicate gradations of green, and its mossy lawn, and its perfectly placed sundial), and instantly her cares would fall away. There was harmony, serenity, in every corner of her house; it soothed both the heart and the senses.

Not today, however. Not sufficiently, at any rate.

When the phone rang, Avril was hard pressed to answer it civilly. And when she heard Celeste's voice, the effort required to remain civil became even more burdensome. Celeste didn't just request Steven – she demanded him. She was more than peremptory. She was downright rude.

'I'm afraid Steven isn't here,' Avril replied, as quietly as possible.

'Where is he?'

'I'm sorry. I don't know.'

'Well – tell him I've got to talk to him. Tell him it's important.'

'I shall.'

'Tell him to call me this morning. And if he can't call me this morning, tell him to call me at this number after half past one – I'll give it to you – have you got a pen?'

Avril recorded the number on a pale yellow Post-it Note. As Celeste abruptly terminated the conversation, it crossed Avril's mind that she would dearly love to tear up the yellow slip and throw the pieces into the rubbish bin.

If she did, of course, there would be hell to pay. Steven wouldn't return the call, and Celeste would be *most* offended.

Most offended.

Avril fingered the little yellow slip. Lifting her gaze, she stared out the window, noting that her foxgloves were progressing nicely. Sunlight sparkled on the dewy lawn. A pair of magpies ambled across her field of vision, searching the ground for insects. It was going to be a beautiful day.

Steven wanted her to get out and do something. Well, she would take his advice. She *would* do something. She would act. She would make an effort.

With quick, neat movements, she tore up the Post-it Note. Then she dropped the pieces into her recently disinfected pedal-bin. Then she went to the phone, and called George Lovecek.

He seemed delighted to hear from her.

'Hello, Avril! How's it going?' he said. 'Are you out in the garden? It's a beautiful day.'

'Beautiful.'

'Aren't you well? You sound a bit . . .' George hesitated, '. . . down in the dumps,' he concluded, lamely.

'Actually, George, I was wondering if we could get together for lunch today. Just you and I. Is that possible? There's something I want to discuss.'

During the brief silence that followed, Avril carefully wiped some dust (how had it been missed?) off the corner of a picture frame. She stared at the damp-spotted nineteenth-century engraving – *John Wesley visits his mother's grave* – that was sitting behind the glass. Such a lugubrious scene.

'All right,' said George, in a hesitant manner. 'Where?'

'Not in a cafe.' Avril was firm on this point. 'I'll bring a picnic lunch, and we'll go and sit in a park somewhere. It's such lovely weather.'

'All right,' George said again. Then he added shyly: 'Is something wrong, Avril?'

'I'll talk about that when we meet. About half past twelve?'

'Fine.'

'Good. See you then.'

A picnic lunch, Avril thought, as she hung up. It had better be an impressive one. Artichoke hearts? I think I have some. The last of the brie. Some of my relish, perhaps . . .

She went off to search the pantry for provisions.

They ate their picnic at the Everglades, amid Paul Sorensen's dry-stone walls and grassy terraces. Because they were both Friends of the Everglades, they were not obliged to pay entrance fees; George carried Avril's wicker basket down the sweeping gravel driveway, past banks of Japanese windflower and azalea bushes, until they reached the studio terrace, where they arranged themselves on chairs placed in front of the garden theatre. It was all very satisfying: the cherry trees were a riot of colour, the bluebells were out, and a smoky vista of the Jamieson Valley was framed by a brick pergola draped in wisteria vines. Avril loved the Everglades. She felt at home in such elegant surroundings. She could sympathise with the millionaire who had commissioned the garden's creation, and admire the genius of its designer, who had so skilfully combined its wild, bushy aspects with a formal nucleus of clipped hedges, smooth turf and carefully constructed stonework.

She knew that she always appeared to advantage against spacious and civilised backdrops of this kind; the wilderness was not her natural milieu. Aware that George was a little unnerved, she wanted to tackle him in a place where she felt at the same time relaxed and competent. Besides, it was the perfect environment in which to consume brie, water biscuits, and little cream cakes.

The food complemented the scenery in a way that Avril found aesthetically pleasing.

'Some of those borders are a bit of a mess,' she observed, after familiarising George with the contents of her picnic basket. 'Am I imagining it, or is this place becoming a little shabby?'

‘I think it is,’ George agreed. He was concentrating on his tea, and on the salmon-and-cucumber sandwiches. ‘They can’t get enough volunteers.’

‘I wish I had the time. If only I had the time. I’d love to take care of this garden.’

‘Me too.’

‘We’d learn a lot. It would be very useful. But I’m so busy . . .’ Trailing off, Avril wiped her fingers on a paper serviette. ‘I suppose you know about Steven,’ she sighed, gazing dreamily at the sandstone arch that formed the backdrop of the little outdoor theatre. ‘I suppose he told you he has seven votes now.’

George mumbled an acknowledgement. Looking at him, Avril saw that he was fiddling unhappily with his plastic teacup, eyes downcast.

‘Do you think he’s really going to be elected, George?’

‘I don’t know.’

‘He thinks he is. He’s sure he is.’

‘He might be.’

‘If he’s elected, I don’t know what I’ll do. I just don’t know how I’m going to cope.’ Speaking in a small, thin, weary voice, Avril tried not to plead. ‘I don’t know how he thinks we’re going to carry on. Sometimes I wonder if he’s trying to escape from the business – if he doesn’t want to deal with it anymore. I don’t know.’ She sighed again. ‘He probably thinks I’m neurotic, worrying like this. I daresay he feels that we'll muddle through somehow. But muddling through just isn't enough – not in this business. Not when so much rides on your reputation.'

George said nothing.

'I'm sorry, George. It's not fair of me to bail you up like this.'

'No, no . . .' He was almost incoherent. 'Not a bit . . . don't worry . . .'

'I just – I just wanted to know if you could tell me . . .' Avril was uncertain as to how she should proceed. He seemed distressed, genuinely distressed, but was it on account of her own distress, or because he didn't actually want to be there? 'Isn't there someone else?' she said at last. 'Isn't there someone else who would make a satisfactory mayor? Someone you both respect, like Pat? Because maybe if *you* talked to Steven, George . . . he won't listen to me – he thinks I'm being silly.'

'*Me?*' George exclaimed. 'God, Avril – I mean –'

'No, no. I'm sorry.'

'Of course I sympathise, of course I do.'

'I shouldn't have asked.'

'No, it's not that! Don't feel like that!'

'It's an imposition.'

'Not at all.' George leaned forward earnestly. He had recovered something of his aplomb, and was clearly anxious that she should not think too badly of him. 'I understand your position,' he said. 'Of course

I do. And look – I'm not all that fussed, one way or another. I think Steven would make a good mayor. Certainly better than Finlay would. But I don't know that he'd be faultless. I don't know that he's irreplaceable. I just don't know.'

'And what if I end up as mayoress?' Avril said mournfully. 'What if I have to open flower shows? I'll keel over and die.'

'Is that what you think?' George eyed her doubtfully. 'But you seem like just the sort of person to open a flower show. In a big hat.'

'Goodness, George. I don't know whether to take that as a compliment or not.'

He offered her an awkward smile. 'What I mean is, you've always struck me as being . . . well, being a real lady,' he said. 'In the nicest sense of the word.'

'Oh. Thank you very much.'

'Like the lady of the manor sort of thing.'

'Oh.'

'Elegant.'

Avril smiled.

'But it wouldn't be fair,' George stumbled on, 'asking you to be mayoress if you were very busy.'

'No. And even if I wasn't, I'd be hopeless.'

'Surely not.'

'Oh yes. Quite hopeless. I just lose my voice in public. Go all to pieces. Forget people's names . . .' Avril drooped a little, then rallied as something occurred to her. 'Now *Dianne* would make a good mayoress,' she remarked. 'Dianne would be excellent. Why don't you run for mayor, George, and let Dianne be mayoress?'

George laughed.

'It'd be right up her street,' he agreed ruefully.

'And you'd make a *wonderful* mayor, George,' Avril continued, with enthusiasm. 'You're so sensible and compassionate and even-handed. You're so clever. I'm sure you'd be excellent.'

He laughed again. 'Well, thanks,' he said, 'but I don't think you'd get anyone to agree with you.'

'Why not?'

'Because I don't have the charisma.'

'Nonsense.'

'Really, Avril – it wouldn't work.' He smiled placatingly. 'Besides, I don't want to be mayor. It's bad enough being a councillor.'

Avril, surprised, peered at him over the top of her sunglasses. 'What do you mean?' she said. 'Don't you like it?'

'Not much.'

'*Really?* How amazing. Steven *loves* it.'

'Yes. I know. It's incredible.'

'So you won't be running for election next year?'

'Not a chance.'

'Goodness.' Avril absorbed this revelation in silence for a while. There was no sound except the rustle of leaves, as gentle breezes made the treetops dance. She smeared brie onto a biscuit.

'I don't like the politicking,' George continued, in pensive tones. 'I didn't realise there'd be so much of it, you see. Not at this level of government.' With a half-smile, he added: 'I suppose I was being naive.'

'Steven seems to be in his element,' was Avril's response. 'But then he always did like networking.'

'Oh, Steve knows the score. He's sussed it out, no problem.'

'He's very outgoing. Not like me. We're opposites, in a way.'

'Yes. I realise that.'

'I suppose I'm more like you, George. Gardening and things . . . I like a bit of peace.' Avril made a vague, sweeping gesture that encompassed the plunging shrubberies, the rolling lawns, the distant crags, the empty sky. 'Not that I could cope with a computer shop. Not that I could cope with anything much, except housework. I'm good at housework.'

'Don't sell yourself short, Avril.'

'I'm not,' she said, her gaze on the horizon. 'Steven says it'll be good for me, if I'm forced to deal with new things. Which means he obviously doesn't like me the way I am now.'

'Avril –'

'But I haven't changed.' Her voice became hoarse;

with one finger over her mouth, she cleared her throat before continuing. 'I was the same when we married. So was he. I don't understand what the problem is.'

'Not you, I'm sure.'

'Maybe it's the business.'

'Maybe.'

'He seems to be looking for any excuse to get out of the house.'

Again, silence fell. Avril made a point of looking away from George; she studied instead the bronze relief behind the theatre pool. Who was it supposed to represent? Apollo, perhaps? With neat, firm movements she extracted a handkerchief from her skirt pocket and blew her nose.

'Listen,' George said, then hesitated. She turned towards him. He was wearing a very unhappy expression. 'Listen,' he repeated, 'I'll – I'll have a think about this.'

She waited, wide-eyed.

'It doesn't seem right to me – perhaps he doesn't realise how miserable you really are. Perhaps if you told him.'

'I have told him.'

'Yes. Well. Maybe if he realised that you'd come to me for help . . .' George didn't finish his sentence. He was now fiddling with the silverware. 'Maybe there is an alternative,' he said. 'Personally, I've no objection to Bert Plummer as mayor. And his wife's a real committee woman.'

Avril held her breath.

'I don't think Pat has any particular problem with Bert, either,' George went on. 'And Chris *must* prefer him to Finlay. So perhaps, if we could line up six votes behind Bert – seven, if you count Celeste – well, it would be a big shift, but it might be possible. If Steve agrees to pull out.'

'Oh, George.' Avril's eyes filled with tears. 'Do you think so? Oh George, if only he would . . .'

'I'll – I'll put it to him,' said George. 'If you'd rather I did it . . .'

'Oh, please!'

'I mean, just as a suggestion. Since you did come to me. But of course it's for him to decide.'

'Yes, of course. Oh, George, you're so wonderful! How ever can I thank you?'

'Don't – don't.' He flapped his hands, shrinking with embarrassment. 'Please. It's nothing.'

'I'm so sorry to get you involved.'

'Avril, I'm honoured that you chose to confide in me. Really.'

'Really?'

'It's very flattering.'

Avril, her heart brimming with gratitude, gazed at him fondly. He sat there in his cheap shirt, his brown eyes blinking behind his steel-rimmed spectacles, and she wanted to plant a kiss on his plump, guileless cheek.

But she couldn't do that. So she did the next best thing, picking up a Tupperware container.

'Cake, George?' she said.

Saturday was glorious, fine and clear, with a touch of summer warmth and a sky of intense, cloudless blue. Leura began to fill up quickly; by noon the Sydney tourists were pouring in, and Steven had his hands full, turning down telephone requests for accommodation. Every single Getaway establishment was full to the brim, so he couldn't even refer the callers to another guesthouse. 'If only Natasha weren't here,' he lamented, 'we could have hired out her room!'

Avril ignored him. She would never have considered hiring out Natasha's room. For one thing, she didn't fancy sharing a bath with a stranger; for another, she regarded such an action as a form of betrayal, a kind of rejection, and feared that Natasha might feel the same way. She did, however, worry about Fergus. If he was coming up to confer with them, where would he be staying? Had he booked a room in advance? When Avril asked her daughter this question, Natasha simply shrugged. 'I told him he wouldn't be sleeping here,' she said. 'If he's too stupid to think ahead, that's his lookout.'

Natasha seemed quite untroubled by the prospect of an emotional confrontation with Fergus. The meeting between them, which was scheduled for 8:30 p.m., appeared to concern her less than the fact that she had somehow mislaid an earring. As for Steven: upon being reminded that his presence would also be required that evening, he groaned and looked cross. 'Oh Christ,' he protested. 'Is that tonight?'

'You know it is,' said Avril.

'Has it occurred to you that we're full up here? You realise we'll probably be in and out the whole time, showing guests how to work their electric blankets?'

'Most of the guests will be at dinner.'

'You hope.'

They still weren't communicating with any kind of ease, but since they were both extraordinarily busy, it didn't seem to matter much. Every time the phone rang, Avril's heart would leap in her chest; she was expecting George to call, and, while to some degree dreading the inevitable fallout, she was also disappointed when, time after time, the callers identified themselves as hopeful tourists. Where, Avril wondered, was George? Had he changed his mind? On one occasion, while Steven was out meeting the 11:29 train, Celeste rang. She wanted to know why Steven hadn't returned her call. Avril assured her, untruthfully, that the message had been passed on. But they were very busy, the place was full, and Steven had so much on his mind . . .

'Tell him to call me when he gets beck,' Celeste insisted. 'Tell him it's *urgent.*'

'I shall.'

'Tell him he has to *make* the time. If he can't find time for a phone call, how's he going to find the time to be mayor?'

'I'll tell him.'

Despite her assurances, however, Avril neglected to acquaint Steven with Celeste's demands. Instead she scribbled a note on a scrap of white paper, and pinned it to the cork board in the kitchen. She was aware that, unless alerted to the presence of a written message, Steven was unlikely to check the cork board. He had always been hopelessly remiss when it came to things like that. 'Details, details' was how he dismissed them.

Sure enough, he didn't glance at the board all day. He barely even entered the kitchen. When he wasn't cleaning bathrooms, he was talking on the phone or sitting hunched over the computer or charming the guests as he gave them directions. It was Avril who, at half past four, finally answered the long-awaited call from George Lovecek. Steven was outside, vacuuming his car.

'I'll get him, shall I?' Avril asked George.

'Yes, um . . . yes. Hang on, though. Have you said anything?'

'No. Not yet. We haven't really been speaking.'

'Oh.'

'I will, though. If you want me to.'

'No. I mean, it's up to you. Whatever you want. I thought Steve and I could have a drink tomorrow. At a pub somewhere. Just him and me.'

'That sounds nice.'

'A civilised discussion.' There was a brief pause. 'At least, I *hope* it'll be civilised.'

Avril considered the possibility of a pub brawl involving George Lovecek and her husband. It seemed an unlikely scenario. Apart from anything else, Steven had a civic reputation to uphold.

'I'm sure it'll be fine,' she said soothingly. Then, having fetched Steven, she proceeded to eavesdrop, quite openly, on his conversation with George – which was brief and to the point. A meeting was arranged. A venue was agreed upon. Steven spoke pleasantly, breezily, laughing several times and making a joke. But he avoided Avril's eye, and, upon hanging up, offered her no explanation. Instead he went straight back outside. Pretty soon she heard the whine of the vacuum cleaner – which was preferable, she thought, to the sound of Steven yak-yak-yakking away on the phone. At least he was *doing* something, for once.

She had been relieved to learn that George didn't intend to tackle her husband until both men were in the same room together. If he had broached the subject of Bert Plummer's possible candidacy over the phone, Steven would have been in no fit state to confront Fergus that evening. He would have been too busy fretting over tactics and votes and who preferred whom. He might even, in a fit of pique, have taken himself off to discuss the matter with Bert or Pat or someone else whose opinion really counted with Steven. He might have refused to help Avril at all.

Avril herself was beginning to worry about Natasha. She had been gone since lunchtime, and had given her mother no indication of where she was, or when she was expecting to return. (By half past eight, surely?) At ten past six, Natasha called to say that she wouldn't be home for dinner; she was eating out. But she'd be back in time to welcome Fergus, she said.

'Eating out?' said Avril, stupidly. 'Why?'

'Because I fancy Thai tonight. Sorry, Mum. Hope you haven't gone to any trouble.'

'Have you met up with friends? Is that it?'

'Don't worry. I'll be back in time.'

As Avril had expected, Steven reacted badly to this news. Moodily prodding his beef Wellington with a fork, he observed that Natasha would probably be out partying all night, while he and Avril dealt with

Fergus. 'I bet she arranged it all beforehand,' he said, 'as a way of giving Fergus the finger.'

'Nonsense,' Avril replied.

'Fergus'll throw a fit, but what does she care? *She* won't have to cope with him.'

'She'll be back,' Avril said coldly. 'She promised.'

Steven grunted. As the evening advanced, he grew more and more morose, while Avril grew more and more nervous. Where *was* Natasha? Why didn't she come? At twenty to nine, having finished her ironing, Avril was making herself a cup of tea when she heard the sound of raised voices.

It seemed to be coming from the garden.

'What the hell is that?' Steven demanded. He had been reading a paper in their sitting room; now he was standing at the kitchen door. 'Do you hear that?'

'Yes,' said Avril.

'Bloody hell.'

'I think it's out front . . .'

'Bloody hell.'

Steven hurried down the corridor, with Avril at his heels. As they advanced, the shouting became louder; one of the guests, who was hovering apprehensively around the front door, remarked that he had been watching television in the drawing room, and had looked out the window, and had seen some sort of conflict happening just up the driveway . . . there were a couple of cars out there . . .

'I've been eating takeaway,' the guest – a Mr Dyster – remarked. 'I hope you don't mind. It's just that there's a show on the ABC that I hate to miss – I spread a towel over my knees, so nothing would fall on the couch . . .'

From the smell, Avril deduced that he had been eating chips. Chips! In her beautiful drawing room! Not that there were any rules posted about eating in the drawing room, but still – it had cost a fortune to have that couch re-covered.

Steven flung open the front door.

'My wife will be back from dinner soon, with her friends,' Mr Dyster continued. 'I hope they don't walk into all this . . . whatever it is. Those cars,' he added, 'are blocking the driveway.'

One of them, Avril could see, was Natasha's car. In the light of a nearby streetlamp she could also make out the slightly battered outline of another vehicle, parked behind Natasha's – an elderly red sedan that stood with its driver's door open. The driver himself wasn't in it. The driver, Avril deduced, was probably the thin man haranguing the blond man who had apparently just emerged from Natasha's car.

The thin man was wearing a goatee. It occurred to Avril that he looked like Fergus – that, indeed, he probably was Fergus. She had only a vague memory of Fergus, but she did recall the goatee. And the black clothes.

There was someone else in Natasha's car, sitting behind the wheel. Was it Natasha? In the darkness, Avril couldn't tell. She moved forward a little.

'You're a fucking nutter! A fucking *nutter*!' the blond man was shouting.

'She asked me –' Fergus began, in equally heated tones, but was prevented from continuing.

'Bullshit!' the blond man roared. 'She asked you what? To fuck off and die?'

'She *wanted* me to come!'

'*Bullshit!* She doesn't want you anywhere near her, can't you get that into your thick skull, you fuckwit?! She's *finished* with you!' The blond man was skirting Natasha's bumper, closing in on Fergus, who stooped to address the person in the driver's seat.

'What the fuck is this?' he wailed. 'I thought we had a date – you tell him!'

'Get lost,' said the blond man.

'Natasha –'

'*Get lost!*'

'Fuck *off*!' Jerking upright, Fergus bared his teeth at the blond man, who was now standing beside him. 'I'm not talking to you!'

'You're not talking to her, either.'

'This is none of your business!'

'If you don't go, I'll call the police.'

'I was fucking *invited*!'

'Just *go*!' cried a voice that Avril recognised as

Natasha's. It was thin and high and unsteady. 'Please! Can't you leave me alone? I don't wanna *see* you!'

'Then why did you fucking invite me?' Fergus raged. 'Just so I could watch you and Fuckface necking in your car, you *bitch*?'

'Back off,' said the blond man.

'You back off.'

'I mean it. I'll call the cops.' The blond man advanced on Fergus, who was the smaller of the two. Fergus, his personal space invaded, pushed the blond man.

The blond man pushed him back.

'Hey!' Steven shouted. 'That's enough!'

Two pale faces turned towards him.

'What the hell's going on?' Steven demanded. 'Who *are* you people?'

'It's all right, Dad.' Natasha stuck her head out of the car. 'It's under control. Fergus is just leaving.'

'Oh, yeah?' said Fergus.

'Yeah,' said the blond man.

There was a tense silence. Then, slowly, Fergus stepped back.

'All right,' he growled. 'Fine. You don't wanna see me, I don't wanna see you.'

The blond man snorted.

'I don't know what you're fucking playing at, Natasha,' Fergus went on, 'but I'll tell you one thing – you're fucking crazy.'

'*You're* the one who's fucking crazy!' Natasha's defender spat. 'We could have you arrested, mate! Stalking's a bloody crime, you know!'

'*What?*'

'So just piss off!'

'What's she been saying about me? What have you been saying about me, Natasha?'

'PISS OFF!'

'Asshole.' Fergus retreated to his car. 'You fucking deserve each other,' he said. Then he climbed into the driver's seat, shut the door, and turned his key in the ignition.

After a couple of false starts, his engine roared to life.

'And if you come near her again, I'll fucking rip your head off!' the blond man yelled, over the noise. Whether Fergus heard him or not was impossible to say. His car lurched backwards, careering up the driveway, then jolted onto the road and screeched to a halt as he paused to change gears.

Everyone watched with bated breath, silent and motionless, until his car had barrelled off down the street, its full-throated howl indicating a faulty muffler.

Only when this howl had faded into the general hum of the highway traffic did Natasha emerge from her own car, and collapse into the arms of the blond man.

They clung to each other.

'What the hell is going on?' Steven groaned.

'Don't you know any of them?' Mr Dyster queried – whereupon Avril suddenly realised that he'd been hovering behind her during the whole incident. Steven, realising the same thing, turned to address his guest with all the civility that he could muster.

'Just my daughter,' he said. 'Boyfriend problems.'

'Ah.'

'I hope that's Malcolm Busso,' said Avril, whose gaze was fixed on the blond man. He was tall and well groomed, and seemed nicely dressed; surely he wouldn't have picked up Natasha in a bar that evening? He was embracing her now with a great deal of passion.

'Can you tell me what the hell is going on?' Steven requested of his wife. 'Who's Malcolm Busso? Who invited him here?'

'No-one. But –'

'I think I'll return to my program,' Mr Dyster broke in. 'If that's all right by everyone.'

'Oh – yes – but wouldn't you be more comfortable eating in the dining room?' Avril said, sweetly and persuasively, as Mr Dyster turned to go. 'I can bring you a plate. Cutlery.'

'No thanks. I'm practically finished.'

'Oh, but –'

'Did Fergus do something out of line?' Steven interjected, allowing his guest to slip away. 'I don't understand. Did Natasha invite him or didn't she?'

'I'm not sure. I –'

'*Natasha!*' Steven raised his voice. 'What's all this about? Come here!'

Natasha lifted a hand. Then, to Avril's astonishment, she conversed quietly with her blond companion for a while, before kissing him, patting him, and pushing him towards her car. He got in. While Natasha was walking down the driveway, he started the engine; by the time she had reached her parents, he had backed into the street.

'For God's sake!' Steven protested. 'Are you giving that guy your *car*?'

'He came up on the train,' Natasha replied. 'He couldn't bring his own car.'

'Where the hell's he going with it?'

'Nowhere. I mean, we're both going. Back to the Fremont. I just came to collect my gear.'

Steven and Avril exchanged perplexed glances. They were completely at sea.

'It's Malcolm,' Natasha explained. 'You know about Malcolm, Mum, I told you.'

'Yes, but –'

'He's got a room at the Fremont tonight, and he's taking me back home tomorrow.' Natasha's head suddenly darted forward as she kissed Avril with cool, dry lips. Her mascara had run. 'Thanks for having me. I really enjoyed myself.'

'But what about this Fergus character?' Steven wanted to know. 'Weren't we all supposed to meet with him? Talk with him?'

'Oh, that's off,' Natasha replied, smiling. 'It was a dumb idea, and anyway, Malcolm's taken care of Fergus. Excuse me – I've just got to throw all my things in a bag.'

'Oh! Wait!' Avril followed her daughter into the house. 'Some of your underwear's in the laundry! Hang on . . . Natty, wait . . . Steven . . .' She drew him towards her, and said in a low voice: 'Could you see what Mr Dyster's up to? I don't want him dropping ketchup all over our beautiful rug.' Then, confident that Steven could handle Mr Dyster without giving offence, Avril went to retrieve Natasha's skimpy satin knickers from the laundry basket.

Fifteen minutes later, Natasha left. As they stood on the front verandah, listening to her car speed off towards the Fremont, Avril and Steven breathlessly speculated as to what it was that they had just witnessed. Shock had, to some extent, forced them to declare a truce. Once again, they were talking to each other – albeit with restraint.

'So you've no idea what that was all about?' asked Steven.

'Not really.'

'Smelled like a set-up.'

'I don't know what you mean.'

'Why bring her new bloke here if she knows that the old one's going to show? Bound to cause friction.'

'Perhaps she wanted Malcolm's support.'

'While she was talking to Fergus?' Steven made a sceptical noise. 'If you ask me, Malcolm didn't even know that Fergus had been invited. You could tell by the way he was talking.'

'We don't know what really happened, Steven.'

'No, but we can make an educated guess. Necking in the car? What was she up to? Was she *trying* to start a fight?'

'You're being ridiculous,' Avril said reprovingly.

'No I'm not. I'm being realistic. The whole thing's suss.'

'Fergus is a liar. He lies.'

'And he's not the only one.'

Disgusted, Avril turned away from him. She went back to the kitchen, furious that he always had to think the worst of Natasha. What kind of a father was he? Fergus had obviously upset the poor girl. If there had been some confusion regarding tonight's arrangements – well, that wasn't necessarily Natasha's fault. And in any case, she had a right to follow her own heart. Perhaps she'd found that she couldn't face Fergus, with or without her parents' support. Perhaps Malcolm had taken the matter out of her hands. He seemed very protective. A little overprotective. But at least he'd demonstrated his commitment to Natasha.

Avril told herself this, as she threw out her cold tea. While making herself a new cup, however, she couldn't help remembering certain inflections that Fergus had employed. Certain chilling little traces of astonishment in his tone. Genuine astonishment? Surely not.

Oh, well, she thought. If Natty has been a bit of a naughty girl, I'm sure they both deserved it. Drunks and philanderers don't merit much compassion.

# CHAPTER EIGHT

Steven met George for drinks at the Alexandra Hotel. Jammed between the highway and Leura station, it was an unexpectedly stylish place – a big, lavish, turn-of-the-century pub, beautifully renovated, with a popular and elegant little cafe, a lively bar, and a view over the Jamieson Valley that wasn't entirely obstructed by railway fences, station signs or large weeds. Despite its position it was for the most part pleasant, peaceful, and curiously detached from the roaring traffic on its northern side and the clattering trains on its southern doorstep.

Steven and George took their beers onto the front verandah, which overlooked a narrow band of rose garden. To their left, a crumbling, shaded path skirted the railway cutting, rising up to furnish those climbing it with a magnificent view of Katoomba, whose roofs and treetops tumbled down from the Carrington Hotel's boiler chimney to the very edge of a jagged escarpment in the most picturesque manner imaginable. To their right, a rubble pit of an unpaved car park was scooped out of the earth, stopping short at the weather-beaten boundary fence of a very shabby old brick cottage.

It occurred to Steven that one often had to wear blinkers in the mountains. Even when you were enjoying the panorama from, say, the Gordon Falls lookout, you had to make sure your eyes didn't stray down to that portion of the valley occupied by the sewage works.

'Well,' he said, settling onto a slighty uncomfortable cast-iron chair, 'how's it going, George?'

'Oh, fine.'

'Been reading the business papers for Thursday? What do you think about Ken Bribie's application?'

'Ken . . .?'

'You know. The car dealership that wants to move onto the highway.'

'Oh! Right.'

'I don't know.' Steven took a deep and satisfying swig of beer. It was a lovely afternoon to be drinking with a chum on an airy verandah; he felt good. Contented. 'Staff say no, of course, but that seems a bit . . . well, I can see their *point*.'

'Yes,' said George.

'And I s'pose we can take what Ken says with a grain of salt. I mean, not being able to expand where they are – having to close down if they don't move . . .' Steven snorted. 'Why not move to another sidestreet? What he wants is exposure, I reckon. But then again, why shouldn't he? He's a businessman. And that place seems to have a big impact on the local economy. I don't know. The mountains *are* a tourist destination, and tourists don't want to be driving along a Magic Mile of Motors when they get here, but it'd be just down the road from a petrol station, after all. I mean, you couldn't say that area was a jewel in our crown, could you? Not exactly a highlight of the scenic route.'

'But why make it worse?' George suggested diffidently.

'I suppose so. I suppose that's one way to look at it. That's certainly going to be Vera's take on things.' Steven swallowed another mouthful of beer, and wiped the foam from his upper lip. 'Still, the poor bastard. Ken, I mean. Anywhere else he'd be in like Flynn. If you ask me, he ought to tone down his design a bit. Go for a compromise. Get a deferral.'

'Yes.'

'Do you think so?'

'Yes. I think so.'

'After all, we're not on council to run everybody's

lives, no matter how much we'd like to,' Steven declaimed. He was feeling statesmanlike – on account of the beer, he assumed, not to mention the sunshine and the majestic view and the fact that the kid at the bar had recognised him from a photograph in the paper. Not that she'd read the accompanying article, of course: it had been about the Bus and Coach Subcommittee of the Highway Revitalisation Taskforce, and kids weren't much interested in things like that. 'We've got to think of the community as a whole,' he continued. 'Not everyone here makes a living out of tourists.'

George grunted. He was looking, Steven thought, decidedly uncomfortable for a man taking his ease with a mate and a middy. Had he arranged this happy interlude with a more specific purpose than the usual one of discussing tactics for the next council meeting? Was there something else on his mind?

'What's up, mate?' Steven asked, deciding to grasp the bull by the horns. 'You seem a little glum.'

George rubbed his chin distractedly.

'Troubles?' Steven pressed him, wondering if the cracks that he'd witnessed in the Dianne–George conjunction had widened until they'd finally brought the whole edifice down. For some time, Steven had been taking note of passing remarks, fleeting grimaces and brief hesitations that seemed to suggest the bonds uniting George and Dianne were under stress. Not that he was surprised. In his opinion, Dianne treated George like a dog, or a dopey kid. Scolding him in public. Rolling her eyes whenever he offered up an opinion. Putting him down even when she was being indulgent.

Steven had never cared much for Dianne. She struck him as being a tough little cookie. On the ball, of course – and George certainly needed someone to organise his life for him – but unnecessarily sharp about it.

No-one could deny that George needed to be taken in hand. But it had to be done gently, as a mother would. Not as a cow of a superannuated primary-school teacher would.

'Business okay?' Steven probed, kindly desisting from making the more obvious inquiry. At that moment, however, George seemed to come to a decision. He straightened in his chair, set down his glass, and lifted his owlish gaze.

'Look,' he said, 'this is difficult for me, and I don't want to do it, but you're both my friends, you and Avril, and I feel like I should make an effort. For both of you.'

Steven stared at him in astonishment.

'Avril came to me yesterday,' George went on, 'because she's really unhappy. *Really* miserable. Steve, I know it's not my place, but the fact that she came to me, the fact that she was *that desperate* –'

'Hang on a minute.'

'Wait. Just let me tell you. Steve, I know she's a fragile sort of person, I know she's not Dianne, but that's part of her charm, eh? If it was Dianne – well, Dianne would be running for mayor herself by now, and so would a lot of women. But Avril's not like that. I'm not trying to tell you how to run your business – for all I know everything's fine – but Avril doesn't think so. She's scared, Steve. She's scared that the whole thing's going to collapse, because you'll be off doing whatever a mayor has to do, and she won't be able to cope on her own.'

Steven's fury hit him hard and fast, like a runaway semitrailer. One moment he was serenely and affectionately surveying his good friend George, who almost certainly had relationship problems; the next minute, he was hot with rage, choking on it, so overwhelmed with wrathful disbelief that he couldn't utter a single word.

He was able to gasp, however, and he knew that he must have turned bright red, because George was eyeing him uneasily.

'I didn't want to approach you like this,' George concluded, faltering a little, 'but she sort of asked me to. She came to me and wanted to know if there was anyone else we could vote for. She was that upset, I – look, I said I'd sound you out. Because I have to say, Steve, if your being mayor is going to cause even one person – your wife – so much misery . . . well, you know. Is it really worth it?'

This appeared to be a question to which George genuinely required an answer. He stopped and looked at Steven, pushing his glasses back along his nose.

Steven took a deep breath.

'I don't believe this,' he managed to enunciate, in accents of outraged incredulity.

'Look –'

'I can't believe you had the gall to come here –'

'Hey. I'm trying to help.'

'You're trying to *bollocks*. Okay. Okay.' With a change of tone Steven withdrew his last comment, lifting his hand as George frowned. 'I know where you're coming from. I know you think you're doing the right thing. But this has nothing to do with you, George. This is between me and Avril.'

'Yes, I know. I know that,' George stammered. 'And I'm sorry. Like you said, it's none of my business. But I didn't know if you realised just how unhappy she is. Just how scared she is. I thought, well, maybe she doesn't want you to think she's inadequate, you know. Because she can't deal with it all . . .'

Bitch, thought Steven. Conniving little bitch. But he tried to speak calmly.

'Avril is scared of one thing,' he announced. 'She's

scared that she won't get her way. Look, George – since she's dragged you into this, well, I'll give you the lowdown.' He leaned across the table. He fixed George with a compelling glare. 'My wife comes across as being very dainty. Like you said, it's part of her charm. And she's got a lot of good points, I'm not saying she doesn't. God love her, she's a terrific housewife, a terrific cook, a terrific mother, she always looks terrific – I mean, if you'd seen her when she was young, George, she was a stunner, and she still is – she's got taste, she's got dignity, she's got brains, she's got . . . oh, I dunno –'

'A beautiful voice,' George interrupted quietly, fiddling with his beer mat.

'A beautiful voice, she can sing, when she laughs it's like watching the sun come out, blah blah blah.' To fortify himself, Steven drained his glass. 'But what you've got to understand, George, is that she *has* got brains. And she uses 'em. And it took me years to work out how she did it. You see, she comes across all helpless. All delicate. Makes you feel sorry for her. I'm not saying she does it on purpose, I reckon it's what her mother probably did, but she *manipulates*. That's what she does.' Seeing the shocked look on George's face, he added: 'I'm not trying to bad-mouth her, George, I'm just stating a fact. It's what she does. And I've come to terms with it. Hell, it makes me laugh. I get a kick out of catching her at it. But not,' he finished sourly, '*not* when she starts doing it to friends, instead of to me or the bloke at the petrol station.'

There was a pause. Leaning back in his chair, George folded his arms and stared at Steven, though his mind seemed to be elsewhere. Steven didn't like the almost mulish set of his mouth.

'What I'm saying,' Steven reiterated emphatically, 'is that you shouldn't worry about Avril. She's not as upset as she wants you to think. Really. I know her. She's trying it on.'

George blinked. He raised his eyebrows. 'Trying it on?' he repeated, and slowly shook his head, blowing puffs of air through slack lips. 'I don't know . . .'

'That's right. You *don't* know. But I do, see. I'm her husband. We've been married twenty-five years, or whatever it is. And this is like – this is Avril not wanting to give way. This is Avril digging her heels in. The business won't belly-up, of course it won't. She'll just have to stop making her own lemon drops, is all. And what's so bad about that?'

Slightly out of breath, Steven stopped abruptly. He decided to fetch some more beer. Rising, he began to work his fingers into one of his jeans pockets. 'More of the same?' he inquired, with as much conviviality as he could muster. George was watching him with a dark, level gaze, and Steven was surprised at how quietly formidable that gaze was. Coming from a man who normally looked like a dishevelled King Charles spaniel, it was slightly unnerving.

'I just think,' George said, 'that you perhaps ought to consider the possibility of Bert Plummer as mayor.'

Steven's jaw dropped.

'Because he's a decent bloke,' George continued, 'he takes his job seriously, and he's an old hand.'

'Are you *joking*?' Steven spluttered.

'No, I'm not.' George looked annoyed. 'It's a perfectly reasonable suggestion. If you were to pull out, I know he'd be Pat's next choice. That means he'd have all the Labor votes, yours, mine, Pat's and Celeste's. Which is seven.'

'George . . .' Steven was overcome by a sudden desire to burst into hysterical laughter. 'Excuse me, but fuck that.'

'I'm just –'

'There is no reason for me to pull out.'

'I still think –'

'Bert's an old stick-in-the-mud. He's got no idea.'

'Now that's not true.'

'It bloody is!' Steven leaned forward, placing both hands on the tabletop. He was finding it hard to control his temper. 'What's your problem, George? Is it Avril, or is it me? I'm beginning to smell something, here.' Envy? Discontent? Veiled resentment? 'Is there something you want to tell me? Are you having second thoughts about me being mayor, for some reason?'

George sighed. He brought both hands together, as if he were praying, then began to chop them up and down for emphasis. It was an infuriating gesture.

'I just think,' he said, with strained patience, 'that if it's a toss-up between your wife's peace of mind and whatever unique contribution you might make to the mayoral office – which after all isn't exactly of earth-shattering significance, in the bigger scheme of things –'

'You'd come down on Avril's side. Is that it?'

'I just think you should give it some thought, Steve.'

'Oh, you do?'

'Yes.'

'And this wouldn't,' drawled Steven, 'have anything to do with the fact that I'm not supporting you for deputy mayor?'

Again, George blinked. Then he grimaced.

'No. It wouldn't,' he said flatly.

'You sure about that?'

'*Quite* sure.'

'Because it seems to me that ever since I told you it wasn't an option, you've been kind of sulking in a corner –'

'Oh, what crap!' George suddenly lost control. He leaned forward, his eyes narrowed. 'If you want to know why I've been less than enchanted with you lately, it's because you're so bloody high-handed!'

'*Me?*'

'Yes, you! You didn't even ask if you had my vote – you just assumed you did. You offered my vote to Allan without consulting me first –'

'Oh, come on.'

'. . . and now, when I make a perfectly sane and reasonable suggestion, you act like it's not worth a second thought!'

'Because it's not!'

'*Wrong*, Steve! It's worth some very serious consideration! Because if this is the way you handle my feelings, then perhaps you ought to question your attitude towards your wife! Perhaps you ought to wonder if you really know what's going on with her!'

'Believe me, I know exactly what's going on with her.' Realising that they had both raised their voices, Steven lowered his, with a sideways glance through the hotel window. Fortunately, no-one seemed to have overheard them. 'She's casting a line for you, my friend, and you're too thick to realise what's happening,' he said quietly.

George recoiled.

'She's done it before, and she'll do it again. As long as there are idiots like you who get sucked in by her little performance. You'd better watch yourself,

George.' Steven tapped him on the breastbone. 'She'll do you like a dinner, mate.'

George's features were tense with disgust. He shook his head.

'You're unbelievable, you know that?' he growled. Then he got up, slapped a bill on the table, and walked away.

Steven sat down again. He wanted to calm himself before he ordered another beer. And he *would* order another beer. Why let George dictate his actions? He didn't have to worry; he was going to be walking home. Anyway, he needed a little fuel with which to stoke his righteous anger.

Avril, he thought. So she's out recruiting supporters, is she?

I'll give her supporters.

Avril was clearing up dirty teacups when Steven returned to the Bella Vista. She was in the drawing room with the Dysters and their friends; the Dysters had come up from Sydney with a pair of sisters, Gwyneth and Doreen, who were obviously great mates of Jill Dyster. Steven couldn't understand why Jill's poor chip-eating husband had been dragged along too. Ned Dyster had barely left the house since reaching it – spent all of his time on the couch, reading newspapers – while 'the girls', as he called them, were off visiting craft shops and cafes. But he was a hopeless old fart, was Ned, with his slack, mottled face and his stained trousers. Perhaps he couldn't be left by himself. Perhaps Jill had to draw his bath and make his meals and put his clothes out in the morning.

Anything was possible.

'Ah! There you are!' Jill exclaimed, when Steven walked in. She was a game little matron, with dyed hair and a bright smile; good company, on the whole, though perhaps rather exhausting if you had to put up with her all day long. 'We need your advice about bushwalks,' she trilled. 'Avril says that you're the one to talk to.'

'Oh yes?' Steven murmured. Though he kept his gaze fixed politely on Jill, he was conscious of Avril sliding off into the kitchen. Sneaky bitch.

'We thought we might take a little walk tomorrow,' Jill informed him, turning to her friends for confirmation. They both nodded vigorously. 'Something nice and easy. We're not as young as we used to be, you know!'

The three women laughed; Ned smiled vacantly; Steven tried to look agreeable.

'Well – there's an easy walk at Govett's Leap,' he said. 'Very easy going. It's accessible to wheelchairs.'

'Oh!' More laughter. 'Well, I don't know if we've quite come to *that*.'

'Or there's the Prince Henry Cliff walk. That's not too hard.'

Fluttering a map at him, Gwyneth requested guidance, and Steven was forced to point out very carefully where the Prince Henry Cliff walk was in fact located. He then made his escape, retreating with a suitable show of reluctance to the kitchen, where Avril was donning her rubber gloves.

He shut the door behind him.

'You bitch,' he said.

She turned.

'You unholy bitch.'

'I think you'd better keep your voice down.' She spoke coldly. 'We don't want the guests to hear.'

'I've just had a drink with George,' Steven hissed. He approached her, and wrapped his fingers around her upper arm. 'I'm guessing you know what we talked about.'

'I can't imagine.'

'Shut up.' He squeezed, applying the pressure until she winced. 'You are not going to do this to me. This is not going to work. Understand? No matter what little fuck-ups you arrange along the way, you're not going to stuff me around.' There was a tap on the door. 'Yes?' he said, in ringing tones. 'What's up?'

'Oh – I'm sorry, Steve.' Jill's voice was tentative, but cheery. 'I don't want to be a bother . . . there's just one more thing . . .'

'Hang on a minute!' Steven thrust his face into Avril's as he released her. 'You take care of whatever this might be, all right?' he muttered. 'I've got some phone calls to make.'

Slowly, without taking her eyes off Steven, Avril peeled the gloves from her hands. Then she flung them, with a fair degree of force, into the dish drainer. Her heels struck the polished floorboards with a *rap-rap-rap* as she made her way to the door.

'I shall take care of it,' she said softly, pausing with her hand on the doorknob, 'because you're obviously not in a fit state to confront our guests.'

She didn't wait for a reply. Instead she whisked out of the room, closing the door very gently behind her, as if to emphasise her ability to keep calm.

Steven picked up the cordless phone. He took it into his study, where he tapped out Allan's mobile number. He'd had sufficient time to think, on his way home, and knew that he had blown it. He had lost his temper, and offended George – the dozy bastard. Now he would have to make things right again, before George got hold of Bert and started making dangerous suggestions.

Fortunately, Allan answered on the third ring.

'Ah,' he said. 'Hello, Steve. How are you?'

'Fine. Well, no, not fine, actually. In a bit of a mess, if you want the truth.'

'Oh.'

'George has done the dirty on me. Or at least, it looks as if he might.' When Allan failed to comment, Steven elaborated. 'He's been talking about Bert Plummer being a good candidate for mayor. Can you believe it?'

Allan was briefly silent. Then he said: 'What brought this on?'

'I don't know,' Steven lied. 'Though I do think he's annoyed that I didn't offer him my deputy vote.'

Another silence. Steven, who had been juggling names in his head, decided to press the point home. 'Just say Bert did decide to stand,' he postulated. 'See, right now, I've got you, Sue, Pat, Maeve, George and Celeste. That's seven votes, including mine. But if Bert stands, I reckon Celeste will vote for him. And if George switches sides, that means Bert'll have brought two votes on board – which is the same as what Finlay's pulling, now that Maeve's in our camp.'

'Yes,' said Allan, thoughtfully. 'I see what you mean. Labor might switch candidates.'

'Bound to. Because Chris likes Bert a hell of a lot more than he likes Finlay – and I know that Finlay isn't a favourite with the branch membership either. Now, whether he decides to break ranks and stand, or whether he doesn't, is immaterial –'

'. . . because he'll only have three votes,' Allan finished. 'And Bert will have four, and you'll have five.'

'So Finlay has to realise it's not worth the flack

he'll get for breaking ranks. He'll go over to Bert, which will give Bert five, too. Then it's a matter of who Vera and Gareth will go for. And if you ask me, Gareth will go for a Ward Two candidate.'

'Hmmmph.'

'Especially if they offer him deputy.'

Allan sighed. 'So what are you saying, Steve?' he asked.

'I'm saying that if you want to head this off – because I know you don't want Bert as mayor, Allan – if you want to head it off, you're going to have to join me in offering George our deputy votes.'

Allan seemed to think for a while. Steven, noticing a jumble of teacakes in a Tupperware bowl, helped himself.

'I take your point,' said Allan at last. He sounded tired. 'And even if George did get our votes, no-one else would vote for him. Not even Pat, I shouldn't suppose.'

'Exactly.'

'But there's got to be something in it for me, Steve.'

'Pardon?'

'I said there's got to be something in it for me.'

Steven nearly choked on his teacake.

'What are you talking about?' he demanded, spraying crumbs. 'Isn't a non-Labor mayor good enough for you?'

‘Ah, but can you give me any guarantees on that?’ Allan replied, almost playfully. ‘People can change their minds, you know. Alliances can shift. I’m giving up something concrete – your vote. And mine. Would it be asking too much to request that, in return, you’ll support Ken Bribie’s application?’

For one confused moment, Steven had no idea what Allan was talking about. Then he remembered. Car dealer. Highway. Eyesore.

‘Oh. That,’ he said.

‘There’s nothing wrong with Ken’s proposal, Steve. It’s a perfectly reasonable request. Have you looked at the car dealership at Medlow Bath recently? *Right* on the highway, let me remind you.’

‘I know, I know.’

‘Ken is a real pillar of the community. A responsible man. He shouldn’t be penalised because certain people don’t approve of the internal combustion engine.’

Grimacing, Steven frantically scratched his head. What to do? He’d always sympathised with Ken Bribie. It was a bit rough, expecting a car dealer to behave like a vegetarian restaurant owner. But still . . . ‘What about a deferral?’ he suggested feebly. ‘If he takes another look at his plans . . . perhaps amends them a bit . . .’

‘Oh, come on, Steve. You know that’s just dithering about. Putting off the evil moment.’

Steven didn't like Allan's tone. It was too peremptory. Should he tell Allan to stuff this rather dubious little deal up his fundiment? It might cause offence, but what if it did? Allan's choice of mayor was very limited; he could choose either Steven or a member of the Labor party. And he wouldn't be choosing a member of the Labor party.

'I'll think about it, mate,' Steven remarked diplomatically. 'I'll give it my earnest consideration.'

'Will you? I see. Well, then, I'll give my earnest consideration to whether or not I should release you from your promise.'

'You'll have to, Allan. I'm going to ring up George tonight, and offer him my vote.'

'But not mine,' Allan said, in tranquil tones. 'Or Sue's. Or anyone else's. You might find, Steve, that he wouldn't want to face the embarrassment of such a miserable show of hands – not as a matter of public record. And of course it's bound to come out that you've been offering your deputy mayor vote to all and sundry. People might not believe you're a person to trust, if they hear about that.'

He was right, of course. It would look bad. It would look . . . desperate.

Steven felt an urgent desire to kick the wall, but restrained himself.

'Oh, all right!' he snapped. 'What the hell. Ken's going to lose out anyway.'

‘I hope not. But if he does, at least we’ll know that we’ve made a valiant effort to save the life and work of a struggling small businessman.’ Allan chuckled quietly. ‘Thanks anyway, Steve. Good luck with George.’

In your arse, Steven thought, as he hung up. What a bastard Allan could be. Surely he must realise that nobody *else* would vote for him? Except Sue, of course: Sue, The Doppelgänger.

Breathing heavily, Steven called George Lovecek. When a machine answered, he left a detailed message. He urged George to reconsider ‘that decision about Bert’. He offered George his vote, and apologised for being ‘so high-handed’. He promised that Avril would not be made to suffer, that they would work something out – extra staff, perhaps – and thanked George for bringing the matter to his attention.

‘I used to be a bank manager, George,’ he finished. ‘I wouldn’t be considering this move if I saw it as a threat to my business. I know what I’m doing here; Avril can’t even read a profit and loss statement.’

George’s tape ran out before he had time to unburden his heart fully, but he was certain that he had made his point.

Now he would just have to wait, and hope. Hope that George responded as any intelligent man *should* respond.

Hope that his entire mayoral campaign wasn't going down the gurgler.

Dinner that night was a very unpleasant experience. As he distractedly waited for the phone to ring, Steven decided that it would be a waste of time trying to speak to Avril. There was no reasoning with her. Furthermore, any argument that they might engage in was bound to get noisy – and noisy arguments would damage the reputation of their guesthouse more efficiently than ants in the jam. So he held his tongue. The only words that he uttered were 'thank you', and these words were delivered in exactly the tone normally employed by Steven when he was addressing the dog that sometimes crapped on their front lawn.

Avril was also silent. Never garrulous at the best of times, she made a point of expressing her displeasure by ceasing to speak at all. Instead she rattled her spoon violently in her teacup, and clashed plates together in the sink, and didn't offer Steven any dessert. That was a pity, because Steven had been intending to take one bite of whatever she might have presented him with, before pushing it away with a half-concealed grimace.

He did manage, however, to use the last of the dental floss, and derived a fleeting satisfaction from the fact that Avril had forgotten to include it on their shopping list the previous week. Serve her right; it was her own fault. The shopping list, as she so often pointed out, was one of the jobs that she was lumbered with.

But this pleasurable moment was very brief. On the whole, it was an evening of unremitting gloom, because George didn't call. He didn't call the next morning either. Steven cleaned the bathrooms with manic energy, his ear cocked the whole time, but only once did the phone ring – and that was because someone in Sydney wanted to speak to Jill's friend Gwyneth. The Dysters and their companions were leaving that day; they had stayed an extra night so as to avoid the Sunday afternoon traffic jam. Only one guest was booked in for Monday, and that was a woman from Sydney called Gillian Rivers. She was due at around half past three.

The Dysters and co. left at nine. Elspeth, the cleaner, arrived at ten. Elspeth came once a fortnight to give the whole house a basic scrub-and-vacuum, so that Avril could concentrate on fancy things like dusting the picture rails, polishing the mirrors, and cleaning the grates – tasks that no-one else would have worried about doing, for the most part. With Elspeth in the house there was no opportunity to engage in any sniping or wrangling. Steven and Avril were forced to restrict their displays of feeling to stony looks and long-suffering sighs.

By the time Elspeth departed, at a quarter past twelve, Steven was desperate. Sneaking into his office with the cordless phone, he rang George at the shop. But it was Kyle who answered.

'Sorry, George isn't here,' said Kyle.

'What do you mean? Is he off sick today?'

'Nah. He just popped out.'

'For how long?'

'I dunno. He's the boss.'

'Well – would you tell him Steve called?'

'Okay.'

Stupid young punk, Steven thought, as he signed off. Always sounds as if he's chewing gum, even when he isn't. Steven wondered if he should call Bert, just to sound him out, but decided not to. He considered calling Pat – would she speak to George on his behalf? – but realised that he would come across as feeble if he asked her to do anything like that. And mayors weren't supposed to be feeble. Mayors were supposed to be authoritative.

Then the phone rang under his hand. The shock was such that he nearly dropped the receiver as he put it to his ear.

'Hel-hello?' he gasped. 'George?'

'No.' A constipated female voice. 'It's Celeste here.'

'Oh. Celeste.' Steven's heart sank almost to his knees. 'How's it going?'

'Well, Steven, it would be going a lot *better* if people would return my calls.'

'Pardon?'

'We're *all* busy, you know. It isn't jest you. I'm *extremely* busy, but I still menege to be polite. I still menege to return phone calls.'

Steven was lost. What on earth was she twittering on about?

'I'm not sure I follow you, Celeste.'

'I've called you four times in the last few days. Why didn't you call me beck?'

'But –'

'At any rate, it doesn't metter. Because Bert reng me last night and told me he's thinking of running for mayor. Instead of Finlay. So if he does, I'll be voting for him.'

Steven, who had been standing, abruptly sat down. Horror had rendered him speechless.

'He's not sure yet. He has to discuss it with Chris and Finlay,' Celeste continued. 'Then he'll tell me what they decide. So I thought I'd give you fair warning.' Her tone became waspish. 'Even though my views don't seem to metter much to you.'

'But . . . but . . .' Steven tried to organise his thoughts. 'But Celeste, don't you think – I mean, Bert's a great bloke, don't get me wrong – but don't you think he's a little old to be burdened with the kind of responsibilities that you have to take on as mayor . . .'

'He's *experienced*,' Celeste interrupted witheringly. 'And he's wonderful with the old people.'

'But he's affiliated with a political party, Celeste. The Labor party. You know how you feel about them.'

'Thet doesn't mean he's not a Christian. And a gentleman. At least *he* always returns my phone calls.'

'What are you talking about?' Steven spoke sharply. 'What phone calls?'

'I called you. Four times.'

'Well, I didn't know that.'

'Your wife said she wrote down my messages.'

'Oh did she?'

'She said you were very busy, but thet you were going to call me as soon as possible . . .'

With the phone jammed against his ear, Steven hurried into the kitchen. He ran his gaze down the cork board. He flicked up an electricity bill that was pinned there, and found four half-concealed notes. *Call Celeste. Celeste rang. Please phone Celeste* . . .

That bitch. That *fucking* bitch!

'. . . she said she told you . . .'

'She didn't tell me,' Steven interrupted, aware that his voice was trembling. 'I didn't know you called, Celeste.'

'Oh. Really.' It was clear that she didn't believe him. 'Well – whatever you say, Steven.'

'It's the truth.' (You cow.) 'Somehow she . . . somehow she forgot.'

'Well, anyway, it doesn't metter now. Things have changed since then.'

'Celeste –'

'I've got to go. Someone's picking me up.'

She broke the connection. With the dial tone humming in his ear, Steven ripped Avril's notes, one by one, from the cork board. Then he put down the phone, marched out of the house, and descended on Avril, who was pegging wet laundry onto the clothes line.

She must have heard him approaching, but didn't turn. Steven stopped a couple of metres away. He was afraid to move closer; he was afraid that, if he did, he would belt her across the earhole.

'What the fuck are these?' he demanded, with suppressed fury.

She bent down, plucked a damp sock from her wicker laundry basket, and straightened. He knew that she was expressing her displeasure at his use of a certain word. She wouldn't reply until he asked 'nicely'.

'Has Celeste been calling? Over the last couple of days?' he inquired, with remarkable self-control. Avril turned her head slightly, and her gaze fell on the white and yellow slips in Steven's left hand.

'Oh. Yes,' she said.

'And you didn't see fit to tell me?'

'I forgot.'

'You forgot.'

She sighed, stooped over her basket again, and pulled out a pair of jeans. 'The last time you mentioned Celeste,' she said, with weary patience, 'you told me that if she called, I was to say you weren't here.'

'But I didn't say not to tell me.'

'It slipped my mind. I didn't think it was important.'

'Bullshit.'

'Don't take that tone with me, Steven.'

'Do you think I'm *stupid*? Do you think I don't know what you're *doing*?'

Avril narrowed her eyes at him. 'If you can't be bothered to check the cork board,' she said quietly, 'then that's your problem. I'm not your receptionist.'

'No! You're my bloody *millstone*, you vicious *cow*!' Steven screwed up his slips of paper and threw them at her. They scattered like confetti in the breeze. 'If you lose this for me,' he gasped, 'if you lose this for me, you're going to suffer! I mean it!'

She said nothing. Purse-lipped, she continued to jab pegs onto the line.

'*Are you listening to me?*' Steven yelped, whereupon the dogs next door began to howl and yammer. The slightest noise always set them off. '*And you can shut the fuck up too!*' he bawled at them.

'Oh, stop it,' said Avril, in disgust.

'No! You stop it!' He shook a clenched fist. 'You

back off, Avril, or I won't answer for the consequences! Understand?'

Then he went inside, took a corkscrew from the kitchen, and dragged it, very firmly, across the glossy bottom shelf of Avril's early Victorian whatnot in their sitting room.

He felt much better after that.

# CHAPTER NINE

Avril noticed the whatnot on Tuesday morning. She was dusting the sitting room when she saw a deep, pale scratch on the dark mahogany shape in one corner. The sight of it made her feel fleetingly ill, as if she herself had been scarred.

With trembling hands she removed the lustre bowl and silver pillboxes that normally graced the whatnot's bottom shelf. She examined the scratch, which gaped like a wound. It was deep. Very deep. Not something you could disguise with a dab of polish.

Sitting back on her heels, she whimpered in pain. Steven had done it – of course he had. He had done it and said nothing. All last night, all that morning, he hadn't said a word. He had held himself aloof. He had even slept in Natasha's bed. And he must have been waiting, watching, listening for her cry of dismay when she discovered this – this *desecration.*

There was no other way of describing it.

At least she hadn't given him the satisfaction of witnessing her horror. He was out now; having cleaned the bathrooms with savage thoroughness, he had driven off without consulting her. She didn't know where he had gone. She didn't know when he'd be back. He had abandoned her, knowing full well that there was a guest to be met at the station after lunch.

I need baking powder, she thought. I need baking powder to make scones. What does he expect me to do? *Walk* all the way up to the shops?

Avril rose stiffly, then lost heart and slumped into her chaise longue. It was a beautiful thing, Edwardian, with the graceful lines of a swan and the solid, reassuring legs of an efficient hospital nurse. Would it be safe from Steven? Would he start spilling wine on upholstery and treading golden syrup into the rugs? What would he do to her crystal? To her china figurines? To her silk cushions?

'He's sick,' she said aloud, into the silence. 'He's gone mad.' Only a madman would do such a terrible thing to an early Victorian mahogany whatnot.

Avril went to the phone. She dialled George's number. When he answered ('Hello, G. L. Business Systems, can I help you?'), she said, 'George. It's Avril.'

'Avril . . .'

'Are you busy? Can we talk?'

'No. I mean, yes. We can talk.' He sounded breathless. Distracted. 'Is something wrong?'

'It's Steven. I'm worried about Steven. He's gone all . . .' Hopelessly, Avril racked her brain for the right word.

'Crazy?' George supplied.

'Odd.'

'I know.'

'I'm afraid of what he might do,' Avril went on, thinking about her porcelain Staffordshire dogs. And her glass paperweights. 'He's so cross that I talked with you, George. He's being impossible. So *violent* . . .'

'Why? What's he done?'

'Oh . . .' Avril gave a watery laugh. 'Just made himself obnoxious.'

'Avril, I – I can't talk now. I've got customers.'

'Yes. I'm sorry, I'll –'

'Can we meet for lunch? Is that possible? In half an hour, say?'

'I can't. He's taken the car. I don't know where he is.'

'Then I'll pick you up. Shall I bring you a sandwich? A meat pie or something?'

Avril grimaced. Meat pies, in her opinion, were just marginally preferable to dog food.

'A chicken sandwich would be nice,' she said faintly.

'Chicken sandwich it is. I'll see you soon. If . . .' George hesitated, then continued. 'If Steven arrives in the meantime, could you give me a call? You've got my mobile number.'

'You mean you don't want to –'

'I'd rather not –'

'. . . meet him?'

'I'll explain when I get there.'

Which would be in half an hour. As Avril put the phone down, she calculated that she would have enough time to change her clothes. (She was wearing one of her shabbier outfits, to match her feather duster and her polish-stained work gloves.) Would George give her a lift to the shops, perhaps? So that she could buy baking powder, and make scones for the guests' afternoon tea?

She would have to ask him.

Having finished dusting the surfaces in the sitting room, Avril changed into a pale dress and linen jacket. She put on fresh make-up and rearranged her hair. She made coffee, which she poured into a Thermos flask. Then she went outside to wait on the front verandah, seating herself on a wooden pew of some antiquity, her back straight, her ankles crossed. She liked that pew. Although it gave a welcoming appearance to the house, it was so uncomfortable that it discouraged guests from sitting about on the verandah, smoking and drinking. Large groups of sloppy, noisy people, permanently ensconced beside the front door, would, she felt, have given her house entirely the wrong tone.

It was a pleasant day – a little windy, with high clouds scudding in front of the sun occasionally – but pleasant enough. Avril's pink hyacinths looked beautiful. They set off the pink of the peach tree on the nature strip. Her daffodils also looked beautiful. But the rose beds were a mass of weeds; the azaleas, which were continually attacked by lace bugs, had to be sprayed again; the honeysuckle was creeping back into her garden. Those people next door! They didn't look after their own garden, so everyone else had to suffer! Avril wondered what would happen if she were to sneak in there one day, and spray herbicide all over the rampant ivy and honeysuckle on her neighbours' side of the fence.

They probably wouldn't even notice.

George arrived ten minutes late, apologising profusely. A last-minute phone call had delayed him; he'd managed to buy the sandwiches though. Avril assured him that it didn't matter, that she'd been surveying her garden, perfectly content. She waved her Thermos as she climbed into his car, and George looked relieved. 'I forgot about drinks,' he confessed. 'Though I did pick up a couple of fruit salads.' He was looking even more dishevelled than he normally did, and his car was a mess. That was one thing you could say in Steven's favour: at least he always kept his car spotless. Not that he had any choice, of course. With so many guests to be picked up and dropped off, he couldn't afford to let his car become dirty.

George drove down to the stone amphitheatre near the Toy and Railway Museum, talking about the weather and other inconsequential things: tea-trees; Katoomba cafes; compact-disc players. Although a little hesitant, he didn't seem particularly disturbed. But as he pulled over and parked, he became silent; instead of pulling his keys from the ignition and opening the door, he simply sat, his eyes fixed on the steering wheel.

Avril waited.

'Steven came to the shop yesterday afternoon,' he announced, without looking at her. 'Did you know that?'

'No,' she replied.

'He offered me deputy, and I turned him down. Anyone could see that it was an out-and-out bribe. When I told him as much, he gave me an earful. I think he would have punched me in the face, if Kyle hadn't been there.'

Avril said nothing.

'It's all because of this stupid election. God, I don't know. Why did I get myself into such a mess?'

Avril cleared her throat.

'I'm sorry, George –'

'It's not *your* fault! Here.' With some effort, he leaned over and retrieved their lunch from the back seat. 'Come on. Let's go and look at the view. I hate talking in cars.'

They got out. George was wearing an unappealing beige pullover; his straggling fringe was blown back to reveal a very broad white forehead. Avril, who used hairspray and just a few carefully positioned Lady Jayne bobby pins, didn't have to worry about the wind at all. She put on a pair of sunglasses.

'I don't know if Steve ever told you about our little talk the other day,' George remarked, as they set off across the grassy slope that separated the road from the amphitheatre.

'Not really,' Avril replied. 'But I get the impression that it wasn't very friendly.'

'It wasn't. Not at all.' George's cheeks were red. 'And I must say Steve was bloody offensive. *Bloody* offensive.'

'I'm sorry.'

'Don't be. It's not your fault. He can be very high-handed – which is what I told him. I suppose he really rubbed me the wrong way on Sunday.' George sighed. 'That's why I went home and called Bert Plummer. Maybe I shouldn't have. But I was under a bit of stress at the time.'

'Oh dear. Really?'

'Dianne and I haven't been relating very well.'

Reaching the edge of the amphitheatre, George stared blankly across it, as if oblivious to the hazy view of receding blue–green valleys and golden cliffs. 'Where shall we sit? At the top here?'

'I think so. You should have brought a hat.'

'It doesn't matter. We can't be long – I have to get back to the shop soon.'

'I'm so sorry.'

They sat down on the edge of a stone step. George passed Avril her sandwich; Avril passed George his coffee, which she had poured into the outer lid of the Thermos flask. She herself drank from another, inner lid.

'I asked Bert if he would consider running for mayor,' George remarked, as pieces of chopped chicken spilled clumsily out of his sandwich. 'That was after Steve had rejected the entire notion. I didn't realise this business had . . . well, had got such a *grip* on Steve.'

'It has,' Avril agreed sadly.

'He wouldn't hear of it. Just . . . exploded in my face. Which put my back up, of course. I mean, it's bad enough at home . . .' Stopping suddenly, George tackled his sandwich. He wrapped his mouth around one end of it in the most ungainly way, like a carp trying to suck up half a slice of bread. Avril averted her eyes. 'You know,' he continued, his voice half muffled by a mouthful of food, 'I was only trying to help you, Avril, but I think I've made things worse.'

'Oh no.'

'Oh yes. Steve's not going to vote for Bert. Not in a million years. He's going to fight him every step of the way, and make both our lives a misery in the process.' George paused, presumably to take another bite of his lunch. (Avril wasn't looking.) 'I should never have called Bert,' he said at last, thickly and gloomily. 'I should have tackled Steve again. Let him get used to the idea. Mind you, we don't have much time before the election.'

'George, *please* don't blame yourself. If it's anyone's fault, it's mine.'

'No.'

'It is. I've ruined everything. Just look at what I've done! You and Steve are fighting, he's in a rage, you're miserable.'

'That's not why I'm –'

'And God *knows* what this has done to our marriage!' Avril whipped a filmy white handkerchief out of her jacket pocket. She pressed it to her nose. 'I'm sorry. I'm so sorry. He – he scratched one of my antiques, last night. Deliberately. Gouged a hole in the finish. Just because he – because he knew how much it would upset me. I think he hates me, George.'

'Oh, no.'

'He called me a millstone.'

'Jesus,' George sighed. He swallowed the last of his

sandwich before crumpling the greasy waxed paper in which it had been cradled. 'It's all right,' he said. 'It'll be all right.'

Avril sniffed.

'He doesn't hate you. How could he hate *you*? He'd have to be out of his mind,' George said.

'If only I wasn't so useless.'

'You're not useless.'

'If only I was more like Dianne!'

George made a breathy, scornful noise. 'Dianne!' he exclaimed. 'Believe me, you're better off as you are.'

'But –'

'Dianne is bone selfish. I have come to that conclusion. She is bone selfish, so she takes me completely for granted. The way you take a fridge for granted. Or a doormat.'

'Oh, George,' Avril said sorrowfully. Wiping her eyes, she gazed at him in consternation. 'Is it – is it really that bad?'

'Worse.'

'But you seemed so . . . so . . .'

'Happy?'

Avril thought for a moment, knitting her brow. 'Entrenched,' she said at last. 'I mean . . . established.' Happy was not exactly the word. Dianne didn't exude happiness; she was labouring under far too much work-related stress. And George, on reflection, had seemed more resigned than anything else, as he obediently opened bottles of wine or changed compact discs during Avril's rare visits to his house. 'Perhaps she's just very *stressed*, George.'

'Because she chooses to be. She allows that job to dominate her life. She treats me like one of her staff. And I'm sick of it.' Plunged into gloom, presumably by his memories of Dianne's behaviour, George folded his arms across his knees. He sat hunched and disconsolate, his nose reddened by the wind.

'Oh dear,' Avril murmured. She fumbled for something consoling to say. 'But you know, George, a long-time partnership – I mean, everyone has to be careful. About taking their partners for granted. It happens a lot.'

'So I've noticed.'

'I'm – pardon?'

'It seems to me that Steve takes *you* for granted.' George was gazing moodily off down the Great Dividing Range, which was being rapidly swallowed by clouds. 'If you ask me, we're both in the same position.'

He sighed, and fell silent. Faintly, in the distance, a white cockatoo screeched. The sky was becoming overcast, and Avril was growing chilly. She wrapped up what was left of her sandwich.

The fruit salad remained untouched.

'Fruit salad, George?' she asked quietly.

'No, thanks.'

'You should take it home.'

'I will.'

'So what do you think I should do?' she said in a very small voice. 'He thinks I'm his enemy now. He thinks I'm plotting against him.' Sighing, she added, 'Which I suppose I have been, in a sense. Oh dear. How silly I've been.'

'You're not silly.'

'Is it possible – I mean, I know it's a lot to ask – but if he didn't feel threatened anymore – if you were to reconsider . . .' Avril trailed off under George's searching gaze. 'I shouldn't have come to you in the first place,' she finished, hopelessly. 'I should never have interfered.'

Slowly, George pushed his glasses back up his nose.

'Could you still vote for him, George?' Avril queried. 'Do you still think he'd make a good mayor?'

George turned away. He was speechless for a while. Then he said: 'I don't know.'

'Oh dear.'

'I'll think about it.'

'Even if I could tell him that I'd asked you –'

'Yes. I understand.'

'It would make things easier. At home.'

The wind was now faintly damp, the south-western sky a bruised and threatening colour. Avril climbed to her feet. She brushed down her skirts, which were becoming unmanageable, flapping and billowing like a flag. George also got up.

'Looks like it's going to rain,' he murmured.

'Yes.'

'Well, you know what they say: if you don't like mountains weather, just wait ten minutes.'

'I must get home. I've left the washing out.'

'You'll be all right. It's quite a way off, still.'

They returned to the car in silence. On their way back to the Bella Vista, George made some observation about a very beautiful flowering cherry, and confessed, in a melancholy way, that he appeared to be 'coming down' with something. Avril commiserated. When he stopped in front of her house, she thanked him, with feeling, for granting her so much of his time. He assured her that his whole day would have been at her disposal, if it weren't for the fact that he had a shop to attend to.

'Anything you need, just call me,' he said. 'Anytime, Avril. I mean it.'

Dear George, she thought, as she returned to the sanctuary of her beautiful home. He's such a comfort.

By five o'clock that afternoon, Steven still hadn't returned. Avril had been forced to walk to the shops, *buy* scones for afternoon tea (something she was almost ashamed to do), and hire a taxi for the guest who arrived on the 3:22 train. This woman had just bought a house in Leura, but her furniture wasn't yet installed, because she wanted the carpets ripped up, the floorboards polished and the interior painted. Therefore she had come to the mountains for a couple of days to secure quotes from the local tradesmen.

She was in her thirties, young and dry, with a long, pale face and a long buff-coloured raincoat. Her hair hung straight and limp from a centre parting; she wore a pair of steel-rimmed accountant's spectacles.

Avril didn't warm to her.

'Oh – thanks, but I won't,' the woman said, when Avril presented her with a plate of scones. 'I'm trying to lose weight.' She did, however, accept a cup of camomile tea, before trudging off into the drizzle under a large black umbrella. She said that she had to meet a floor sander, who was due at her new house in an hour or so. She'd be back after dinner, she said.

Avril envisioned her hunched over a bowl of noodle soup at the Chinese cafe, her wet hair dripping onto the linen tablecloth. (It was not an attractive picture.) She would need a roaring fire when she returned – and where was Steven, for heaven's sake? Would Avril have to light the damned fire now?

At half past five the telephone rang. Anticipating some pathetic excuse from Steven, Avril answered it with rather less warmth than she usually employed.

But the voice that addressed her was female, and instantly recognisable as Janelle's.

'Mrs Lockhart?'

'Yes.'

'This is Janelle Pearce.'

'Yes.' Avril wasn't about to make it easier for her. Coolly, remotely, she said: 'What can I do for you, Janelle?'

'Is she there?'

'Who?'

'Natasha!'

'No. She's not.'

There was a pause. Avril waited. Finally, Janelle said, 'She is, though, isn't she?'

'*No*,' Avril replied, in steely tones. 'I do not *lie*, Janelle, not even for my daughter.'

'Then where is she?'

'I've no idea.'

'She's gone away. With Malcolm.' Janelle's voice was tight and hoarse with suppressed feeling. Rage, perhaps? Despair? It was hard to tell, over the phone. 'She's got him stashed away somewhere.'

'I'm sorry, but I can't help you. Is that all? Because –'

'I'm going to have an abortion.'

These words shot out of Janelle like bullets. They were wielded with explosive force, and were obviously designed to inflict a wound. Avril caught her breath.

'If Natasha doesn't fuck off out of our lives,' Janelle

went on, 'I'm going to get an abortion. I'm not going to be a single mother. It wouldn't be fair on anyone.'

Avril was speechless.

'Malcolm has to make a choice,' Janelle concluded, on a rising note. 'It's either Natasha or the baby. He can't have both. That's what I'm going to tell him. That's why I have to find him.'

Avril cleared her throat. She knew that some kind of response was called for, but one that wouldn't involve her in an argument. Such a confrontation, she knew, would be pointless.

'Well – as I said, I can't help you,' she declared.

'I've made the appointment. For the day after tomorrow.'

'I don't know where Natasha is.'

'You should have aborted *her*, you know. That's what you should have done.'

'Goodbye, Janelle.'

Avril hung up. She wouldn't allow herself to be heckled and insulted. On the other hand, she couldn't prevent herself from feeling increasingly flustered. What on earth was going on? Was Janelle *insane*? How could she go about blithely making such terrible, obscene threats? Avril began to fear for Natasha's safety. Anyone willing to abort her child if she lost her boyfriend would surely be capable of going to even more extreme lengths.

Avril rang Natasha's mobile number. To her

profound relief, it was her daughter who answered the call – through a storm of interference.

'Natty?' she said. 'Is that you?'

'Hello?'

'Can you hear me?'

'Mum?'

'Yes.'

'I can't hear you very well. Hang on.' There was a pause. Then the interference subsided somewhat, although the line still crackled and hissed. 'I just stepped outside. That's better, isn't it?'

'Where are you?'

'In Sydney, of course.'

'But you're not at home.'

'No. I'm house-sitting. A very nice place in Neutral Bay. Harbour views.'

'Are you with Malcolm?'

Another pause. 'Why?' Natasha said at last.

'Is he there?'

'What's up, Mum?'

Avril closed her eyes. She could imagine Natasha on a balcony overlooking Sydney Harbour, neon lights flaring in the dusk, reflections rippling on the oily surface of the water, a distant siren blaring.

It seemed a suitable backdrop, for some reason.

'Janelle Pearce just called me,' Avril sighed. 'She was looking for Malcolm.'

Silence.

‘She wanted to tell him,’ said Avril, ‘that she’s going to have an abortion unless he gives you up. She’s made the appointment.’

Natasha said nothing.

‘I told her I didn’t know where you were,’ Avril went on. ‘She was incredibly rude.’

‘She’s a lunatic,’ was Natasha’s contribution.

‘Is he with you, Nat?’

‘Yes, he’s with me. Because she’s driven him out.’ Natasha’s voice was impatient. ‘*You* try living with a raving lunatic. Poor guy, he’s at his wit’s end.’

‘Perhaps you should tell him –’

‘About the abortion? Why should I? He thinks her whole pregnancy is a fake.’

It took Avril a moment to absorb this, during which time Natasha continued.

‘She’s incredibly manipulative. She’ll try anything. Well, I don’t have to tell *you* that, do I? Malcolm fucking *ordered* her not to contact you again. So what did she do? She’s a total cow. Doesn’t care what she says. Before I even met Malcolm, she used to insult me behind my back. I’d go out to lunch with her one day, and the next day she’d be calling me a bitch and a nymphomaniac and I don’t know what else.’

‘But – I mean – she’s not violent, is she? She wouldn’t try to hurt you?’

‘Oh no. That’s not her style.’

Avril put a hand to her forehead. It was all too much to deal with. And Steven still hadn't come home.

'Listen, Mum, don't worry,' Natasha said. 'Janelle's just trying it on. She isn't going to abort her kid. She isn't even pregnant.'

'Are you sure?'

'Sure I'm sure. Malcolm didn't hear about this baby till after he got involved with me. A bit of a coincidence, don't you think?'

'Well – all right. As long as you're not worried.'

'I'm not worried.'

'And everything else is all right?'

'Perfectly fine.'

'Good. That's good.'

'Bye, Mum.'

'Oh. Yes. Um . . . goodbye, Natty.'

And that was that. Natasha offered no apologies. No expressions of regret. No inquiries into Avril's state of mind. But perhaps it was just as well. What could Avril have said in response? That Steven had vanished? That she didn't know what to say to him when he returned? Natasha wouldn't have wanted to hear about it, in any case. Though Avril had expressed nothing but sympathy and concern when it came to Natasha's emotional entanglements, dutifully reporting to her every development in the Janelle Pearce–Malcolm Busso conflict, Natasha didn't have the grace to repay her with even a show of fellow feeling.

But that was children for you. They always regarded their parents as impermeable, God-like providers of money, food and accommodation. One had to accept it, and look for a sympathetic ear elsewhere.

One also had to accept the fact that Natasha was coping with a lot at the moment. Avril just hoped that the whole affair wouldn't get too messy. An aborted foetus was . . . well, it was something beyond a normal lovers' spat. Quite simply, it was macabre.

At half past six Avril began to prepare dinner. She diced carrots, peeled potatoes, pounded, rolled and tied chicken fillets. Vic Rebke called; Avril took a message. Carla McGuigan, the lank-haired guest, returned to her room after a solitary meal at a Leura cafe. Avril boiled and mashed her potatoes, steamed her other vegetables and fried her chicken fillets. She arranged the cooked food on two plates, and put one plate in the fridge, under a transparent sheet of Gladwrap. She picked at the other plate, listening to the radio as she did so. When she'd eaten all she could – a few mouthfuls of carrot, half the potato, a bite or two of chicken – she made herself a cup of tea, which she drank in the sitting room.

There wasn't a sound from Carla. Obviously she didn't intend to watch television or seek out a hot drink. Avril didn't even hear a toilet flush; it was as if she were all alone in the dim, sprawling house, whose front door key had been made available to any number of people over the past five years. Outside, a gusty wind rattled the branches of the apple tree, so that they clawed at the slate roof in a threatening manner. Stray draughts whistled through warped window frames.

Avril retired to bed at half past nine, with a book and a glass of water. Shortly thereafter she must have dozed off, because at one-fifteen she woke with a start, propped uncomfortably against a stack of pillows, her bedside lamp shining, her glasses, which were attached to a chain, twisted around her neck.

Steven still hadn't returned.

Carla McGuigan didn't require a large breakfast. She wanted only cereal, toast and orange juice. Stoically, Avril served up this scanty fare in solid silver and Royal Doulton, providing a choice of three preserves (as well as honey and marmalade), freshly squeezed juice, perfect curls of butter in a chilled dish, and toast that reached Carla when it was still piping hot. Carla's response was to eat far more than she had intended, and afterwards complain about her lack of self-control. She read while she ate, stuffing food into her mouth without lifting her gaze from the *Sydney Morning Herald*.

At nine o'clock, wearing her buff-coloured raincoat, she left the house. Avril heard her heavy rubber soles grinding up the gravel driveway, and was relieved. She didn't want to cope with guests that morning. She had enough on her plate already, what with the bathrooms to clean – only one bathroom, happily, but one was enough – and the china to wash, and the laundry to do, and Steven to worry about. She was frantic about Steven. Of course, he had probably stayed away to punish her, but what if he hadn't? What if he'd crashed his car? What if he'd drunk himself into a coma? What if he'd been mugged? Muggings did happen in the mountains. They were regularly reported in the *Blue Mountains Gazette*.

Avril didn't know whether she should start making phone calls. If she did, and Steven was absent purely from spite, then their marital difficulties would soon become public knowledge. On the other hand, if he had paid for a bed the previous night, their problems would be public knowledge already – for Steven was acquainted with most of the hotel proprietors and guesthouse owners in the Upper Mountains. Unless he had gone further afield? Unless he had met with foul play, or become involved in an accident? But if he'd had an accident, the police would surely have phoned her.

Providing, of course, that he hadn't driven his car

off a secluded cliff somewhere. Out around Mount Hay, perhaps.

All morning, Avril fretted and fumed. She was at the same time angry and anxious, though as the day wore on, her anxiety began to outweigh her anger. People called, wanting Steven. He wasn't with Maeve. He wasn't with Allan, or anywhere at the council chambers. Finally, Avril rang George. She rang him at the shop, and began to weep into the receiver.

'I don't know where he is,' she sobbed. 'I don't know what to do.'

'I'm sure he's all right.'

'But where's he gone?'

'Did he take anything? Clothes, or anything?'

'You think he's *left* me?'

'Oh, Avril. I don't know.' George sounded sad. 'I doubt it.'

'Should I call the police?'

'No. Don't do that. Even if he is missing, they won't do a thing till he's been gone a while. At least a day, I think it is.'

'We're all booked up for the weekend. How am I going to cope? He's got the car.'

'I'm sure he'll be back by then.'

Avril sighed, and sniffed. 'What if he isn't?' she quavered. 'Oh God, I'm so sorry . . .'

'It's all right.'

'I'm so sorry, George.'

'Don't apologise.'

'It's so silly of me.'

'It's not.'

'I *must* pull myself together. What if Carla comes back? Oh dear. Oh dear.'

'Listen.' Suddenly George sounded firm. 'I'll come round. I'll come round this afternoon. We'll work out what to do then.'

'Will you? Oh, George . . .'

'Sit down. Take it easy. Have a cup of tea and a chocolate biscuit. Let me sort things out.'

'Oh, George . . .'

'If you ask me, he's staying away on purpose. To upset you. But we'll see what happens.'

With this, and with many other expressions of support, George tried to put Avril's mind at rest. After he'd hung up, she followed his advice; she had a long, hot bath, made herself a cup of tea, and treated herself to a handful of after-dinner mints. She also put on her favourite outfit, a long tunic jacket over floppy trousers, made of dull silk dyed a smoky mauve. It was a beautiful suit, beautiful but comfortable, like Chinese pyjamas – the sort of thing you could wear on any occasion, formal or informal. It always made Avril feel good.

And she certainly needed to feel good now.

'I'm coping,' she told her reflection in the mirror. 'I'm coping perfectly well. If Steven wants to upset me, he'll have to try harder than this. I'm sober. I'm groomed. I'm relaxed. I have a fantastic collection of antique silver. Nothing bad is going to happen to me, because I won't let it.' The very contents of her bedroom – all of it starched or inlaid or beeswaxed or hand-quilted – seemed to guarantee protection from the colder, crueller world outside. Her silver-backed brush and hand-mirror were so solid, so traditional, that they were utterly incompatible with a shaky, ephemeral marriage. Gazing about at her exquisite possessions, Avril was once more reassured. In such a setting, even heartache and loss must take on a more dignified, classical, aesthetically pleasing character.

Then George arrived, and she went to let him in. The sun was already low in the sky; flame-tinted clouds, fluffy and benign, drifted overhead. The garden was in shadow. Currawongs called plaintively from the crests of tall, dark pines. George entered without wiping his feet – although there was a perfectly good mat on the doorstep.

'How are you?' he said, fixing his earnest gaze on Avril. 'You look good.'

'I am good.'

'No news yet?'

'Nothing.'

'I was thinking – maybe you should call the bank. Check your credit-card records. Your savings-account records. If he stayed somewhere, he must have paid for it.'

'Unless he stayed with a friend.'

'What friend?'

'I don't know.'

Avril conducted George into her private sitting room. She offered him a cup of tea but he declined it. She suggested coffee and biscuits. Alcohol. A sandwich. He smiled gently and took her arm.

'Don't worry about me,' he said, drawing her onto the chaise longue. 'Stop worrying about other people. I didn't come here to be fed.'

'I'm sorry.'

'Don't be sorry. There's nothing to be sorry *for*. How are you managing? All right?'

'All right. Do you think I should call the bank?'

'You could try. But it's probably a bit late in the day now. Maybe tomorrow – if he isn't back . . .' Seeing Avril's face, George himself grimaced and hastily added, 'But he probably will be. I'm sure he will be.'

'If he misses the council meeting, I'll know that something's wrong.'

'He won't miss it. He won't miss the election.'

'Unless something's happened to him.'

'You would have heard, Avril. By this time you would have heard.'

Avril stared at the empty grate in the fireplace. She

thought: I'd better turn the heater on. But she felt too drained and sluggish to move.

'You're right,' she said dully. 'I would have heard by now.'

'The police would have contacted you.'

'Yes.'

'He's just in a rage. I'm sure that's it.'

'Yes. You're right. He wants to punish me.' Looking down at her hands, she confessed, 'He's always trying to punish me.'

There was a long silence. Avril was conscious of George's warm, solid shape beside her. She was conscious of his breathing. He seemed to radiate warmth, perhaps because the room was growing chilly.

'I'd better put the heater on,' she remarked. 'It looks as if it's going to be a cold night.'

'Would you like me to stay?'

Startled, Avril turned her head, drawing back in order to examine George's expression. His cheeks were flushed. His gaze was alert, direct and unflinching. His lips were pressed firmly together.

'Stay?' she said. 'Here?'

'Yes. If you want me to stay, I'll stay.' George spoke with slightly unconvincing carelessness. Then, in more sombre tones, he added: 'Dianne's moved out, you know.'

'No!' Avril exclaimed. She put a hand to her throat. 'I didn't! When?'

'Day before yesterday.'

'You didn't tell me . . .'

'No. It wasn't the time.' Lifting Avril's other hand from where it lay, upturned, in her lap, George pressed it between both of his. Avril noticed how stumpy and thick his fingers were. She also noticed how well they matched his short, fleshy, polyester-clad thighs. 'So I guess we're in the same boat,' he went on. 'More than ever now.'

'But do you know where she is?'

'Oh, yes. At her sister's. I know that much.'

'I'm so sorry. I'm so sorry, George. If I'd realised, I wouldn't have –'

'Bothered me? You're not bothering me. Far from it.'

'The last thing you need is this. My problems.'

'Your problems are worse than mine. You've been married – what? Twenty years? Dianne and I were together less than six. We aren't married. We don't have kids. There's no comparison.'

'Oh, George.'

He looked at her, his eyes spaniel-soft behind his glasses. Then he raised her captive hand to his lips. 'Poor Avril,' he murmured. 'He doesn't deserve you.'

It was at this point, as Avril struggled with many conflicting emotions, that her husband walked through the back door. They heard his key in the lock; they heard his heavy footsteps in the kitchen. George had barely stood up before Steven appeared, framed in the sitting-room doorway, large and lean and uncharacteristically rumpled. He hadn't shaved.

'Well,' he said, with heavy sarcasm, 'this *is* unexpected.'

Avril didn't know whether to laugh or cry. She felt as if she were in some horrible bedroom farce, with half-clad people popping through windows and scrambling under beds. At least that must have been what it looked like to Steven, who had such a suspicious attitude towards these things.

She cleared her throat, and didn't get up.

'Avril was wondering where you were.' George spoke carefully. 'She was worried.'

Steven snorted. He advanced a step, looking sullen and dangerous. He scowled at his wife. Then he turned his attention to George.

'You'll be pleased to know,' he announced, 'that Bert Plummer's going to run for mayor. Chris and Finlay have given him the go-ahead. Who'd have thought it, eh? Who'd have thought that Finlay would back down? Not me, that's for sure.'

George said nothing. His complexion had become mottled, red patches alternating with white.

'So what are you going to do, George?' Steven continued. 'Where do your interests lie, I wonder? Of course, you'd like to do the dirty on me, I realise that. But if I become mayor, it'll be open slather back here. I'll be gone all hours. Very convenient, I would have thought.'

'You'd better calm down, Steve.'

'I'm perfectly calm. Considering.'

Aware that the tension between the two men would have to be defused – and quickly – Avril found her voice, at last. 'Where have you been?' she inquired shrilly, wondering if Steven had in fact spent the day in a public bar. He certainly looked as if he'd been drinking.

'Around and about,' her husband rejoined.

'I was going to call the police.'

'But you called George instead.'

'I didn't know what to do.'

'Oh, I doubt that very much.'

'Listen. Steve,' George interrupted. 'I don't know what your playing at, but let me assure you that Avril's been –'

'A perfect lady? Of course she has.'

'She's been *worried*. Bloody worried.'

'George.' Steven approached him, and placed a heavy hand on his shoulder. 'Can I make a suggestion, George? Can I ask you, as a friend – a good friend, George – can I ask you to do us a favour, and piss off out of here? Please?'

George looked at Avril. He didn't have to explain himself. He was waiting to be told what she wanted.

'It's all right, George,' she said faintly. 'I think we'd better – I think Steven and I should try to work this out by ourselves.'

'Are you sure?'

'Yes. I think so.'

George hesitated. He eyed Steven doubtfully, cautiously, as one might eye a chained but growling Rottweiler.

'Well?' said Steven. 'She asked you nicely, mate.'

'Would you like me to wait in the car?' George inquired, pointedly addressing Avril. Whereupon Steven folded his arms with calculated aggression.

'Why?' he asked. 'You going to whisk her off when we're done?'

'I'll be all right, George, really.'

'If you're *sure* . . .'

'I'm sure.'

'Well. Okay.' With obvious reluctance, his gaze still snagging on Steven's crumpled shirt and scrubby cheeks, George made his way slowly from the room. He left through the back door, pausing there for a moment. But no sounds of discord reached his ears. No shrieks or crashes summoned him back. So with dragging feet he returned to his car, which was parked in the front driveway.

Only when they heard his engine roar did the Lockharts recommence their heated exchange. Steven, who had been contemplating the cornice, suddenly pushed himself off the doorjamb and approached Avril. She, in turn, raised her eyes and straightened her back.

'So,' he said, 'it didn't take you long.'

'Where were you, Steven?'

'Taking a breather.'

'Which is to say, dodging your responsibilities.'

'Who did you get dressed up for?'

'I'm not dressed up.'

'Bullshit.' He stepped forward and seized a handful of her mauve silk tunic. With a yank, he pulled her upright.

'Be careful!' she exclaimed.

'Why? You said you weren't dressed up.'

'The buttons . . .'

'Oh Jesus! If I pull them, I might tear them off!' They were self-covered buttons, which Avril regularly had to re-attach. Her firm, competent sewing meant that when his fingers clamped onto one of them, and he headed towards the bedroom, she was forced to follow him on clumsy, faltering feet, or run the risk of having him rip a hole in the silk tunic.

'Stop!' she cried. 'Stop it, Steven!'

'Why? It's just an old rag. You said so yourself.'

'I did not, I –'

'So you *did* dress up for George?'

'This isn't dressed up!'

'No. It's dressed down. It's so dressed down it's almost not there.'

'Oh, what rubbish.'

'I can see right through the fucking thing!'

'I'm wearing a *slip*, Steven!'

'A slip? You mean one of those slippery little satin things? One of those slippery little satin-and-lace peek-a-boo things that slip off *so* easily – whoops! And there goes the top button!'

'Stop it!'

'Better take these clothes off, or we'll lose the next button too. Shit, I *know* you don't want to tear your nice little fuck-me outfit, do you? Hmmm? You'd rather do *anything* other than damage all these lovely clothes . . .'

'You've torn it!'

'I have.'

'You animal!'

'If you say so.' He threw her onto the bed, and pinned her there. 'You think you've won, don't you?'

'I know you scratched the whatnot!'

'I know what you've been doing with George.'

'I haven't *touched* George!'

' "I haven't touched George!" ' he fluted, mimicking her. ' "I'm so pure! I'm so put-upon! My husband is such an ape!" '

'You *smell* like an ape!'

'Then hold your breath.'

'Wait.' She struggled futilely. 'Wait. I need to –'

'Do what you're bloody well told.'

Later – much later – after Steven had stained the sheets and the rug and the piece-quilt cushion on the rocking chair, knocked over the glass of water on his bedside table, torn a button off his own shirt and left marks on the William Morris reproduction wallpaper behind the bedhead, he looked down at one of the garments strewn like bomb wreckage across the floor and said: 'That top of yours is ruined.'

Avril stirred beside him. She didn't bother to open her eyes.

'It doesn't matter,' she murmered lazily. 'It's pretty old.'

Besides, she thought, it's served its purpose.

# CHAPTER TEN

Steven sat down to breakfast the next morning scrubbed and shaved and feeling surprisingly tranquil. He had one day – just one – in which to foil Avril's plans. Tonight, the councillors would be electing their new mayor; at the last count, only five (Pat, Allan, Sue, Maeve and Steven himself) would definitely be voting for Steven – unless George changed his mind, of course. But that seemed unlikely, now that Avril had George twisted around her little finger. Looking at Avril as she stirred the porridge, a purple bruise already blossoming on her upper arm, Steven felt almost indulgent. She was bloody sly, he had to admit it. Cunning as a fox. He remembered her comment from the night before, a drowsy comment that seemed to come out of nowhere – 'Did you know that Dianne's left George?' – and it occurred to him that this heavily veiled threat was also an explanation. He hadn't factored Dianne into his calculations, when he'd first dismissed Avril's attempts to win George over. He hadn't realised that the Dianne–George alliance was on its last legs.

Well, he'd made a mistake. And he'd paid for it. And now he had one day in which to salvage something from the wreckage.

What he needed to find out was where Vera and Gareth stood. Bert had five votes: his own, Chris's, Finlay's, Celeste's, and probably George's. But who would be his choice as deputy? One of the Greens? Gareth, perhaps? Surely not Vera. Though people might question having a mayor and deputy mayor from the same ward.

It was possible, of course, that Bert had promised Labor's support to Finlay, as a sweetener for losing out. Which would put the Greens' backs up no end, if they heard about it. No – Bert wouldn't be that stupid. And George didn't want to be deputy. And Celeste wouldn't need encouragement to vote for Bert. No, Gareth was the obvious choice. He had a track record, for one thing. And he was in Bert's ward. And trying to win over Steven's power base wouldn't work, because Maeve, like George, didn't want to be deputy, Pat was bowing out of as much as she could, and Allan wouldn't be able to countenance a Labor mayor at any price.

But where did that leave Steven? Was he really going to have to offer his deputy vote to *Vera*, of all people? And not even for a win, mind you – just for a draw. Just for the chance of having his name pulled out of a hat.

God, no. There had to be another way.

The phone rang. Steven answered it, because Avril was in the dining room, but as soon as he spoke there was a click, and then the dial tone.

He snorted as he put down the receiver.

It had probably been George, wanting to talk to Avril. Well, he wasn't going to get the chance. Let him sweat a bit, Steven thought. Let him sit there wondering what I might have done to her last night. Wondering if I beat her up, or chucked her out, or stabbed her to death.

Or even worse, if I fucked her until she was limp and moaning, until she was sore and submissive, until her pale, supple whippet's body was wrung absolutely dry.

Tick option D, thought Steven, and grinned smugly as he dropped his dirty plate and knife into the dishwasher.

'Carla's checking out soon,' Avril announced from the doorway. 'Would you take care of it, please?'

'Sure. Does she want a lift to the station?'

'I don't know. I'll ask.'

You think you've won, Steven decided, watching his wife disappear into the dining room. Perhaps you have, but not yet. Not quite yet. Glancing at his watch, Steven saw that it was eight-fifteen. Probably late enough to ring Allan.

He retired to his office, where he was guaranteed at least a vestige of privacy.

'Allan. Hi. It's Steve,' he said, when Allan answered the phone. 'Just a quick word. Did you know that Bert's definitely going to run for mayor? I heard it yesterday.' In fact, Steven had called Bert several times on Tuesday and Wednesday, finally pinning him down at around nine o'clock the previous morning. Steven had been waking up in a cheap Lithgow hotel room at the time; he had spent Tuesday night there, drinking Guinness draught and eating corn chips in bed until the early hours, while he watched the kind of American sitcoms that always made Avril wince. But he wasn't about to go into that with Allan. 'Somebody must have pulled rank on Finlay, and got him to concede. Don't ask me how.'

'And George?' Allan asked, quietly.

'George turned me down. Doesn't want to be deputy after all.'

'Then what's his problem?'

'Me.' Steven sighed. 'I am. We've had a few disagreements lately.'

'On policy issues?'

'Sort of. He doesn't think I'd make a good mayor.'

'I see. Well.' There was a brief silence. 'I hope this doesn't mean that you've changed your mind about poor Ken. You should see his premises – talk about a can of sardines.'

Steven replied obliquely. 'I was thinking about offering Celeste our vote,' he said, and grimaced at the splutter that greeted this suggestion.

'*Celeste?* Are you *joking*?'

'Bert didn't tell me his choice for deputy, but it's gotta be Gareth. He wouldn't be thick enough to field Finlay. And I'm sure he couldn't stomach kissing up to Vera.'

'Who could?'

'Right. God knows who she's going to vote for. She hates us both.'

'But she's in your ward.'

'Yes. That's one thing.'

'Celeste isn't.'

'No. But she likes me. If I offered her three deputy votes, she might change sides.'

'Vera doesn't have a side. Yet.'

'No, but –'

'Steve, I realise there's no point in offering to endorse Gareth. If he's got support from both sides, he could go either way. But surely Maeve would vote for Vera as deputy, instead of Gareth? Didn't Maeve and Vera run for council on the same ticket? That would make four votes you could promise Vera – plus her own.'

'Yes, but –'

'Frankly, Steve, I think Vera would be a better bet than Celeste. It would consolidate your hold on Maeve, it would build on this friction I've been seeing between Gareth and Vera, and – well, let's face it, Steve, Vera might be a 24-carat bitch, but at least she's a player. Celeste is ludicrous. She's a joke. I'd be *embarrassed* to vote for Celeste. Wouldn't you?'

Steven sighed. 'I know,' he said, 'but *Vera*, Allan . . .'

'She won't win. Pat's bound to vote for Gareth. And if Bert's mob fall into line, that's seven votes.'

'Yes, but –'

'Just think, Steve: would you *lose* anyone, if you voted for Celeste? I think you might. And Celeste is just the sort of person to blab about any deals she's got going. Before we all cast our votes, I mean.'

Steven considered Maeve. He summoned up a mental picture of her earnest, frowning face. And he capitulated.

'All right,' he groaned. 'I'll ring Vera. But you can nominate her, Allan.'

'Ask Maeve to nominate her. Maeve can ring her, and then you won't have to talk to her at all.'

'Of course I'm going to have to talk to her! If it's a trade-off –'

'Steve, Vera's not a total moron. If she's told that she'll have your support, she's got to know where you're coming from. I mean, in the circumstances. Why else would you be voting for her?'

'I suppose so.' The more Steven considered it, the better he liked Allan's plan. It didn't look too obvious. Well, it didn't look *as* obvious. It was obvious, but in a subtle sort of way. 'All right,' he said. 'I'll ring Maeve.'

'You do that. And I'll see you tonight.'

'Okay. Thanks.'

'And may the best man win.'

'Right. Absolutely.'

Allan was barely off the line before Steven began to punch out Maeve's number. She lived with her parents, and it was her father who answered the call; apparently Maeve was already at work. So Steven had to phone Katoomba Cabs, leave a message for Maeve – which, he was assured, would be conveyed to her within minutes – and wait for her to respond. He wondered if she had a mobile phone handy.

'Steven.' Avril's voice sounded muffled through the door. She turned the handle, and gave the door a shove, but it was stubborn, and wouldn't yield. 'Steven, Carla would like a lift to the station.'

'Right. Okay.'

'She's catching the 9:29.'

'Sure.'

'Are you finished in there?'

'I'm finished.' Wrenching the door open, Steven gave Avril a bit of a start. She fell back, placing her hand to her bosom.

'Oh,' she said. With a sense of satisfaction, Steven noted that she wasn't looking quite as well groomed as usual. Not that her hair was untidy, or her clothing in disarray. But her lips were slightly grazed and swollen, there were bags under her eyes, and she walked as if she were a little stiff.

Before she could withdraw from him, he pinched her bottom.

'Oh, stop it,' she said. Her tone was unconvincing.

'Fancy a quick one?'

'Don't be obscene.'

'I've only got one bathroom today.'

She pretended to ignore him, stalking off into their bedroom. Steven considered following her, but decided against it; instead he went and introduced himself to Carla, who was sitting, drab and sallow, at the dining table. Dear me, he thought, as he jauntily offered her his name. What a dreary sight, first thing in the morning. Enough to put you off your food.

'I'm sorry I wasn't here yesterday,' he said. 'But I'm hoping that my wife took care of you.'

Carla, who had raised her eyes at the sound of his greeting, grunted something incomprehensible. Her resigned air told Steven that she was dying to return to her book.

'More juice?' he asked.

'No thanks.'

'More toast?'

'No thanks.'

'Did you say you were catching the 9:29?'

She nodded.

'In that case, we'll want to leave here by quarter past. Are you all packed up?'

'Not quite.'

'Just give me a yell when you're ready, then, and I'll carry your bag to the car.'

Lesbian, he concluded, as his most winning beam was answered by another unsmiling nod. Glad that *she's* taking off today. He returned to his office, and busied himself with his GST files until the telephone rang.

He pounced on it.

'Hello, Bella Vista Guesthouse?'

'Steve?'

'Maeve! Hello! Look, I'm sorry to bother you at work –'

'It's okay.' She sounded rather cool. 'What is it?'

'I'll be as quick as I can.' Steven found himself on his feet, heart pounding. All at once he felt uneasy. 'The thing is, I was wondering who your choice might be for deputy mayor.'

There was a brief silence. The line crackled and hummed.

'Well . . . I don't know,' Maeve replied at last. 'It depends on who's nominated.'

'You hadn't thought of nominating anyone yourself?'

'No. Not really.'

'Vera, for instance?' Steven waited, but, upon securing no immediate response, added, 'I don't know what relations between you are like these days, after all the changes that have taken place – I mean, after that business at Gareth's house . . .'

'They're all right,' said Maeve. She paused. When she resumed speaking, her tone was flat. 'Vera called me last night, as a matter of fact. She told me that Bert's decided to run for mayor instead of Finlay.'

'Yes. So I've heard.'

'She told me that Finlay called her with the news. She was very pissed off at him.'

'I'm sure.'

'He said he was doing it because George Lovecek wanted Bert for mayor. Is that true, Steve?'

'Well, I'm – I'm not sure. It's possible. We had a bit of a row.'

'He said that Labor's going to endorse Gareth for deputy – as a trade-off sort of thing, you know –'

'Yes, of course.'

'. . . and that George told Bert that you'll be supporting Allan. As deputy mayor. Is *that* true, Steve?'

Her voice was sharp. Steven couldn't believe it. George! That son-of-a-bitch! That *dirty* son-of-a-bitch!

'Actually – actually, no,' he stammered.

'It's not?'

'No.'

'You mean George was *lying*?'

'Not exactly.' Steven was beginning to sweat. He couldn't bear the pure, clear note of accusation in her query. 'Possibly he got hold of the wrong end of the stick. As a matter of fact, Maeve, I was considering Vera.'

'*Vera?*'

'If you were going to nominate her, that is. I thought I'd second your nomination.'

'Why?' Maeve demanded. 'So that she'll vote for you?'

Steven, who had been retreating in shame, suddenly took a stand. What a bloody ridiculous question, he thought. I mean, for Christ's sake, what does she think this is? We've both been councillors for three years. We both know the score.

'Let's not be naive,' he said. 'As far as Vera's concerned, Bert and I don't constitute much of a choice. And since Bert's tried to get Gareth's vote by offering him deputy, I thought I'd do the same with Vera.

I thought it would please you, Maeve. If nothing else.'

There was another silence. Biting his lip, Steven stared out the window. He wondered why he hadn't anticipated this particular development. Because his domestic troubles had interfered with his powers of reason? Avril had a lot to answer for.

'Well,' Maeve finally remarked, sounding tired and discouraged, 'I wouldn't object to nominating Vera, except that I'd like to see a Lower Mountains deputy. It would make things fairer, I think.'

'That's true,' said Steven, rolling his eyes. 'But what kind of a choice is there? Who would you suggest?'

'I don't know. Chris, perhaps . . .'

'Chris? Well, yes, I've no problem with Chris. But you've got to factor in the party line, Maeve. If Bert's trying to get Gareth's vote, he'll be wanting Chris to vote for Gareth too. You know how it works.'

'Yes. I suppose so.'

'It's up to you. If you don't want to nominate Vera, I'll do it myself. I'll tell her that Allan's willing to get behind her too. And Sue Schaarf.'

'*Allan* is?'

'Yes.'

'But why?'

'Why do you think? Allan doesn't want a Labor mayor, Maeve.'

Maeve sighed. She cleared her throat. She sighed again. Steven waited, holding his breath.

When she eventually spoke, her words were halting and indistinct.

'Well . . . I've got to get back to work,' she said. 'I'll . . . I'll talk to Vera, if you want. I'll see what she says.'

'Great. Thanks.'

'But maybe you ought to talk to her yourself as well. Maybe I should ask her to ring you.'

'Whatever you think, Maeve.'

'I don't know. This is . . . I don't know.' Her lack of enthusiasm was disturbing. 'Anyway, I'll see you tonight.'

'Maeve . . .'

'Goodbye, Steve. Gotta go.'

She hung up. The sound of it jarred Steven; he frowned as he let the receiver drop. That hadn't gone as well as expected. In fact it had positively unnerved him. And because it had unnerved him, he had begun to sound dodgy. Shifty. No wonder Maeve had been unimpressed.

But there wasn't anything much he could do about it now – except ring Vera, perhaps. Not that he wanted to. Not that he needed to, just yet. He would wait for a while, to give Maeve a chance. To see whether Vera, once informed of his intentions, would ring *him*. After all, it was still early.

Steven glanced at his watch. Five past nine. More than ten hours to go until the election.

The Blue Mountains City Council held its public meetings in a large, windowless, oval-shaped room that seemed utterly insulated from the outside world. Purple carpet covered the floor, and ran up the walls to a height dictated by the tops of the doorframes. An electronic digital clock sat between two Australian flags, enabling every speaker to watch his or her allotted three minutes rapidly diminish as the clock performed its inexorable countdown. A series of modular tables forced the councillors to sit in a circle, facing each other, beneath the city shield – which featured a representation of that peculiar rock formation known as the Three Sisters. The press occupied chairs beneath the honour board; group managers and Speaker Registration were placed opposite the press; and the public was crowded into a semicircular space at the bottom of the room, from which position it was possible to see only the backs of four of the twelve councillors.

Steven liked this room. He felt at home in it. Before his arrival in the mountains, his experience of council chambers had been confined to great echoing nineteenth-century structures full of scuffed wooden panelling and melancholy oil portraits. This room was different: with its low ceiling, bland decor, recessed lighting and artificial, electronically charged warmth, it reminded Steven of bank premises. It had a reassuringly corporate feel to it. Upon his first visit, as a member of the public, he had thought to himself: I could make my way, here. The very smell of the stale, filtered air was invigoratingly familiar – unlike the chilly, dusty, public-school smell that characterised so many more ancient government buildings.

Steven liked the room, and he liked attending meetings there every fortnight at 7:30 p.m. He enjoyed the exciting, muted, purposeful buzz that preceded meetings. He appreciated the sense of importance bestowed on all those participating by the fact that there was a security guard posted by the door (as there had been ever since the 1992 bombing of the council chambers). He savoured the highly structured nature of the proceedings, which made him nostalgic for the highly structured life of a bank manager. And he loved the conspicuous role in these proceedings that was his by right – the role of councillor. Elected representative. Guardian of the community.

He felt that the role suited him rather well.

Avril, of course, had never attended a council meeting. She had offered 'the business' as an excuse, but had expressed no regrets that she was (for some reason) prevented from witnessing Steven at work. She was entirely ignorant of his talents as a public speaker. She was obviously not interested in the fact that he could think, very incisively, on his feet, or that he was a favourite with the public gallery. Such things meant nothing to Avril. The things that mattered to Avril were dovetailed drawers, handmade lace and Laura Ashley catalogues. She had no sense of civic responsibility. No grasp of the wider issues. She was utterly focused on her petty domestic sphere, and expected Steven to exhibit the same lack of vision.

Well, she wasn't going to drag him down to her level. Not even if he lost his bid for mayor – an outcome that seemed almost certain, in light of the fact that Vera hadn't called him yet. Of course, she might have been still in the process of considering his offer. She might have been giving herself until the very last moment to make a decision.

On the whole, however, it wasn't an encouraging development.

'Well,' he said, rising from the table after he had consumed, at top speed, his wife's lamb casserole. (One of her grudges against the fortnightly council meeting was that it obliged Steven to bolt his carefully prepared dinner as if he were guzzling fast food.) 'I s'pose I'd better get going.'

No response from Avril. She was sitting opposite him, lips pursed, daintily sawing at a piece of boiled potato.

'Don't wait up for me, will you?' he said, perfectly aware that she had never once felt constrained to do so in the past. 'If Peter calls, tell him I picked up those pamphlets that I was telling him about, and I'll drop 'em in the mail tomorrow.'

Still she said nothing. So Steven pulled on his jacket and went outside. The sky was clear, illuminated by a full moon; the breeze was mild enough to lift his spirits. Spring is in the air, he thought. A new beginning. A good omen. As he drove down the highway towards the council chambers, he listened to a vigorous and optimistic piece of Baroque music on the car radio, and felt as if the power of governance was coursing through his veins.

But when he arrived at the council building, his confidence began to ebb.

It was partly because he met up with Gareth near the lift. Gareth was a hard man to talk to. He seemed impervious to Steven's charm; Steven's jolly salutations would bounce off his armour like pebbles bouncing off a cliff face. Gareth's voice was dry and flat, his smile a slight elevation of one side of his mouth, rarely witnessed. Upon Steven's joining him at the after-hours entrance, he simply nodded. When Steven asked him gaily if he was all toned up for the fight, he expelled some air and shook his head. Then Chris Diacopoulos joined them, and Steven began to feel even worse.

Not that he disliked Chris. On the contrary. Chris was a very likeable fellow, because for all his dark and glossy good looks, for all his wit and style and confidence, he never put on airs, threw his weight around, or failed to respond genially to a friendly greeting. The only accusation you could make against Chris was that he sometimes seemed a little too sharp for his own good. His clothes were a little too crisp, his remarks were a little too pointed, and his arguments cut a little too close to the bone. Even this quality, however, marked him as a man with a future. And Steven, who had once been just as good-looking as Chris – who had once been impelled by a modest ambition, and had honed his tongue and his brain in an effort to attain his goals – Steven was always cast down when Chris was in the vicinity. For some reason, Chris made him feel . . . well . . . not *inferior*, exactly, but depleted. Worn out. As if he were past his use-by date.

Sometimes it was all he could do to dredge up a smile when Chris approached him (as he did now) and, with carefully judged force, slapped him convivially on the shoulder.

'G'day, Steve.'

'How are you, Chris?'

'Not bad, not bad. And you?'

'Fine.'

'Big night, eh?'

'Big night.'

'Bit different from the usual run of things.'

Gareth grunted. Then the lift arrived, and the three of them piled in. Steven noticed, in the confined space, that Chris's cologne was just a little too intrusive.

But he's young, Steven thought glumly. When he gets a bit older, he'll have smoothed out all those sharp edges.

The lift hauled them up to the first floor, where most of the other councillors were already milling about in a serious fashion, flipping through their business papers and talking in low voices to each other, to the staff, or to select members of the public. Pat wasn't present; Steven concluded that she must be in her office. George didn't seem to be there, but then he always cut it pretty fine. Vera was there. She was already seated, poring over her business paper, her fuchsia mohair cardigan clashing horribly with her lipstick.

Steve decided to bite the bullet.

'Vera!' he said, approaching her. Looking up, she greeted him with the severe expression of a magistrate quelling a public outcry.

'Yes?' she said.

'Did you get my message?'

'Yes,' she said.

'And?'

'And?'

'What's your decision?'

'You'll know soon enough.' She spoke in an undertone, turning her attention back to her business paper. 'I don't think we ought to discuss things here.'

Bitch, thought Steven. He strolled over to where Vic Rebke was accepting nominations, and checked that Pat had done the job for him. She had. Then he retreated to his usual seat, which gave him a fairly good view of the public gallery. Stella Swann was there, of course; she never missed a meeting. Ken Bribie was there, deep in conversation with Allan Purchese. Vera's moth-eaten boyfriend was planted right in the front row of chairs, wearing a thin, ragged sky-blue jumper and looking uncomfortable. Steven sucked in his breath. Why would old Hairy Harry be present, unless Vera was anticipating a moment of glory?

This was good. This was *very* good.

Electronic chimes announced that the meeting was about to begin. People slipped into their seats; there was a rustle of paper. To Steven's right, Sue Schaarf settled herself with a great deal of fuss into her customary chair, adjusting her contoured backrest, arranging piles of documents, removing her tailored jacket, pouring herself a glass of water, clearing her throat, adjusting her collar, smoothing her hair, and blowing her nose with a single, ladylike snort into a wispy handkerchief – which then had to be restored, fussily, to one of the numerous compartments in her handbag. Steven despised Sue Schaarf. She was a forty-ish bottle blonde, divorced, a legal secretary, with one child – a son – and absolutely nothing to say for herself. All her energy seemed to be expended on grooming; nevertheless, despite her thickly applied cosmetics, her burnished hair, her glossy nails and her beautifully pressed suits, she always looked tired and faded.

When she did speak, her voice was high, nasal and deeply irritating, like the sound of a distant chainsaw.

'Good luck, Steve,' she said.

'Oh. Thanks.'

'Where are my cough drops? Damn. They must be in my purse.'

More craning and delving and fiddling. Steven turned away, just in time to see George sliding into the seat on his left-hand side. They had been sitting next to each other ever since their first council meeting. Now they were stuck with each other – unless Steven won the election – because it was considered disruptive to confuse everybody by changing places.

'Hello,' Steven drawled.

'Hello.'

'So you made it.'

'Yes.'

'Didn't drop in to see Avril on your way here?'

George delivered himself of a long-suffering sigh. Pointedly, he fixed his attention on the business paper in front of him. Then Vic Rebke called the meeting to order.

'Please be upstanding for her worship the mayor,' he intoned.

Pat Baldwin entered, all in grey, like a mouse. Having thanked the general manager, she reeled through the usual apologies and prayer-cum-reflection before surrendering the chair, once again, to Vic Rebke. 'First item on the agenda,' she said, 'is the election of mayor and deputy mayor for the next year – until September next year. Traditionally, the mayor now joins the other members of the council and leaves the general manager to conduct the election. So I now call upon you, Mister General Manager, to . . . um . . . conduct the election.'

Moving awkwardly, Pat retired to an empty chair placed conspicuously beside Gareth's. Vic Rebke thanked her, and donned his reading glasses. He was quite a small man, nondescript, with a developing paunch. The strength of his booming voice never failed to surprise Steven.

'Em,' he said. 'Right. As the mayor has pointed out, first item on the agenda is the election of mayor for the next year, and I have two nominations.' He consulted the slips of paper in his hands. 'Councillor Diacopoulos has nominated Councillor Plummer, and Councillor Plummer has consented. Councillor Baldwin has nominated Councillor Lockhart, and Councillor Lockhart has consented.' Looking up, Vic removed his glasses. 'The situation with voting is that we have a show of hands among the councillors, and the nominee who receives the lowest count is excluded from the vote. Since I received Councillor Lockhart's nomination first, I'll call for a show of hands in his favour. All those in favour of Councillor Lockhart for mayor, please raise your hands.'

Steven raised his hand. His heart was pounding. Glancing around the circle, he began to count along with Vic. Sue, one; Allan, two; Pat, three; Maeve, four – thank Christ! Her brow was furrowed, her expression was stern, but her hand was raised. And Vera! Hallelujah! Vera had come through after all! Thank you, God, he thought. I don't believe it.

That was six votes altogether, including his own. Six. An equal split.

'Six,' Vic declared. 'Hmm. All those in favour of Councillor Plummer as mayor, please raise your hands.'

It was a pointless exercise. Six hands went up – including George's. He wouldn't look at Steven, the dirty traitor. Steven made a loud, wordless, disgusted noise.

'All right,' said Vic. 'We have an equal number of votes for each nominee. And it's customary, in this kind of situation, to draw the names out of a box. Um . . . I believe we have a box, here . . . thank you, Anna.' A white cardboard box was produced from under a table. 'Now. I'll put the two names into this box, and I'll ask a member of the public to come up here and draw out a name. Any takers? Yes sir. Thanks very much.'

A pale, solid man with thin red hair rose to his feet. Self-consciously he crossed the room; awkwardly he positioned himself beside the white cardboard box. Steven folded his arms and attempted to watch the proceedings with a detached expression, though he could feel the pinpricks of sweat breaking out all over his body. Pat Baldwin caught his eye, and smiled her encouragement in a weary fashion. There was a murmur of voices from the public gallery, as one slip of paper was drawn and surrendered.

'All right,' said Vic. 'We have a name. Thank you, sir. A name has been selected, by due process, so it's the determination of this ballot that . . .' (A pause. Steven looked down at the table in front of him.) '. . . that Councillor Plummer is now elected mayor of the Blue Mountains . . .'

Steven missed the rest. There was a buzzing in his ears. With an enormous, convulsive effort, he raised his eyes, plastered a rueful smile across his face, and slowly shook his head. He knew that everyone must be looking at him.

Bert. Bert was rising. Steven could hear a spattering of applause, and glanced around to see that Bert's wife was sitting with a couple of silver-haired cronies. Well, at least Margaret looked pleased. She'd be in her element as mayoress. She was already involved with the Girl Guides and the CWA and every other volunteer association you could think of.

Steven turned back to Bert, and leaned across the table, smiling.

'Congratulations,' he said, raising his voice.

'Thanks.' Bert spoke gruffly. 'Thanks, Steve.' Vic was muttering in his ear, drawing him towards the seat vacated by Pat Baldwin. They conversed briefly. Steven turned to George, and said in a low voice: 'I hope you're satisfied now.'

George continued to stare at the papers lying in front of him.

'Well. Thank you, um, Mister General Manager,' Bert declared. His voice was hoarse and gravelly. He sounded almost embarrassed. 'I'll . . . it's now my duty to conduct the election for deputy mayor. So, without further ado – what? Oh.' A rustle, as he was handed the nomination forms. 'Thanks. We have . . . a-hmm . . . we have two nominations. Councillor O'Meagher has nominated Councillor Rudkowski, and Councillor Diacopoulos has nominated Councillor Cleves. So if we could have a show of hands for Councillor Rudkowski as deputy mayor . . .'

Gritting his teeth, Steven raised his hand. Beside him, Sue did the same. He saw Vera, her face bright, putting her hand up. Allan, expressionless, following suit. Maeve. Celeste . . .

*Celeste?*

Steven couldn't believe it. Why would Celeste be voting for Vera? Bert wasn't. Bert was voting for Gareth. So why? Because Vera had a cat? Gareth didn't like cats. He'd made that abundantly clear. Vera, on the other hand, was a little less than hardline when it came to cats (as long as they were desexed, microchipped and under strict curfew). She was also surprisingly reluctant to air her views on white jasmine (classified as a weed), slow combustion stoves, the keeping of hens . . .

Suddenly, Steven realised that George had raised his hand. George! Had *raised his hand*! Steven stared at him, slack-jawed. What –? How –? It was impossible. No. It couldn't be true.

'I count seven votes for Councillor Rudkowski,' Bert said, frowning as he scratched the side of his face. 'Could I see a show of hands for Councillor Cleves? Thank you, that's . . . two . . . five. All right. I declare Councillor Rudkowski elected as deputy mayor for the next year.'

'Woo!' cried Hairy Harry. There was some scattered, tentative applause from the public gallery, and a ripple of exclamations from the councillors. Allan was shaking his head, his pudgy fingers clamped across his eyes. Chris looked stunned. Vera was struggling to suppress a grin, as Finlay congratulated her.

Sue nudged Steven.

'Steve,' she said. 'You can put your hand down now.'

Slowly, Steven lowered his arm. Slowly, he turned to glare at George. He discovered that George was watching him, with a provocative smile glinting deep in his brown, spaniel eyes.

'What the fuck . . .?' Steven spluttered. 'What the hell do you think you're playing at?'

'Just following your example, Steve.'

'For Chrissake!'

'There isn't much to choose between them.'

Steven was gobsmacked. He slumped back into his chair. He sighed in disbelief. He tried to imagine a year during which Vera would be filling in for Bert, and was overcome by a yawing, spinning sense of vertigo.

This is my doing, he realised in despair. This is *my* bloody doing!

Then it occurred to him that he was wrong. It wasn't really his fault. It was Avril's.

Good Christ, he thought grimly. Good Christ, that woman has a lot to answer for.

Good Christ, but she's going to pay for this.

# CHAPTER ELEVEN

Natasha had come up from Sydney for the weekend, in a surprisingly mellow mood. Almost immediately upon arriving, at around eleven o'clock, she had whisked Avril off to the Mall, where they had both indulged themselves by purchasing some extremely expensive, extremely beautiful English shirts – on sale. Natasha had also persuaded Avril to buy a pair of linen trousers to match her shirt. Finally, having run up a large bill among the racks of high-priced wool serge and silk chiffon clothing, they had repaired to a cafe for lunch; Natasha had ordered a bagel and salad with iced coffee, Avril the leek-and-potato soup, with tea.

Upon sampling the soup, Avril decided that it wasn't as good as her own.

'Well of course not,' said Natasha, when Avril had delivered herself of this opinion. 'Everyone knows that you're a champion cook.'

'Well – I have my specialties,' Avril admitted. 'Not exotic cooking. Just traditional European dishes.'

'Right.'

'It's very hard to find a good roast nowadays. Or a good Irish stew.'

'People have probably stopped looking.'

'I notice that puddings have been coming back into style, but half the time they're not done properly, either. The bread-and-butter pudding I've been served in restaurants lately . . .' Avril shook her head. 'The consistency is all wrong.'

'A farce.'

'And I always think that puddings are better served in a dish. Not sitting on an enormous white platter in a puddle of Cottees' strawberry conserve.'

Natasha laughed. She was looking very well, Avril thought. More relaxed, somehow. Less drawn.

'So . . . Malcolm couldn't come up with you this time?' Avril inquired delicately. Natasha smiled. She was sitting with both elbows on the table (as Avril had noticed with an inward sigh) and was pinching small pieces off her bagel as if she were plucking petals off a flower. As each piece went into her mouth, her tongue flicked out, just a little, to receive it.

'Malcolm and I aren't seeing each other anymore,' she said, after a moment's reflection.

'Oh dear.'

'It's no big deal. It was bound to happen.'

'Because of Janelle, you mean?'

'What? Oh God, no.' Natasha snorted. 'He didn't go back to her, if that's what you're talking about. They're well and truly finished. When he found out that she'd had the abortion, he –'

'*What?*' Avril exclaimed. 'You mean there *was* a baby?'

'Oh, yeah.'

'And she got *rid* of it?'

'Oh, yeah. Gross, eh? Malcolm certainly thought so. He was shattered. It was his kid too, you know.'

'But – but you said that there wasn't any baby.'

Natasha shrugged.

'I was wrong,' she conceded. 'So was Malcolm.'

'How awful.'

'Yeah. Poor guy. But that's what you get for taking up with a neurotic, manipulative little bitch like Janelle Pearce. You get totally screwed.' Putting down her bagel, Natasha dragged her iced coffee towards her and began to jangle the long silver spoon around the glass, breaking up two full scoops of ice-cream. 'I warned him,' she continued. 'I said to him: "What did you expect?" And now he can't stop talking about it. On and on and on about what a cow she is and how much he did for her. I mean, I hate her too, I think she's pond-scum, but even *I* can get sick of hearing him slag her off. So I told him to hit the road – at least until he can get his act together.'

'Goodness,' said Avril. She was awed by Natasha's sublime indifference to another person's pain. But in many ways it was self-defence, of course; one couldn't allow oneself to become used as a kind of receptacle for somebody else's misery and regret.

Besides, maudlin men *were* very dreary.

'Well,' Avril remarked, after a pause. 'How – how very sad.'

'Oh, yeah. Really sad,' Natasha agreed, in careless accents.

'And you haven't heard from Janelle?'

'No, thank God.' Natasha's crimson lips puckered around her straw; she sucked up a mouthful of iced coffee, swallowed, and sighed. 'But she deserved it. I mean, she 100 per cent deserved it. And now she has to find herself another flat – or another flatmate.' Smiling slightly, Natasha picked up her bagel again. 'With any luck, she'll choose some kind of psycho. Someone who'll smash the place up, or cut their wrists all over her duvet, or something. That would be poetic justice.'

Avril didn't see how, but remained silent. She didn't want to antagonise her daughter, just when they were getting on so well. Scraping the soup from the bottom of her bowl, she consumed the last, slightly oversalted mouthful and announced that they would have to be getting back. Steven had some kind of civic function to attend, at half past one, and Avril would have to be home to welcome the new guests.

'Oh, right. The guests,' said Natasha. 'I suppose you'll be glad to get rid of 'em, won't you? In a way.'

Avril blinked. 'What do you mean?' she asked.

'Well . . . I dunno.' Natasha's blandly good-humoured expression slumped into discontented lines. She began to riffle through her bag, in search of her wallet. 'When you close down, or whatever it is you're doing.'

'Close down?' Avril echoed. Suddenly she realised that Steven must have tackled their daughter while Avril was changing her clothes, that morning, and she laughed a tinkling laugh. 'Oh, goodness,' she said. 'Has Dad been telling you about his silly idea? It's just because they didn't elect him mayor – he's a bit demoralised. That's why he's talking about going and getting a job somewhere else. Outside the mountains. But of course he won't.' (And if he does, it'll be over my dead body, Avril thought.) 'Of *course* we won't be selling the Bella Vista. It's such a success, we'd be mad to do anything of the sort.'

'Whatever.'

'Can you tell me exactly what he said, Nat? Do you know if he's actually applied for anything?'

'Sorry.' Natasha slapped down a $10 note. 'I don't get involved, remember?'

'But Natty –'

'Can you take care of this? I'm dying for a smoke, Mum.'

She practically bolted out the door, leaving Avril to settle the bill and calculate an appropriate tip. Even as Avril laughed with the waitress over their shared mathematical incompetence, she was fuming about Steven. So he still had *that* bee in his bonnet, did he? Obviously he intended to deprive Avril of her beautiful home, simply because he was jealous of the love and care that she had lavished upon it. Well, he wasn't going to succeed. They wouldn't be going anywhere. And if he was deluded enough to think that by getting a job *in* the mountains he could force her to close the guesthouse by denying her his full-time assistance, then he was sadly mistaken. *Sadly* mistaken. No doubt he was hoping, at the very least, to close the guesthouse; then he would argue that the house needn't come first, because it was no longer a business.

A manager, Avril decided. I'll suggest a manager – and not a female one, either. There has to be a way around this.

She emerged from the cafe to find Natasha slouched near the entrance, puffing away at a cigarette as she exchanged stilted remarks with George Lovecek.

'Oh!' said Avril. 'Hello, George.'

'Hello, Avril.'

'What are you doing here?'

'I was just up at the woodcraft shop. Looking for a present.' He was all windblown hair and rumpled clothes; Avril noticed that part of his shirt had managed to work its way out of his jeans. 'Natasha's been telling me that you were having lunch together.'

'That's right.'

George nodded. He adjusted his glasses, and shifted his weight. 'Well,' he said awkwardly, 'we'll have to do that ourselves, soon. Catch up a bit. Next week, perhaps?'

Oh dear, thought Avril. She'd felt rather guilty about George ever since their last, disastrous encounter in Avril's sitting room. Though Avril hadn't once, by word or deed, encouraged George to think of her as anything more than a friend, he had obviously misread the situation. Not that this was her *fault*, of course – how could it be? – but she felt a little guilty, all the same.

He'd been such a good friend, and now circumstances had forced her to distance herself somewhat. Just in order to drive her message home. She didn't really want to *spell it out*, because so blunt an approach would place both of them in a very undignified position. But if he continued to press his company upon her, she might have to take more drastic steps.

I'll see how things go, she decided.

'Yes,' she said, in pleasant but not overly affectionate tones, 'it's been a while, hasn't it? But we've been absolutely frantic, I'm afraid. Maybe when things settle down a bit. I'll have to see.'

'Oh. Well . . . all right. That's all right.'

'Or perhaps we can all go out to dinner somewhere,' Avril went on. 'That cabaret on Friday nights, perhaps. Anyway, we'll think of something. Sorry we've got to fly, but Steven has some council thing – well, you probably know about it – and there are guests due. Sorry. I'm sorry. I'll see you later. Goodbye.'

'Goodbye,' said Natasha, before following Avril down the street. Avril headed for her daughter's car; upon reaching it, she slowed, and turned, and caught sight of Natasha's face – which was wreathed in a huge knowing grin.

'God, Mum,' Natasha drawled. 'You're worse than I am.'

'What do you mean?'

'Come on. You know what I mean.'

'I certainly do not.'

Natasha regarded her for a moment, as the last of the cherry blossom drifted down around them. Avril, noticing for perhaps the millionth time that Natasha's eyes were exactly the same shape – and colour – as her own, wondered what she herself would look like with black hair. Would it be worth considering? Probably not.

'Right,' said Natasha, exhaling a lungful of smoke. 'Okay. You win.'

Then they got in the car, and drove back to the Bella Vista.

Also available in Penguin

LITTLE WHITE SECRETS

Catherine Jinks

*Gossip, gossip, gossip. Alice had been fending off inquiries for days: it was out in the open now, with a vengeance. People were talking about David all over town…*

David French leaves Sydney to work in Sable Cove, a small Canadian fishing town, convinced that a year away from his lover will repair their failing relationship. But he's not prepared for life in a community where everyone has something to hide – and where it's always a fight to keep your secrets to yourself.

At once poignant and entertaining, and full of the razor-sharp perception that has become Catherine Jinks's signature, *Little White Secrets* takes us behind the façade of a place that isn't quite what it seems.